GOLDEN HORIZON

GOLDEN HORIZON

This is a work of fiction. names, characters, and incidents either are the product of the author's imagination and or are used fictitiously. Any resemblance to actual persons, living or dead, events is entirely coincidental.

First Published in paperback in 2020

This paperback addition published in 2020

Book cover design by Gene du Plessis

ISBN 978-1-5272-6461-8 (paperback)

www.nickbohnet.com

For BB,

Without whom this book would have been nothing more than a collection of disjointed ramblings.

GOLDEN HORIZON

by

NICK BOHNET

PROLOGUE

No amount of skill, training, or luck could have saved him. Not the thousands of hours spent cramped in familiar cockpits either too cold, or more often too hot. Nor the hard-earned knowledge accrued from flying mission after mission; fear and heat trickling rivers down his spine, probing the physical and mechanical limits of his profession. Not even his intuitive, deceptively casual connection to this vibrating, whining amalgam of man's best efforts to beat the air into submission, counted for anything when faced with this particular law of physics. A simple failure of the tail rotor, trained for over and over again, might have given him some chance. Lightning reflexes and immediate entry into autorotation may have at least delayed his demise, but catastrophic damage to the tail boom and total detachment of the entire tail rotor assembly gave him no such options.

***

The flight had started strangely, even for him. Over his long career as a pilot he had done pretty much everything that could be done with a helicopter, except steal one. And to be fair, the technical aspects of the theft had been taken care of by his boss's right-hand man. His role had been merely to slide open the hanger door once the alarm was disabled and pull the trolley laden with the familiar outline of the Hughes 500 helicopter out into the night. The dark clad figure who had overridden the hanger's security system clapped him on the shoulder before closing the helicopter's door.

"See you at the estate," Vladimir said.

Remembering instances of ruthlessness that he had witnessed from this man, the pilot shook off a feeling of unease as Vladimir vanished into the night. Diverting his focus to the instrument panel, he began rapidly deciding which parts of the pre-flight checklist could be skipped. All of them as it turned out. A sudden flare of lights from an airport security car washed over him, reducing his small window of time to a minimum.

With a frustrated sigh, knowing full well that cutting corners and helicopters were not a good mix, he flicked on the master battery switch, rotated the twist grip on his collective to start fuel flow and hit the starter. A faint series of clicks reached his ears before being drowned out by the whine of the turbine coming to life. Almost immediately the five rotor blades began to sweep across his vision, each revolution faster than the last.

His attention turned back to the instrument panel, interrogating every dial in a sequence which came to him as easily as breathing, no conscious thought required. This time though he didn't register the details flickering before him. What they would tell him was largely irrelevant at this point. Either the machine would come to life correctly and in the time available before the approaching car reached him, or it wouldn't.

It did. Barely. Hands were reaching for the latch on the cockpit door by the time he had enough rotor RPM to lift the helicopter off the trolley. Wide eyed security staff disappeared below him in a blast of rotor wash as he cleared the perimeter fence and aimed the helicopter loosely in the direction of his boss's country estate.

Two hours later, the second take off of the night - and his last, had been more controlled. Adjusting to the weight of the cargo he now carried, the absence of authority intent on pulling him out of his familiar seat gave him the luxury of time to remain momentarily in a low hover, a meter or so above the wet grass.

'Temperatures and pressures in the green arcs, fuel on and sufficient, no warning lights, centre of gravity feels good.' Satisfied, he simultaneously applied pressure to the cyclic and lifted imperceptibly on the collective. His feet unconsciously countered the resulting yaw created by the increased power demand. The machine pulled itself through the night air, vibrating briefly as the rotor disc reacted to the change in angle of airflow as the helicopter picked up forward speed.

The final forty-five minutes of his unconventional life were mostly spent in deep concentration. Tree tops and power lines reaching up to pluck him from the sky were evaded, in some cases by mere inches. As the coastline passed beneath him, he applied a slight pressure on the cyclic, heading in a more south-westerly direction before descending yet further towards the greyness below.The helicopter noisily ate the miles, and he had begun to relax- if a minute reduction of his grip on the controls could be called relaxing- when the brief flicker of yellow light on the instrument panel caught his eye.

'Tail rotor transmission warning.' His brain had little time to process this information as the sudden vibration thudding up through his legs from the anti-torque pedals met the shiver of fear that ran down his back.

Just before dawn, with wind driven clouds periodically blinding the moon and the white capped sea below shrugging its indifference, the black Hughes 500 helicopter pitched nose down and slammed violently into the cold, uncaring waters of the English Channel. Screams of terror and anguish, if time and character had allowed for them, diluted to silence by the ocean.

ONE

TWO MONTHS EARLIER

Arriving back in my hometown of Dartmouth after an absence of ten years was dramatic enough in its own way. Tired and eager for my impulsive crossing from the French mainland to be over, I had arrived off the Castle Ledge Buoy at the entrance to the Dart Estuary on the south Devon Coast. My arrival aboard the elderly but solid, forty-foot wooden Thames motor launch '*First Light*' coincided with a strong outgoing spring tide and an equally tenacious South-Easterly gale. These two opposing forces conspired to block the mouth of the estuary with a barrier of standing waves, a foam capped proclamation asserting that visitors by sea were not currently welcome in this picturesque coastal town. 'Come back later after consulting your tide tables.'

Inwardly, I shrugged my shoulders at the chance I was taking. I didn't have the enthusiasm or the fuel for a diversion to Brixham or Torquay after ten hours of pitching and yawing my way across the English Channel. Spinning the helm towards the first wall of water, and pushing the throttles forward a little to lift the bow, I braced myself against the seat behind me. The deck pitched steeply up under my feet as *First Light* reluctantly climbed the nearest wave before bursting through the crest and plunging headlong into the trough behind. Despite my best efforts, the bow buried itself deep into the face of the next wall of water.

It sliced out a hefty wedge which swept back along the foredeck, slamming into the wheelhouse. Briefly entombed in a cauldron of hissing greyness, I watched as the water strained to find access. Defeated, it flowed aft, its power dissipating before finally gurgling through the scuppers and freeing ports, back from whence it came. Seemingly unaffected by my urgings, *First Light* began to sluggishly climb the second, smaller wave. In this manner, with slowly decreasing histrionics, we staggered into the calmer waters of the estuary.

Unclenching my fists from their death grip on the helm and throttles, I glided past the oak laden riverbanks. The familiar sights and sounds of my hometown were only vaguely discernible through the salt streaked wheelhouse windows. With the folly of the last few minutes already fading from my mind, I peered out through the glass.

On my port side, the mud of Warfleet Creek showed itself as the tide receded, small boats of various description laying drunkenly to one side, their support drained out from under them. Through the forward windscreen I could make out the blurred reddish bulk of the Naval college, high on the hill overlooking the river.

A small inflatable work boat with *'Harbour Master'* emblazoned in stark white on its blue tubes, closed-up neatly on my starboard aft quarter, matching my speed and holding station with a skill born of constant repetition.

"*First Light, First Light,* this is Dart Harbour Authority, do you require a mooring? Over."

I grinned at the disembodied voice squawking at me from the VHF marine radio, my old friend Andrew's voice, curt and economic but softened by a west country accent.

"Dart Harbour, this is *First Light,*" I responded, "yes please, somewhere close to town for a couple of nights if there is anything available. And would you sort out the river entrance, it's a bit bumpy."

A short silence greeted me. Then; "Matthew Curtis, I should have known. We saw your approach from the office and couldn't decide if you're stupid or crazy - now we can tick both boxes. Take the berth on the inside of the town pontoon. I'm sure you remember where it is. I will be around to say hello and relieve you of harbour dues later."

First Light slotted neatly into the gap between two scruffy thirty-foot sailing yachts, festooned with drying laundry and with mismatched fenders tugging the slack out of their sagging guard rails. The yachts' occupants, beers in hand, curiously looked on hoping for some minor calamity. This tricky narrow tidal berth was well-known among the locals as a humbling zone for many a weekend Admiral. Disappointed this time, they reluctantly stepped ashore to catch my lines, failure to do so being an unforgivable slight.

In a matter of twenty minutes the deck was rinsed with freshwater and the wheelhouse tidied and wiped down. *First*

Light was gently snubbing at her lines, looking shipshape, and welcoming by the time I spotted my old friend making his way down the dock. Andrew was clearing a path through the last of the season's day trippers as they were being disgorged from the river boats, shielding their ice creams and pasties from the ever-present threat of aerial larceny by ill-mannered, occasionally savage, seagulls.

"Permission to come aboard?"

"None required mate, how the hell are you?"

The two of us shook hands, not for us the fist-bumping, hugging rituals so prevalent, yet so bewildering to those of a more taciturn disposition. I looked at Andrew, his ready grin and ice grey eyes seemingly unchanged under a mop of curly ginger hair.

We had grown up together in this west country town, getting up to our fair share of what the local magistrate charitably described as 'youthful exuberance' before going our separate ways. When Andrew had accepted the Queen's shilling and slid easily into the Royal Navy, I was at somewhat of a loss in the vacuum left by my friend's departure. After a year or so of casual labour on a local fishing boat, I found myself on the train to London, glad to be putting some distance between me and the stench of fish. I had the vague idea of joining the fire service. Or the army. Whichever.

Events fell into place as they sometimes do when confronted with naive optimism, and after three rigorous months of basic training, I was posted to a central London fire station to embark on eight years of what turned out to be *'the best of times and the worst of times.'*

"Good to see you, Matt. It's been a long time. Last I heard, you'd left London, and seemed to have dropped off the radar for a couple of years?"

I left his enquiry unanswered. We made our way into my small wheelhouse, lit by the last of the sun, where a soft insistent *beeping* emanated from the electronic fuel gauge, and the remnants of the ebb tide could be heard softly slapping against the hull. I slouched on the small, leather covered bench which ran along the port bulkhead, while Andrew stood at the helm, casting an interested, professional eye over the limited navigational instruments arrayed in front of him.

"Not much like the bridge of your old Destroyer, is it?" I grinned.

"No, nothing like it, but then I don't suppose you plan on setting sail to impose Her Majesty's will on foreign powers any time soon?"

"Probably not," I concurred, trying to sound disappointed. "Let me show you around."

We descended the three steps leading down from the wheelhouse. The galley took up the immediate space found at the foot of the stairs and somehow between me and Sophie we had managed to make it both functional and homely. A stainless-steel oven and hob were set into a worktop running along the starboard side, before turning ninety degrees and protruding out far enough to be home to a granite sink, complete with an elaborate looking tap. The crumbling remains of a baguette sat on a plate alongside a capsized coffee mug in the bottom of the sink, awaiting my attention. On the port side, another work surface, floral themed tiles overlooked by brightly painted storage cupboards.

Forward of the galley was a compact dining table. The four green leather chairs tucked around it had been Sophie's grudging compromise to masculinity. To one side, a small but comfortable sofa was orientated towards a T.V. which had not been turned on in two years. Pastel coloured curtains hung over the brass portholes and the door leading forward to the main cabin had a framed print of Monet's '*Cliff Walk at Pourville*' screwed to it. The space imbued, for me at least, feelings of sadness and comfort in equal measure.

"Very nice, Matt," Andrew said, sitting down on the sofa. "So, what's the story? How have you filled the last two years?" His gaze was frank and unblinking, requiring of a non-flippant answer.

"Mostly I spent it on the canals of France and the Netherlands cruising around a lot," I replied from my position leaning against the galley work top. "Living the dream. You know."

Andrew looked sceptical.

"And the fire service? The pension?" He paused. "No one leaves the pension."

I was not about to recount the real reason for my departure. "It was time for me to leave. Eight years in the city was enough for me."

The scepticism in his eyes did not go away. I sensed we would be revisiting this conversation, but Andrew seemed content to let it lie for now. He looked around appreciatively.

"Well, I like your choice of boat. Much better than the plastic stuff littering the harbour nowadays. So, you're staying put for a bit?"

"Yes, I hope so. Time to stop moving around for a while and find some gainful employment."

"You know, the local fire station is always looking for recruits," Andrew said, "it is retained, not a full-time station so you respond from your normal job as and when needed. It doesn't pay much, but -"

"I was thinking more along the lines of work on the river actually," I interrupted. "On the subject of the river, who would I speak to about a permanent mooring, somewhere close to town?"

Andrew considered my evasiveness for a moment before replying.

"Well, that would be me," he said, the beginnings of a twinkle in his eyes. "You know I've been working for the harbour authority since I left the Navy, and then last year when Pat, my old boss, retired, the board appointed me Harbour Master. So far no one seems to have realized their mistake." He glanced at his watch. "Come around to the office on Monday morning, eight's a good time to catch me, we'll see if we can slot you in somewhere. In the meantime, you're welcome to come grab a meal with us whenever you want. Anna would love to see you. We live in the flat above my office. Just ring the bell."

***

The following few days were taken up with walking once familiar streets, still crowded with late season tourists staring into art shop windows. There were a few more charity shops than I remembered, and inevitably fewer recognizable faces, but otherwise the town of my youth appeared largely unchanged. Memories abounded at every corner as I revisited old acquaintances before settling *First Light* onto her new deep-water mooring, a short tender ride from the towns landing dock.

I had also spotted a sign in the news agent's window and was now the proud owner of an old, battered, nine hundred CC Honda Fire blade motor bike - not yet road taxed. '*Cutting edge in its day*', I was assured by the seller, and certainly retaining enough of its former glory to scare the hell out of me.

***

'*YOUR COMMUNITY NEEDS YOU!*' was the wording on the banner outside the fire station. In smaller letters beneath, it continued: *'Earn a second income whilst safeguarding your community and learning new skills.'*

I had glanced at it a couple of times now on my trips out of town and was reminded of Andrew's recent words. Each time I saw the single-story red brick fire station with its machines lurking behind the full height sliding doors I was jolted with conflicting emotions. I couldn't deny that I missed the banter, the sense of purpose, even the equipment - bespoke and functional.

But, the nightmare, always the same, would still wrench me awake, sweating and terrified. It was less frequent now, but no lesser in its ability to render me helpless. I wondered though if enough time had passed for me to attempt to function once more in my chosen profession.

My savings were rapidly declining. Two years of cruising the inland waterways of Europe, trying to forget, had made a considerable dent. The mooring fees for *First Light* would steadily eat into what remained. With winter fast approaching, my idea of finding work on the river seemed a little optimistic. But ultimately, it was the unanswered phone calls and texts from my bank, reaching a frequency and tone that could no longer be ignored, which made me decide it was time to take my head out of the sand and face reality.

Early one evening as I returned down the hill from the supermarket, supplies crammed into my backpack, I saw activity in the fire station yard. A fire appliance parked to one side of the yard was being rinsed off with a length of hose connected to a hydrant. Its twin was having a ladder slid back into its housing on the roof and various bits of equipment re-stowed into cavernous side lockers.

I recognized the scene and decided that now was as good a time as any to show my face and see how the land lies.

Parking my motor bike next to a group of others, none quite as decrepit as mine, and removing my helmet, I turned towards the approaching fireman.

"Hello, can you tell me where to find the Boss?"

"We don't have a 'Boss'. We have a 'Station Manager', and you can't leave your bike there, it's in the way," he said jerking his head in the general direction of my motorcycle.

Regarding the figure in front of me for a moment, suppressing a flare of anger, I saw a lad in his early twenties with scuffed boots, fire helmet sat at a jaunty angle, chin strap dangling. Resisting the urge to punch him in the face, I addressed him anew.

"Let's start again. How about we pretend you're a capable, competent member of the emergency services, and I'm, oh I don't know, maybe a member of the public who has asked you a civil question, fully expecting a polite, informative reply."

The young fireman stared back at me and I could see he was beginning to wish he were somewhere else.

"He's in his office, first door on the right."

"Thank you," I responded, but unable to help myself, I added, "and do your chin strap up."

The boy was still fumbling with the clasp when I knocked on the open office door.

"Come in Matt, take a seat."

Surprised at the familiarity, I entered the small room with a questioning expression on my face. Inside, there was barely space for the desk, its two opposing chairs, and the decrepit filing cabinet, top drawer fully open; the whole thing threatening to topple. The walls were randomly patched with fire service posters, old and new, proclaiming the benefits of smoke detectors and the hazards of cooking chips in saucepans. Familiar stuff.

"I'm glad you came. Saved me having to come and find you." From behind his desk, Station Manager Kemp reached out and shook my hand.

"Don't look so surprised, this is a small town. People gossip," he shrugged. "I've seen your service record from London and given your experience it would be remiss of me to not try to recruit you. Some days we've barely got enough crew to put one appliance out of the door. The Harbour Master speaks highly of you, which is good enough for me. There would be some paperwork, of course, and you will need a medical check-up and a short refresher at the County Training Centre. I won't be able to offer you your old rank, but with luck, we can get you through the formalities and riding the pumps within a month. Interested?"

I was somewhat taken aback by Kemp's monologue, which had been delivered staccato, like measured bursts from a machine gun. Mildly impressed at the clout this manager of this small provincial station must possess to have accessed my record, I did wonder though which version of it he had been privy to, to be immediately offering me a role at his station.

I had noticed over my years in the fire service there remained, in rapidly diminishing numbers, a subset of real characters who bridged the gap between yesteryear and the dizzying heights of today's political correctness, health, safety, and empire building. Some of them were ill-informed, bigoted, and dangerous, but the remaining few, pure gold. The unlikely figure sat in front of me showed signs of falling into the latter category.

And so, two months after my roller-coaster return to Dartmouth, I found myself once again responding to fire calls. The question still remained however, whether I could hold my demons at bay long enough to be useful.

TWO

The remotely activated fire-station lights and siren had been demanding attention for two minutes before the first cars started to slew their way into the parking area; driven by dishevelled, sleep slumped faces. Moments later, the car park contained a dozen vehicles of varying quality and vintage - none of which were parked tidily, instead, seemingly abandoned as close to the fire stations front door as was possible.

'*House fire. Persons reported,*' was the line passed on to the latecomers, still squeezing into the small entrance hallway, adrenaline and a sense of purpose palpable in the air.

"Matt, you're in charge of the first breathing apparatus entry team, okay?"

I glanced at the source of this decree. My new boss, Station Manager Kemp, at first glance, was not the sort of person who you would normally expect to hear uttering such phrases at four in the morning. At five foot-seven, Kemp appeared diminutive in every way with his stick-like limbs, *Friar Tuck* head of hair, and recently acquired thick glasses - the arrival of which had nearly ended his fire service career.

Fortunately, with a level of common sense not usually attributed to fire service management, it was agreed that Kemp, with or without glasses, was still the most suitable person to bring together a mismatched bunch of individuals; consisting of builders, fishermen, electricians and the like and meld them into an emergency response team capable, at the very least, of not making matters worse.

"Sure, Boss."

I was already moving toward the nearest of the two machines, which were by now rumbling awake from their slumber and throwing urgent blue flickers across the fire rescue appliance bay and out into the night. Squashed into the rear crew compartment, I shrugged myself into the breathing apparatus set clamped to the bulkhead behind me as the vehicle swung wildly along the road out of town, the wide, easy river of tarmac soon contracting into narrow country lanes, more caution required from the drivers.

The two vehicles hurtled towards a nearby village, the specific address containing, as the radio link from control now relayed: '*Well-developed house fire. Multiple calls. Persons reported.*' Fire Service speak for 'Wake up, switch on. This is not a cat up a tree.'

Kemp, from the front seat: "Control from 241, priority, over."

'Go ahead 241, over,' came the reply over the radio.

"Control from 241, 241 and 242 in attendance, premises well alight, make pumps three for manpower and breathing apparatus, confirm ambulance is mobilized, 241 over."

Climbing carefully backwards out of the now stationary fire truck, I tuned out the radio chatter and the running out of thick red hoses between hydrants and pumps. Ignored also the urgent calls from scantily clad figures, woken from their slumber to face a scene not quite fitting their usual frames of reference. Focusing only on my role in this unfolding drama and trying not to stumble over the hoses, I lead my team-mate to the *Breathing Apparatus Entry Control Officer*, identified by his black and yellow chequered tabard and the rectangular whiteboard mounted on a tripod in front of him. Removing the tab from my Automatic Distress Signal Unit, which held space for a name, cylinder pressure reading, and time of entry, I passed it to the Entry Control Officer.

"Firefighter Curtis, three hundred bar."

While my team-mate, Chris, by day a shop assistant in town more familiar with passing over small change, went through the same procedure, I stole a look across to the house at the centre of everyone's attention. The two-story detached building with a sign indicating '*Bed and Breakfast: No Vacancies*' hanging from an ornate metal gate, was indeed 'well alight'.

Thick black smoke boiled out from the join between the roof and wall along the entire front facade. The upper floor windows were heavily blackened, but a soft pulsating red glow hinted at the conditions inside. Crackling and popping sounds punctuated the scene. The 'no vacancies' sign was likely going to remain in place for some time.

Kemp rapidly approached, nimbly navigating his way towards us over snaking hoses.

"Right, listen up you two. I spoke with the householder. We have at least one person unaccounted for. Adult male, staying in the back bedroom, second door on the left, at the top of the stairs. Kemp briefly paused for breath. "The stairs are immediately behind the entrance door. Go straight up and do a left-hand search. Ignore the first door and search behind the second. I will send the next team in behind you to check the rest of the floor. Understand?"

"Got it Boss." I nodded. "Upstairs, left-hand search of the second room on the left."

Chris and I donned our face masks and checked each other for any exposed skin. I stole a quick searching glance at the small part of Chris's face which could be glimpsed through his mask. Reassured at seeing only a resolute expression staring back at me, and wondering what he saw in return, I took the high-pressure hose reel as it was thrust into my hands. Testing it for pressure and spray pattern, less than two minutes after clambering backwards out of the appliance, we turned towards the front door.

Inside, was other worldly. A thin grey smoke swirled around us in the entrance hallway, the crackling and popping much louder now. Checking Chris was close behind me we set off up the stairs, keeping down in anticipation of the heat. Before we had reached halfway, the smoke had become a thick black veil, which was forcing us to crouch lower in an effort to stay in the cooler, clearer air.

I paused before directing some short pulses of fine spray into the blackness above us. The water would turn to hot steam at these temperatures and drive the layer lower, but it was imperative to dilute the potentially explosive mix of smoke and keep it out of its flammable range as we progressed.

After wiping my face mask with the back of my glove to remove the condensation that had instantly formed, I made sure Chris was still closed-up tight behind, before pressing on to the top of the stairs. Visibility was now zero and heat was already beginning to seep through my fire kit. With my left hand on the wall I found the first door, passed it, then fumbled for the handle of the second.

"You good, Chris?" I asked. "Here's the door, can you take it?" Speech had to be timed between the compressed air hiss of our laboured breathing.

Chris gave a thumbs-up and took control of the door, enabling me to operate the hose reel and assess conditions. He cracked the door open about four inches. I could see that inside the bedroom was much worse than in the corridor. The smoke was barely a meter off the floor while mesmerizing tongues of flame appeared and disappeared in a hypnotic fashion at the bottom edge of the layer. The carpet, the only thing in the room not yet fully alight, was giving off tendrils of smoke. After directing a couple of long pulses of water spray towards the ceiling, I signalled Chris to close the door.

"This room's about to flash-over. I want to give it one more soaking, then we'll go in. The room is small, so we should be able to sweep it in one go." I sucked in another breath before continuing. "It is going to be as hot as hell in there, so let's make this quick, okay?"

Chris nodded and cracked the door open again. Before sweeping the smoke with spray, I noted as much of the layout as I could see. The moment I applied more water, the visibility reduced to nothing.

With the door closed again I fought to dispel my fear with procedure, checking both our air pressure gauges. Not quite thirty bar used, plenty left. I choked down the emotions threatening to overwhelm me, the desire to be anywhere other than here, doing anything rather than stepping back across the Rubicon of a fire compartment door.

"Let's go."

Even with the door fully open, the room didn't want to let us in. The punishing heat was pushing us down, making progress only possible on bended knees. We flailed our limbs around attempting to cover as much space as we could. Familiar, but unseen objects - a table, sofa, what felt like a T.V. - bumped us as we searched. Behind the door. On the sofa. On and under the bed.

"Casualty!"

Chris's call was accompanied by him pulling me off the wall towards him. My heartbeat quickened. I had to work hard to fight back against the images that were inflating inside of my skull. Pictures from the past threatening to push the order and control aside and tip me into the chaos of panic. I forced three deep steady breaths, concentrating on listening to the flow of compressed air as it flowed through the regulator. The memories reluctantly receded into the greyness, held at bay for now at least.

I joined Chris, and we both fumbled around to find the orientation of the unmistakable human form lying on the small bed. Positioning myself to pick him up, my gloved hand sliding under his torso searching for a grip struck upon something small and angular pressed up under the inert form's back. Unthinkingly I picked it up and slipped it into my tunic pocket before reaching under again for a decent hold.

"Okay, I've got the shoulders, take the legs. Let's go."

We rapidly retraced our steps, the sagging weight between us scraping the carpet, and tugging on my lower back. No time for anything now except rapid exit. My fire kit, long since defeated, was now doing little to stop the heat from sapping the strength from my bones. We stumbled awkwardly down the stairs with our burden, tripping over the threshold out into the street.

The sound of squawking radios was louder than before and alien green arms with blue latex gloves reached out to relieve us of any further responsibilities towards our charge. I stole a quick glance down at the casualty before he was whisked away, seeing the burnt remains of underclothes and scorched skin.We reported back to the entry control point, giving our assessment regarding conditions inside for the *Officer in Charge* and in return receiving back our B.A set tallies and a *'good job lads, go service your sets and find yourselves a cup of tea'*.

With fresh, fully charged cylinders replacing our still hot to touch originals, and face masks wiped out with antibacterial wipes, a good enough stop gap until a full wash out could be given, the sets were re-stowed on the appliance; and we went looking for the promised cup of tea. A steaming urn was to be found on the tailgate of a fire service pickup truck, parked a couple of houses down the road. In the back of the pick-up packets of opened biscuits competed for space with towers of plastic cups, standing proud among their fallen comrades.

As usual, milling around this focal point were uniforms of all types - not just fire service personnel, but Police, Ambulance and anyone else whose job decreed that they should be here and who had accepted the trade-off between something warm to drink on a cold night, and the unpleasant reality of fire service tea.

A man, not in uniform, yet somehow not out of place, stood in the shadows to one side of the pick-up truck. He seemed taught and angry, the younger man in front of him slumped in comparison. I tried to place these unfamiliar faces in the context of the night's events but came up blank. Curiously, I looked on, the oldest of the pair turned and melted away into the night.

***

Three hours later, showered but still smelling faintly of smoke, I conceded defeat to any notion of getting back to bed after the intensity of the recent call out and headed to my favourite riverfront cafe. A shabby old Gortex sailing jacket kept the morning chill at bay and nursing a strong black coffee on the terrace, I watched as regulars slowly trickled in, bringing the café alive.

Around me, the town also appeared to be waking up, reluctantly accepting the infusion of weak winter sun, in a lacklustre way, as if not yet sure it was going to be worth the effort. As the day took hold, I felt a sense of satisfaction begin to build. The memories of my partner's death in a London warehouse fire were ever present, but at least I had been able to thrust them aside and function once again. Whether that state of affairs would continue, or the fear and panic would return to crush me, remained to be seen.

THREE

"Where's my fucking helicopter!" exploded Dimitri, slamming his hand down on his desk. Before him stood Vladimir Cuskov, trim and contained in contrast to the incensed bulk of his employer. Vladimir managed to maintain eye contact with his boss, but seriously wished the events of last night had run to plan. Facing the wrath of Dimitri was an unpleasant experience at best, and he hadn't expected to be having this conversation. Didn't expect to have any further conversations at all with this man, if the truth be told.

Dimitri sat at his desk, his back to an ornate French window with the first of the day's many espressos in his grip. A small portion of the Royal Albert Hall was showing itself through the window, poking up over his shoulder. The opulent setting gave no clue that Dimitri's star was falling. Plummeting even, and no one better placed to witness it than Vladimir.

The most likely outcome in the coming months, assuming prison could be avoided, was clear water appearing between

Dimitri and his associates. Business ties vehemently denied, income and influence diminishing to nothing. Some perks would inevitably remain; a villa here, an apartment there, some staff, dwindling as the years crawled by.

As for Vladimir? What? Touting his skills to the highest bidder? Forever marked by association in the murky shadow world in which he operated? 'No,' he'd thought to himself, 'that wouldn't work for him. Much better to jump ship, and why leave empty-handed?'

"I don't know where the helicopter is. It took off as planned from your estate, at 03:00 but didn't arrive at the yacht. The last contact from it was a cell phone call at 04:35 to the yacht, giving an ETA of 05:00 this morning. The call was cut off abruptly and the Captain was unable to re-establish a connection.

"He's working on getting a rough last position based on the time of the call, but since we don't know the exact track the helicopter was following, it will be a best guess more than anything. There is no news about any crash and given the illegal nature of the flight we can't ask the Coastguard to carry out a search. I assume we wouldn't want them finding anything anyway."

Dimitri stared at Vladimir across the desk, anger still flushing across his sagging features.

"You know what was on that helicopter."

Vladimir was well aware what was on board the helicopter, as well as what wasn't. He'd helped carry the boxes over the wet grass of the lawn, his shoes still damp with the memory. Aware, also, of the implications to his employer of its possible loss.

The fact that the pilot, with assistance from Vladimir, had 'liberated' Dimitri's machine from its hanger last night where it had been impounded, would undoubtedly bring the authorities to their door today. And the contents of the sealed boxes strapped into the back were the result of months of painstaking work, researching and purchasing private coin collections, sourcing the finest gold items which could be bought for cash. A surprisingly difficult task Vladimir had found.

However, it was the rugged, black, watertight case which was of far more concern to Dimitri than the other boxes. Crammed, as it was, with documents and recordings stretching back through the years of hard scrabbling and outright criminality that would ensure, in any reckoning before a judge, that Dimitri would not be alone in his confinement. Vladimir's mobile pinged in his pocket. Taking it out he glanced at the screen.

"It's a *WhatsApp* message from the Captain of the yacht, Sir." Vladimir paused as he read the text.

“Well?”

“They are still anchored in Falmouth Bay, waiting for your instructions. Based on the information we have, his best guess is that if the helicopter crashed, and the pilot didn't just head off on his own agenda, then it might have gone down anywhere between Torquay and Salcombe on the South Devon coast."

Vladimir scrolled down through the rest of the message while Dimitri impatiently waited for him to continue.

"He says if the call cut off at the time of the possible crash and the helicopter was following the coastline, then that would narrow it down closer to a headland called *Start Point,* near the town of Dartmouth. There has been no news about any incidents overnight, so he assumes no one saw anything unusual." Vladimir glanced up. "He is keen to obtain your permission to inform the Coastguard, so they can mount a search."

Dimitri sat heavily in his chair whilst he digested this information and began to consider his options. That the pilot could have flown off with the boxes rather than delivering them to the yacht was unthinkable. His loyalty had been tested many times and not found wanting. In his journey with Dimitri from the chaos of Russia in the nineties to the affluence and privilege they had attained, the pilot had witnessed first-hand what happened to those who thought to cross Dimitri. The pilot would recall the noisy blast of hot air as the helicopter's side door slid back high over the dusty terrain of some embattled hellhole, and the wasted pleading and ignored tears, followed by the quickly corrected lurch as the sudden loss of weight and balance was instinctively reacted to.

'No', Dimitri thought, dismissing treachery as an option and given the lack of any news story, he had to assume his helicopter and all that it contained was at the bottom of the English Channel.

A chill ran through him as he realized he was lucky to be sat here with a coffee in his hand, and not being steadily nibbled into bite sized pieces by inquisitive sea life. His last minute decision to send the helicopter on without him had saved his life but presented him with a major problem going forward. Without the 'insurance' which was onboard, contained in that black case, he would be unable to fend off the inevitable attacks on his freedom.

"Tell the Captain to keep his mouth shut. If it crashed into the sea, there is little chance that the pilot would have survived the crash or the water temperature for long at this time of year. Alerting the authorities is pointless and I forbid it."

Vladimir had expected no other response and nodded.

The probable death of his pilot was of little consequence to Dimitri. Years of operating in the vacuum created by the fall of the Soviet Union being lifted by the rising tide of feverish Capitalism, favouring the ruthless and the well-connected, had left him detached from many of the perceived norms of humanity. Too many deals had been facilitated by one-way flights in helicopters and single gunshots in frozen forests for him to think about death in any way other than how it could be used as a tool.

Dimitri wondered how much time he had left before the knock on the door came. The long-running probe into his affairs, instigated by the 'Panama Papers' data release of 2015, had finally gathered enough momentum to allow the British authorities to launch a full-scale forensic investigation into the sources of his wealth, and begin seizing his assets - the missing helicopter a case in point. He had known for some time that he had to liquidate his holdings before the forces of law and order, relentlessly chipping away at his convoluted financial structures, enveloped, and ultimately incarcerated him.

The work was mostly completed. The contents of the helicopter were largely, though not entirely, icing on the cake. He had hoped for a little more time, post *Wimbledon* week perhaps, with his favourite box already reserved; but instinctively knew that with this new development the prudent course would be to distance himself from any repercussions.

At least, as far as he was aware, the powers who were shining spotlights into his shady corners had no knowledge of his yacht, '*Natasha*'. She was registered to a company in the Cayman Islands, which was itself owned by a Virgin Islands corporation whose address was a post box number, and the best of luck trying to contact a director.

"I need that case, Vladimir."

The words were spoken with a finality brokering no discussion.

"Yes Sir."

Vladimir wondered if his boss had any idea of the scale of the task he was proposing. Did he think that in the absence of a full-scale search, backed by significant resources and experts in the field, finding a small helicopter at the bottom of the sea was a realistic goal? Vladimir was thinking on his feet now, damage control coming instinctively to him. Half of his plan was still intact, which was better than nothing.

"I should go down to the yacht and try to sort things out from there," he suggested.

Dimitri thought this over, but was unable to come up with a better idea.

"You do that. I am going to fly out to the villa in Cypress today before last night's activities catch up with us. Get down to *Natasha* in Falmouth. Lay off all the crew whose loyalty to me can be questioned. The wage bill is crippling, and we do not need the full complement anyway. Do whatever you need to do to retrieve my property. I don't care how you do it, but at the very least I want my case back."

Dimitri's voice was cold and dismissive, now back under control after his outburst. The small espresso cup was engulfed in his pudgy hand.

Vladimir's countenance remained unchanged, though his mind was far from still. The soldier in him was well aware that even the best laid plans rarely survived first contact with the enemy, but he was cursing the fickleness which had stopped his boss from climbing aboard the helicopter in the pre-dawn dampness of last night as originally planned. That *empty seat* where the three-point harness had been loosened to its full extent in anticipation of Dimitri's bulk, was without a doubt going to complicate his immediate future.

FOUR

Still sat in my favourite café, watching the day get a grip on itself, my warm satisfaction and cooling coffee were interrupted by Andrew who plonked himself down in the faux wicker chair next to me. His mug, of what appeared to be green tea, clanked down on the glass table in front of us.

"Wow, she is a beauty."

Following the direction of his gaze I saw the shine of *real* wealth gliding through the waters of the river entrance.

About fifty meters of polished perfection with four decks, topped off by two rotating radar antennas; one spinning twice as fast as the other, almost frantic in its purpose to locate and identify. The vessel continued to glide effortlessly up the estuary, past the small car ferry with all eight of its customers out of their vehicles. Taking pictures on their phones as the yacht passed them, they conveyed both admiration and envy in varying measure. Continuing upstream, passing the sailing club with its faded green flag snapping in the breeze, there was still no visible effort from the vessel. Only the two blue inflatable harbour tenders nipping at its heels like over-enthusiastic sheepdogs showed any signs of urgency.

A blast from the yacht's horn signalled a turn to starboard and drew any remaining unaware eyes towards it. The rumble of thrusters reached us from across the water, and we watched as lines were thrown and received, knots tied, winches getting everything '*just so*'. With the yacht now neatly secured between two large yellow mooring buoys, I turned my attention back to Andrew.

"Nice boat, what's she doing here? Don't those things usually winter in sunnier climes?"

"No idea, we got the berthing request late yesterday. She's come up from Falmouth, paid for two weeks here. Seems they have already annoyed the locals having spent several hours steaming up and down off Start Point during the night, through all the fishing gear out there. Hasn't gone down too well with the crabbers. You know what they are like, thinking they own the place."

I smiled. There was always some tension between the various groups of seafarers sharing the oceans. Sailors disliked power boaters; the Navy was disdainful of anything not flying a white ensign. Commercial fishermen just hated everyone.

"You seem tired. Busy night?" Andrew asked, changing the subject.

"Yep, got called out to a house fire in Blackawton village last night, just finished up," I said. "Think I might take *First Light* up the river, if the weather holds off, for some lunch in the Ferry Boat Inn. You want to join me?"

"Sorry Matt, I have a feeling this new arrival will keep me busy, one way or another, for most of the day. But Anna and I want you to come for dinner tomorrow night. Maybe you can tell us then, why you disappeared for two years."

Sensing my reluctance, he quickly added, "Anna's inviting Jess as well, a woman who works for me. I'm quite sure you will get on like a house on fire. Pun intended."

"I'm not in the market for romance, thanks all the same."

"I'm sure you have your reasons, but burying issues from the past doesn't work." Andrew stood and swigged back the last of his tea. "It's just dinner, Matt. See you at seven-thirty. That's not a request."

He clinked his empty mug onto the table before heading off in the direction of his office. It seemed the Navy had added considerably to Andrew's direct, *no nonsense* approach to perceived problems. I had known that he would at some point want a more in-depth explanation of my recent history. Thinking about his words for a moment, I lubricated them with my lukewarm coffee before adding them to the bunch of others on my mental health 'to do' list.

***

The idea of heading up-river for lunch still appealed to me. Walking back along the riverfront, I climbed down the seaweed festooned ladder into my small tender, its seats still damp from the overnight dew. The recalcitrant outboard motor refused to start after ten or so precarious pulls on the starter cord. Conceding defeat and somewhat out of breath I slotted the oars into their rowlocks, resigning myself to a stiff row across the river.

"Need some help?"

A harbour launch came to a flamboyant rest in a foam of white water, the well-timed burst of astern stopping its forward motion perfectly.

The woman at the tiller was slightly built and had tendrils of red hair escaping from under a blue woollen hat. Her expression was neutral, but green eyes held the beginnings of a smile.

I spoke while bracing myself as the wash from her arrival caused my dingy to pitch and roll.

"Well, my crappy outboard needs some attention. Cleaning the plugs usually works for a while but my tools are on my boat."

She looked out across the river.

"Tides flooding," she said, "going to be a struggle to row against it. I have some tools here. We can take a look at it if you like. Or I could tow you across?"

I would rather attempt to swim the distance holding an anchor than be ignominiously towed. Long standing independence issues, *another story*.

"If you have a spark plug spanner, that would be great."

I shipped my oars as the launch came alongside and made fast. She stepped across into my small dingy, a canvass roll of tools tucked under one arm. It was the work of a few minutes before the outboard motor reluctantly spluttered into its usual intermittent form of asthmatic combustion. I could tell she was not impressed.

"Thanks. Matt, by the way." I proffered an oily hand.

"Anytime. I'm Jess." An equally oily hand was offered in return. 'Small world,' I thought.

"Seems like we will be having dinner together tomorrow night."

She eyed me appraisingly before replying.

"Yes, Andrew's told me lots about you."

"Oh dear."

"You're still going to owe me a drink or two though," Jess said, jutted her chin towards the stuttering outboard.

"Absolutely."

She paused momentarily.

"We could knock one of those drinks off of your tab this evening if you like?" Seeming to sense my hesitation, Jess hopped nimbly back into her launch. "Just a thought," she shrugged. "Glad I could help. Here, you better take my number."

She passed me a damp, ink smudged, scruffy card, the numbers barely legible under the harbour authority emblem. "Andrew's going away for a few days soon, so if you need anything river related, give me a call." She winked, before leaning forward to reach for the engine controls.

Jess's departure left my dingy rocking in her wake and a long-forgotten sensation in my stomach.

***

First Light was moored about one hundred meters downstream of the 'new arrival.' I decided to take the opportunity to have a close-up look on my way back - perhaps admire my reflection in the pristine paintwork. Approaching, I saw what looked like an animated conversation taking place high on the bridge with the shaking of heads and a figure pacing to and fro. I guess even when cosseted by vast wealth, smooth seamless living was not always attainable, and stress and drama always a possibility, perhaps even an inevitability.

The deck crew, some hanging from harnesses, were washing the vessel, soaping off the salt, rinsing, and drying the bright work and windows. It seemed like a huge undertaking to me. I wondered how they felt knowing that almost as soon as they had finished, it would require doing again. Still, they were well-paid, I assumed, and getting to travel the world in that way must have its advantages.

The tide carried me down the towering yacht's starboard side, offering me fleeting glimpses through shining stainless-steel portholes into immaculate cabins, cushions being arranged and plumped by a not so plump stewardess. Passing the stern, a large transom door, levered open on hydraulic rams, lay flat just above the water like a raised beach. Inside, racks of water skis, wake boards, and diving equipment filled the space - all pristine and immaculate, looking as if never used. My gawping complete, I let the current continue to carry me down towards my own, more austere abode. While smaller than my new neighbour, and with far fewer cushions for sure, she'll do for now.

***

After making the bed, which was a jumble of tangled sheets and duvet as a result of the piercing four A.M. wake-up call from my pager the night before, I busied myself with more domestic chores until it was time to warm up the engines and slip the lines. Crabbing sideways away from the moorings, I pointed *First Light* in the direction of the village of Dittisham, a few miles upstream.

The River was quiet and cold, pleasure boats of all kinds safely tucked away for the winter months in marinas and shipyards. The *Higher Ferry* plying its trade was my only threat as I headed upstream. Some invisible internal mechanism clawed it along two guide wires, each as thick as a man's arm. Every completed crossing leading to another, the final destination always elusively behind it.

Something was in the back of my mind, tapping away, an omission or oversight. It came to me as I passed the Royal Naval College, perched high on a hill above me from where it commanded an uninterrupted view over the lower stretch of river. I hadn't shown myself as *unavailable* for the next few hours on the fire station's ready board. Hoping to catch someone there who could take me off call, I rooted around on the chart table for my mobile; then the charger, because the phone was inevitably flat. I had to wait for a few minutes for the electrons to do whatever it is they do before dialling the fire station. Fingers crossed, I wouldn't need to turn back and trudge up the hill.

"Yes?"

Knowing the line was rarely, if ever used by the public, Kemp had developed a telephone manner which stretched the meaning of *terse* to its limits.

"Boss, it's Matt. Can I sign off for three or four hours?"

"Let me see." He paused. "Yes, should be fine this afternoon."

"Great, thanks."

I was already lowering the handset away from my ear, knowing Kemp would just hang up, when I faintly heard him continue.

"The police are here with me. The man you and Chris pulled out of that house didn't make it.

"That's a shame."

"There has been a question raised over the cause of death. We need you both to write out a statement for the inquest describing your part in the job last night. The sooner the better. Can you do it this evening?"

"Of course. I will find Chris later, and we will leave it on your desk."

I waited, but this time, true to form, he'd hung up.

My thoughts turned to the man from last night as *First Light* chugged steadily up-river, passing dormant shipyards and getting occasional glimpses of majestic houses interspersed in the trees.

I had purposefully given little thought to any of the casualties I had encountered, whether in fires, car wrecks, or any of the other tragic situations the fire service responds to. You did what you could for them in the moment and then did your best to forget them. For the most part, this technique worked for me, or it had, right up to the point where the sheer horror of traumatic death of someone close to me had shattered my ability to remain calm and dispassionate. From that moment on, I was of little use to anyone when the chips were down, hence two years bumping into the riverbanks and canal locks of Europe.

Although sorry to hear that the casualty had not survived, I was in no small way grateful to him for the part he played in perhaps bringing me closer to some sort of emotional balance. Either that, or I was just getting better at burying my emotions deeper. For the record, I was fine with both.

Lunch was adequate and lengthy. The cosy log fire and picture window looking out over this stretch of the river proved hard to wrench myself away from. Daylight was being replaced by winter evening gloom by the time *First Light* was snugly back on her mooring. My phone was ringing on the chart table when I re-entered the warm wheelhouse; bow and stern lines neatly secured, and the decks rinsed with fresh water. I picked it up, the familiar number on the screen evaporating any contentment which had accrued during the afternoon. With a sigh I stepped back outside into the cockpit, the still ringing phone held unanswered at my side.

A faint hum of generators drifted over to me from my near neighbour. Its cavernous transom garage was now firmly closed, revealing the name, '*Natasha*' emblazoned across the stern. The letters were depicted in what looked like gold and accented with neon lights scrolling through the colours of the rainbow as I watched. I found myself apologizing to *First Light*. Her battered wooden name plate with flaking varnish just didn't cut it now that the neighbourhood had gone upscale. The second project, after the recalcitrant outboard motor.

The ringing stopped. But not for long. The same number repeated itself on the screen as it rang again. Reluctantly I tapped the throbbing green icon and raised the phone to my ear.

"Yes?"

"You need to address this, not ignore it." The voice on the line was dispassionate, the nature of his job infusing his words. Numbers, black and white. No room for interpretation.

"I am working on it," I said, "I know I missed the last three months, but I can catch them up. Can you just give me a little longer?"

"I'm sorry Mr. Curtis, but it's not how this works. The terms were explained to you when you took out the loan and you are behind with three payments already. The bank has instructed us to recover what we can, which means any assets you own, up to and including the boat."

His mention of *First Light* caused an invisible weight to push down on me.

"How long have I got?"

"Someone will be down your way in the next few days. You are going to require at least the arrears for them, or your boat will be repossessed."

I didn't question how they knew where I was. It wouldn't have been too hard to track me down, given the paperwork involved in returning across the channel from France. And it wasn't as if I was trying to hide. He was right, I was well aware the payments for *First Light* had to remain uninterrupted. I had hoped my savings would have carried me a little further towards summer when I might make some more money. But they hadn't.

Like a few other things, the issue of my declining funds had been pushed aside. It had been a shadow lurking in the background of every day, glanced at, but not illuminated with the hard light of reality. Until now.

Sophie and I had bought First Light together and moved straight on board, friends and family shaking their heads in bewilderment. A tidal berth on a Thames backwater had become our new home, the overpriced rented flat abandoned as soon as was legally decent. We became accustomed to having the sounds of the city in one ear, loud, but not enough to drown out the raucous calls of gulls and waders in the other, as they squabbled for morsels in the mud. The tide came and went to a rhythm of its own, alternately exposing, then covering the birds dining table and gently lowering our home onto the mud. Breaking free of its sucking grip with each incoming tide had never failed to make her smile. We loved it, and every spare moment, along with most of our salaries, had been put into First Light. Not one corner of the boat didn't carry some memory of Sophie. The idea of losing my last tangible link to her, was difficult to contemplate.

***

The wind and rain of a fast-moving depression began lashing the town later that evening, a suitable accompaniment for frame of mind. As I walked up the hill towards the fire station to write my report on the previous night's job, the reality of my financial situation finally sank home. No matter how I viewed it, keeping ownership of *First Light* beyond the next few days was looking increasingly unlikely.

With the paperwork completed, a glance out of the station door confirmed that the rain had refused to give up. No lightening of the weather or my mood was in sight, so going to the pub seemed the only realistic option.

FIVE

Vladimir looked morosely out of the window from his lofty perch on the bridge of *Natasha*. Raindrops splattering on the glass partially obscured the yellow lights of Dartmouth and the grey river was corrugated by random gusts of wind. It was now thirty-nine hours since the helicopter went missing. The weather outside did nothing to improve his disposition.

They should've found it last night. But the hydrophone trailing astern of the *Natasha* for much of the night had not picked up anything other than the usual strange clicks and rumbles of marine life going about its business. Certainly nothing like the regular 'ping' they had been expecting.

"The transmitter has an underwater range of up to five miles, and we covered a lot of ground last night. Either the equipment you put onboard was somehow damaged in the crash, or the helicopter wasn't anywhere near where you thought it would be when the charge detonated," Victor said, from his seat on the raised leather bench lining the back wall of the bridge.

Vladimir remained looking out across the windswept river, going over the events of the previous night and wondering what else could go wrong before he replied.

The boxes had been secured onboard. Three had been tied down to the rear floor, a further three strapped to the seats running along back of the passenger compartment. The pilot had remained seated with the rotors turning, his attention focused on a thick manual open on his lap, checking the positioning of the heavy boxes didn't take the machine out of its centre of gravity limitations. Unobserved, Vladimir had slipped backwards into the darkness where he attached the Velcro belt with its slim charge, detonator, and delay timer around the tail boom. Vicious rotor blades had scythed the air inches from his head.

Walking back over the lawn, he was told that Dimitri had changed his mind about going. Powerless to do anything about it, Vladimir had watched as the helicopter noisily ripped itself off the grass, hesitating briefly, as if unsure this was a good idea, before finding confidence from somewhere and tipping forward, clawing its way into the night.

Vladimir sighed at his reflection in the bridge window of the *Natasha*. Not only was Dimitri still alive, but thanks to the lack of signal from the acoustic transmitter, they were now faced with the near impossible task of trying to find a needle in a haystack.

He turned to look at Victor. A comrade in arms from the weeks and months spent fighting in Chechnya, battle hardened and brutal, they had a mutual respect for each other.

Fashioned from countless forays together into the heart of darkness, their experiences and actions served to isolate them in their friendship. When the inevitable war crimes lawyers came too close, Victor sought, and was offered sanctuary by Vladimir and Dimitri. The official position he held on board *Natasha* was as assistant engineer, but his general demeanour and blank stare discouraged any requests for him to assist with oil changes.

"Either way Victor, this is a mess, but giving up is not an option," Vladimir finally answered.

Despite this determined outlook, the only plan they managed to come up with, sketchy at best, was to use the yacht's depth sounders and fish finding equipment to look for possible targets in the admittedly vague search area. Comparing any targets with the known obstructions marked on the charts, a quick dive could be made to investigate. The depths in this part of the Channel averaged around seventy feet and although it had been many years since Vladimir had donned a SCUBA set, the type of training he had undergone in a previous life was not the sort that would ever leave you.

Their search area though, as they had discovered last night, happened to be in a zone of high fishing activity. Long strings of crab pots terminating in bright orange marker buoys. Nearby trawlers occasionally encroaching close enough to these vulnerable traps to elicit loud calls on the radio, warnings to steer clear. It was also a vast area to search with their limited equipment and given that the helicopter might not even be in it, Vladimir realized, unless luck played a part, they could spend months looking to no avail.

He had also been reminded by the Captain of *Natasha,* that Maritime regulations decreed vessels their size were required to continually transmit course and position data when at sea by means of AIS, *Automatic Identification System.* This enabled them to be tracked by the various authorities who regularly monitor the waters. What's more, Vladimir was irritated to learn, they could be seen by anybody else who logged into *marinetraffic.com.*

Last night's repeated heading changes had already piqued the interest of Falmouth Coastguard, with a radio call to check if all was well. He was sure that continued use of the vessel in this manner would result in further investigation into their activities. Yachts like this were usually anchored off St Martin or Nassau at this time of year, not performing grid searches off the south Devon coast.

It was clear to Vladimir, continuing to use the yacht for anything other than a base at this point was not realistic. He knew he had to find another approach and given the amount of fishing gear they had encountered during the night, Vladimir concluded that *fishermen* were the place to start. Surmising that seafarers, the world over would have similar habits when weather-bound, a quick google search informed him there were upwards of ten bars and pubs dotted around the riverfront of Dartmouth, all within walking distance of each other. Vladimir, with enough cash in his pocket, didn't think he would have much of a problem finding someone to talk to.

The tender dropped him smartly on the town quay, fenders barely squeaking with the coming together. After instructing the two-man crew to return and pick him up in a couple of hours, Vladimir headed along the embankment, his head down and coat collar up as some small defence against the rain.

The Pub holding the most promise for him was a short walk down the river front. It occupied the corner of the three-story block with a curved frontage looking out over the estuary and faced the full brunt of any storms with South in the title. The result of years of such storms had left the façade somewhere between weather-beaten and decrepit with the brickwork pointing absent in as many places as it survived. Streaks of rust from the ancient steel swinging sign proclaiming '*The Dartmouth Arms*' to be a free house, dribbled their way towards the ground. On a breezy day, the sign's hinges did a good job of competing with the constant racket from the ever-present seagulls. That said, the interior was warm and welcoming, at least to the locals who tended to occupy the end of the bar furthest from the door and who would cast blank glances at any strangers who might have the temerity to enter their narrow world.

The door squeaked loudly in one direction before banging shut in the other. All eyes turned towards him. The burble of overlapping conversations briefly muted as quick assessment was taken - conclusions jumped to. Dismissed as 'not one of us' the burbling soon returned to its former volume. Vladimir smiled to himself as he edged closer to the bar. Small towns were small towns wherever they happened to be, and to be overlooked as unimportant was a complement in his world.

"Whiskey ginger, *Chivas,* if you keep it, no ice." His Russian accent, little softened over the years, further marked his status as an interloper.

Vladimir looked around while he waited for his drink. The ceiling behind the bar had dozens of personalized pewter tankards hanging from brass hooks. On the wall behind the barman, faded sepia photographs of boats, long since forgotten, shared the space with inverted bottles of spirits and racks of peanuts. Roasted or salted - your choice.

At the far end of the pub sat a dozen or so people at low tables loosely grouped around a blazing open fire. Logs lined up on both sides of the fireplace like dormant soldiers, ready to sacrifice their calories to the room when the call came. A glass was plonked in front of him, payment proffered, change not required. Vladimir eased himself away from his initial perch and took up a position further down the bar. Here, he was closer to both the fire and the patrons whose dress and speech made them a more likely target than the well-groomed set quaffing wine nearer the door.

His eyes passed casually over the nautical paraphernalia affixed to the walls as he tried to tune his ears into the multiple conversations around him. One picture, in particular, caught his eye - an old aerial photograph of a tanker, its back broken on a reef, oil spewing into the sea. A small brass plate at the bottom of the frame identified the vessel as the *SS TORREY CANYON -1967*. The germ of an idea started to form in his mind, still a long shot, but worthy of further thought.

He nursed his drink for a while, the conversations ebbing and flowing around him but affording no access to outsiders. A direct approach would have to be made.

"Excuse me for interrupting," he ventured, "but would any of you be fishermen?"

The group he had selected were nearest the fire, the gap at their table being the main reason for his choice. A short silence followed his words.

"Pretty much all of us mate, except these two light weights, they couldn't hack it."

This from a squat tattooed bear of a man sporting a faded blue cap which gave the impression it was rarely removed. Laughter erupted from Dave's statement, the two in question having the good nature to allow their expressions to concede that this was indeed the case.

I looked with interest at the newcomer standing before us, noticing the compact form, energy contained but confidence not. It dawned on me that he was one of the figures I had seen pacing the bridge of *Natasha* earlier today.

"Take a seat if you want," manners dictated, as I gestured to the empty chair.

"Thank you. My name is Vladimir."

I shook the offered hand, which was firm with hidden strength, fingers reminiscent of the rods found running through concrete.

"Matt," I countered. "This is Chris, Dave, Lucas; I can't remember the others."

More laughter, but not from Vladimir, whose eyes remained expressionless.

"So, you're looking for a fisherman?" I prompted.

"I have an interest in fishing. I like to try to do some wherever I am, if time permits, and find that local knowledge adds considerably to the catch."

"Sorry Vlad, you've fallen in with the wrong crowd at the wrong time of year," I pointed out. "These guys are all commercial fishermen, dragging nets and scooping up sea-life on an industrial scale. The rod and line boys are laid up for the winter. No call for them until the tourists return in the spring."

Vladimir pondered this information, sipping at his drink.

"Nevertheless, I would like to fish." His gazed swept around the table. "Could someone be persuaded to take me, perhaps for some day trips out to Start Point?"

Dave, the pot-bellied Captain of the *Maid Marion,* one of the inshore crabber fleet, piped up again.

"You won't be going anywhere for the next twenty-four hours mate. The shipping forecast is keeping us all tied to the dock until this depression blows through. When it settles down, all the boats will be fully engaged with their own gear."

Another sip, as Vladimir digested this statement.

"Well it seems I must miss out this time. That is disappointing. I would pay well to be go fishing for a few days."

"Hey Matt, why don't you take him in your tub?" Lucas suggested loudly, "You know those waters, or at least you used to, before you decided to go all 'Red Adair' on us."

I couldn't deny that the thought had occurred to me, particularly after the offer of payment was out there, hanging in the air. Still, I hesitated, unsure why my instincts were telling me something was off. It was an odd request at this time of year and any seasoned fisherman would know that. But, mostly, I questioned why someone connected in any way to the pile of floating wealth moored mid river was seeking his solutions in a down market pub. Whatever person or organization was sitting behind *Natasha* surely had access to shore-side agents and a myriad of staff to organize such things as impromptu fishing trips. No, I didn't buy it and was not ready to jump in and offer my services right away. Ignoring Lucas's suggestion, I stood.

"My round, same again everyone?"

Nods of agreement from around the table. Nothing like a spell of bad weather to lift this particular pub's bottom line. The evening crowd was thinning gradually, my route to the bar unimpeded.

"Same again, Pete, except for me and Chris. We are still on call, so we'll switch to your finest orange and lemonade please."

Vladimir appeared silently at my side as glasses were replenished.

"You own a boat?" he inquired.

Hard to deny after Luca's utterance.

"Yes, it's not in quite the same league as yours, but a boat, nonetheless," I replied. I could see him computing the fact that I had connected him in some way to *Natasha*.

"Alas, that fine vessel belongs to my employer, I am merely a guest."

"Can't they take you fishing if you promise not to get blood on the decks?" I suggested. "I'm sure there's even a chef or two on hand to deal with the catch."

Vladimir either didn't recognize my humour or chose to ignore it, not an uncommon reaction.

He persisted, "*Natasha* is not the most suitable vessel for my needs. I require something smaller, and there is also the matter of local knowledge, of which you have some, no?"

"There you go Matt," Pete interrupted, placing a tray of drinks in front of us. "This one's fine, but you should clear your tab before much longer."

I smiled reassuringly at him, reminded for the second time today of my increasingly precarious financial position. *Thanks.* I turned back to Vladimir.

"What exactly do you have in mind, if I decide I can help you?" I capitulated somewhat, deciding not to throw away the chance of some ready cash before hearing this man out. Pete would be happy, at least.

"I would like to charter your boat, assuming she is seaworthy of course- *'ouch,' I thought, 'seems I'm not the only one able to get a dig in'* -for a few days, a week at most. I would like to fish and perhaps some other activities which all are perfectly legal. In return, I can pay you one thousand pounds a day, plus expenses. We would come back to port before dark each evening and I do not need to stay onboard overnight, as you are aware."

Two things became apparent to me as we stood there at the bar, drinks slowly fizzing their way towards flatness. One good, the other not so much. Firstly, here was an opportunity to become financially solvent for a good while which would be a big relief. Secondly, there was not the slightest chance Vladimir's desire to be at sea had anything to do with fishing.

I had no idea what his motives were, but a large financial carrot had been dangled in front of me, and I was leaning towards taking as big a bite as possible. I thought, mistakenly as it turned out, that with the addition of few conditions of my own, I could go along with this pretext for as long as was profitable, and legal.

Picking up the tray of drinks I said, "Let me take this over to the guys, then we can find a quiet table and talk about this a bit."

We relocated to the far end of the pub nearer the door. A table recently vacated, still covered with dregs of *Pino Grigio* in lipstick stained glasses holding down empty packets of high-end crisps. No peanuts down this end. I had done some fast thinking in the short distance travelled.

"Okay, I will take you *fishing*, but here's the deal. Tomorrow's out. The weather is too bad." I continued, "When we *do* get out there, you can do what you want, but the decisions regarding weather and seamanship will be mine and mine alone. Cash payment at the end of each day. The slightest whiff of anything illegal, and we head straight back in. And, you should know I am not a professional skipper. My boat is not registered for commercial use, so this has to be on an unofficial basis."

Vladimir regarded me from across the table, a glint of what may have been amusement in his eyes. The door behind us banged closed behind a departing couple.

"But you do possess some local knowledge, that is correct?"

"Yes," I replied, "rusty, but still there."

"Then I accept your terms. Come alongside *Natasha* the day after tomorrow at 07:00. I will be waiting." Vladimir pushed his chair back, crushed my hand briefly, and was gone.

This time the door didn't bang.

SIX

I woke the next morning with a sense of unease. Halyards clanking against nearby masts and wavelets slapping abruptly and rhythmically against the hull of *First Light* had woken me. The gentle rocking of last night had turned into something altogether less soothing with the Atlantic depression doing its thing, and I was glad to be securely ensconced in harbour.

Coffee from a chipped mug bearing the faded emblem of London Fire and Rescue Service lifted my heart rate but had little effect on my unease as I thought about what I had committed myself to last night.

On the surface it seemed like a good deal, spending a few days cruising in the bay in return for an envelope of crisp notes to plug the leaks in my finances. However, I had got the distinct impression from Vladimir last night, that my 'terms and conditions' where inconsequential to him. Why not allow the 'boat guy' to think he had some control over events if it got Vladimir what he needed? I also realized I would have to square away my absence from the duty board at the fire station for an unknown number of days, not a conversation with Kemp which I was looking forward to.

***

A short distance down river, coffee was also being consumed, albeit in superior chinaware. Vladimir lowered his cup and reached across the table for a croissant, fresh from the galley, as light and fluffy as any to be found in the cafés of Paris.

"Do any of your crew own a drone?" he asked, the question directed at the yacht's Captain, seated on the other side of the glass table in the main Saloon. Impressionist art surrounded them, a combination of the bold and understated.

The Captain stared quizzically across at Vladimir.

"Sure. We have a couple. The crew like to spend their wages on something."

"Tell them I need to borrow one. The best they've got. Buy it if they are reluctant."

The quizzical look remained so Vladimir enlightened him.

"It has occurred to me that any fuel and oils on the helicopter would inevitably leak out. If that process has not already completed, there's a chance of spotting the slick on the surface. It's a long shot again, given the small quantities of fluids involved, but even small amounts may be visible from above. Therefore, the need for a drone."

"I agree," the Captain said nodding, "that might work providing we're not too late. If the fuel leaked only from the tank's breather, it would be a slow process. And a drone will certainly cover a larger area than we can. This weather is not going to help though. The forecast only shows improvement overnight tonight, with a short period of settled conditions for two or three days before the next low tracks in from the Atlantic. Pretty typical for this part of the world in December. Shall I make us ready for sea tomorrow?"

"No, not this time. You will be pleased to know you are 'off the hook' as you English say. I organized a local boat to take me out. I will be taking Victor with me." Vladimir rose, dropping the remains of his croissant onto a plate. "Now I am going to speak with our boss."

The Captain remained seated as Vladimir moved silently across the thick carpet in the direction of the Bridge. His relief was twofold; pleased not to be drawing further attention to the yacht with continued suspicious movements, but even happier to enjoy a few days free from the presence of two people who, quite frankly, chilled him to the bone.

***

The same weather system which was buffeting Dartmouth was also beginning to form early morning puddles in the gutters of Tinworth street, Lambeth, the London headquarters of the Nation Crime Agency.

Deborah Hanse, lead investigator from the NCA's Financial Investigation Unit, sat at a desk with newly formed habits picked up during her recently ended Costa Rica holiday in front of her. Recent enough for her to be still battling jetlag and clinging wistfully to the idea of a healthier lifestyle, hence the Coconut water and acai bowl slowly trickling condensation onto a brown paper napkin on her desk. Across from her sat agent Richard Shepperton, not someone who would ever be caught dead trying to pronounce 'acai' correctly. He looked on with faint amusement, the taste of his full English fry up a not too distant pleasant memory.

"So, bring me up to speed with the Dimitri case," she commanded, anxious to gather up the numerous threads that had been left hanging whilst on obligatory annual leave. '*Take it or lose it,*' came the directive from above, '*no more carrying over.*'

"Not great news I'm afraid, Ma'am," Richard ventured. "Two nights ago, his helicopter, which we had under lock and key in a hangar at Bournemouth airport, was stolen and I would bet my pension that his pet psychopath, Vladimir Volkov had a hand in it-"

"Any way of proving that?"

"It's all conjecture at this point, Ma'am."

Debora frowned. "And where is the helicopter now?"

"We don't know. Southampton flight information service, which provides Radar coverage in that area, had a brief unidentified target in the early hours of yesterday morning. Unfortunately, it was fleeting. They think it subsequently descended to an altitude their equipment can't pick up, which, I'm informed is tree-top height. As you know, Dimitri employs an ex-soviet special forces pilot and I imagine low-level flying on a dark winter's night would be at the lower end of his capabilities."

"Any news on Dimitri?"

"Dimitri flew British Airways first class out of Gatwick to Larnaca, Cypress later the same day-"

"So, Dimitri has left the UK," Debora mused. "I think we have enough on him for me to persuade the Home office to cancel his visa, should he be tempted to return."

She paused. "What I don't understand is why they felt the need to run the risk of stealing back their helicopter."

Debora had eaten a few spoons of her breakfast during the briefing, her tongue now stained bright purple. Richard pondered whether or not to tell her.

"And what about Vladimir?" she asked, "Did you lose him too?"

He made up his mind regarding the purple tongue.

"No, Ma'am. The surveillance team picked him up leaving the Hyde park address yesterday morning. He took the Paddington train down to the West Country. Truro initially, then the connection through to Falmouth. From Falmouth train station he took a taxi to the port and was collected from the landing pier by speedboat, which ferried him out to a rather nice super yacht anchored in Carrick Roads-"

"Does this yacht have a heli-deck, perchance?" interjected Debora with the obvious question.

"It does, but it was empty. The Port Authorities down there say no helicopter has landed on board since she arrived. They also gave me the vessels name."

He flipped open his notebook and continued. "The motor yacht *Natasha* registered in the Cayman Islands. They weighed anchor yesterday, and *Marinetraffic.com* took over surveillance from there. She is currently in Dartmouth, about ninety miles up the coast. The team are looking into the ownership of the yacht, but as you know, that can be a long and fruitless pastime, the way things are in those offshore centres.

Currently, we are working on the theory that the *Natasha* is connected in some way to Dimitri, and Vladimir is onboard. Although, why it would be in Dartmouth is unclear."

Debora sipped her coconut water. The Dimitri case was just one of many she was tasked with overseeing and the resources available to her were spread thinly across all of them. The investigation would continue, but now that he had left the country and would be refused permission to return, Debora would find it hard to justify continuing with expensive surveillance on one of Dimitri's employees. She was loath to stand down the watchers entirely though as the antics with the helicopter intrigued her.

"Who do we have in that part of the world who can keep an eye on the yacht and try to ascertain if Vladimir is still on board?" she asked.

"No one from Financial. I had our team come back up to London when it set sail, and they were re-assigned. But Drugs were running an operation down in the West Country which has just gone tits - sorry Ma'am, gone pear shaped. I could ask them if they can loan us someone if you like?"

Unfazed, Deborah responded. "Do that, ask them if we can borrow someone for a few days at least. Make sure you fully brief them on Vladimir's violent history and capabilities though. They need to keep a respectable distance from this guy."

Richard nodded his agreement.

Before the steady decline in the relationship between the UK and Russian intelligence services, the NCA had requested; and, much to their surprise, received information on Vladimir and Dimitri. By no means complete or comprehensive, the thin files had nevertheless given an insight into the two men.

There was a type of person, not often encountered in civilized western society, who, whether by nature, nurture, or more likely a combination of both, played by a different rule book when it came to violence and evildoing. People who were capable of acts incomprehensible to the general public. During his scramble for riches, Dimitri was such a person - less so now that his wealth allowed him to maintain his distance from the coal face.

In Vladimir however, he had found someone more than happy to take up the slack. A veteran of the fabled 'Spetsnaz', a special forces division of the Russian military not dissimilar in remit to the UK's SAS, Vladimir was highly trained and in no small measure de-humanized by the experience of fighting in the forest's and streets of Chechnya and Bosnia. He was the perfect choice as Dimitri's fixer, with no qualms in carrying out his new boss's often ruthless requests.

Vladimir was approached by Dimitri in early 2010, as the Spetsnaz Units were (briefly as it turned out) being disbanded and personnel reassigned to other units. Dimitri's timing was serendipitous for them both. Not thrilled with the re-organization, Vladimir was also happy to sidestep nascent enquiries into excessive force and brutality during raids he had led in the housing projects of Grozny against Chechen separatists. 'Which must have been saying something', Richard thought, 'given the barbaric reputation of all participants in that particular global flash point.' Respectable distance was undoubtedly the wisest choice, for now at least.

***

Jake's run took him through the southern part of the city, its sea faring tradition apparent at every turn and in every street name. Much of the cityscape was familiar to him, including the navy dock yards, where several his missions had either been trained for or departed from. As he settled into his pace, the inclines of Citadel road deepened his breathing. Rain and wind kept his route clear of pedestrians and traffic was light and mostly avoidable as he paced himself through Millbay park and on towards the Hoe, the frustration of failure fuelling each stride.

'Weeks of undercover work developing contacts, digging for names in a way that didn't result in a bullet in the head, aimed at identifying someone in the underbelly of the region's organized crime who might be turned; who had enough information to balance the risk of trying to turn them.' The operation had, until recently, exceeded expectations. A potential informant, far higher up the food chain than Jake could have hoped for, had made an approach. Details, lots of them, in exchange for immunity and relocation. A deal had been reached, in principle, subject to the information being as described of course.

Jake's now deceased informant had travelled out of Plymouth for the meet-up, his face too well-known to risk contact there. An anonymous bed and breakfast forty miles away in an even more anonymous sleepy village was his choice. A good night's sleep before long held trusts could be shattered in the privacy of the near deserted, floral themed breakfast room. That had been their plan, at least.

The night before the meet, however, with a precautionary surveillance put in place, Jake arrived to relieve his colleague, finding him asleep in the car at the end of the street. Rapping on side window had woken the watcher at about the same time the fire trucks were eagerly turning into the road. And just like that, the inability of a young policeman to keep himself awake had ensured all the efforts, the risks, had been for nothing.

Jake had no doubt the informant had been compromised. He was convinced the autopsy would show a cause of death other than from the effects of fire. There were just too many coincidences for him to believe otherwise. The claim from the house owner that her guest had had a visitor late that evening - her uncertainty as to when he left.

Jake had also walked through the property once the fire service had given him the go ahead. In contrast to the rest of the house, which was immaculate, the room in which his contact had died, gave every indication that it had been turned upside down by someone searching for something. Firefighters could make a mess, there was no doubt about that, but the room had been torn apart before their arrival'.

Digging deeper as the slope of Hoe Road steepened before flattening out into the park, Jake's anger at the constable - given the job of guarding against just such a possibility - resurfaced. He couldn't help but recall a time when he would willingly have sold his soul for the chance to close his eyes for even a minute.

Three days in a shallow scrape in the sand, taking turns to watch the structure five hundred meters in front and slightly below. Cloud cover over the target hampering the preferred use of satellite imagery - boots on the ground the only option.

Three stationary, sun baked days, and freezing nights, drinking little and eating less. All unavoidable movements reduced to slow motion so as not to catch the eye of a wandering goat herd or conscientious guard. Fly covered plastic bags, containing their own faeces lining the extremities of their existence - leaving their shallow indentation in the ground not possible even for their basic needs.

Jake wished he could put the policeman there.

It was on the third day, eyes gritty with windblown dust and sleep deprivation when the three-man patrol literally stepped on them. Two died instantly - the sound from their suppressed Glocks sounding outrageously loud after the silence. The third got closer, shouting in alarm before Jake's knife ended the outburst with a wet gurgle.

Another two days of headlong evasion, the mission fatally compromised. Muscles weakened by the inactivity protesting - struggling to carry them - as they found their way to the extraction point, somehow evading the pursuers who would surely follow.

Compared with that, staying awake for a few hours in the comfort of a car did not seem too much of an ask.

Jake's phone rang, pulling him back to the present.

"I need you to go to the town of Dartmouth, Jake. It's just up the coast from you, as I'm sure you know."

Hearing Richard's voice, Jake stifled his surprise as the depth of his breathing slowly returned to normal. He had expected the call to be an order summoning him back to London for a debrief on the cluster fuck Operation Albion had turned into. And knowing organizations as he did, he was fully expecting that debrief to lead to a desk for him, for some time to come.

"Is it connected to Albion?"

"That operation is shut down. This is unconnected."

Jake stared past the red and white exclamation mark of Smeaton's Tower, towards Plymouth Sound where a grey warship was being unleashed from the attendant tugs. The ship seemed to be sensing its freedom like a dog arriving at the park. Seeing the vessel heading to the sea beyond the breakwater prompted more memories of his past life to jostle for position in his mind. Pangs of nostalgia, however, were easily trumped by a kaleidoscope of images he had no desire to revisit.

Richard continued, "We just need some eyes on the ground in Dartmouth for a day or two. Most likely no longer than that. I'm about to email you a short brief which will bring you up to speed with what we know. Get there today, if you can, but be discreet. We are not sure quite what, if anything, we are dealing with here."

Jake ended the call with an assurance, "I will head there this morning, Sir."

Resigning himself to the fact that the remaining two miles of his run would have to wait, he turned and began to retrace his steps through the puddles, happy that at least the prospect of a desk had receded somewhat, for the time being.

SEVEN

I managed to catch Kemp on his home phone, the conversation going better than expected.

"That's fine Matt, we can do without you for a few days. Try make it to Wednesday evening's training session though. The Area Manager is coming to give us input regarding diversity and equality in the workplace. Wouldn't want you to miss that."

Kemp couldn't understand why the fire service thought that learning about other cultures and their sensibilities was a better use of our two hours a week allocated training time than actually getting hands on with our equipment and procedures. He took people as he found them and was firmly of the opinion that other cultures, for the most part, sucked. Particularly the ones which we were supposed to walk on eggshells around.

I had received plenty of input on diversity and equality when in London. While it had been interesting and informative, I had no desire to sit through another power point lecture. It would be amusing though, to see Kemp being dragged, little by little, into the twenty-first century. Maybe I would try to get back in time.

With my way now clear to taking Vladimir on his mystery mission, I once again slipped the mooring lines, mooching leisurely along the river, engines in dead slow. Rain splattered against the wheelhouse windows. The wiper in front of me provided intermittent glimpses of my goal as I headed unhurriedly in the direction of the fuelling barge.

A battered rusty trawler, flying the tattered remains of the French national flag, was moored on the starboard side of the barge, taking advantage of being weather-bound to top off its tanks. Two of its crew were stood on the fuel barge, sucking on cigarettes directly below a sign demanding in bold red font: '*No Smoking*'. 'The French,' what can you do?

With the port side of the barge and its diesel pump available to me, it was the work of fifteen minutes and an eye watering swipe of my credit card for *First Light* to be similarly replete. Andrew, surveying his fiefdom, must have been watching from his office as I glided, helm fully over, engines in slow ahead, across the tide away from the fuelling barge. My phone, buzzing its way over the chart table, was saved from plummeting over the edge by the charging lead tugging it to a halt.

"Morning, Matt," he said enthusiastically. "There is a berth available on the town quay for the night if you want it. No one will arrive today in this weather. It will be a more comfortable night for you there, and that way you can easily come for dinner without the need for a wet tender ride. I'll come and take your lines."

Highly efficient these navy types.

***

The flat was warm and inviting when I arrived that evening, two bottles poorly presented in a carrier bag hanging by my side. Anna's fragrant hug was followed by Jess's firm handshake and sweet smile.

"Nice to see you again, Matt."

"You two have met?" enquired Anna, before we were interrupted by a medium-sized dog of indeterminate breeding jumping up at me, desperate in its quest not to be ignored by this newcomer. Andrew scooped Bailey up and placed him, still quivering, on a comfy looking armchair; a stern glance and pointed finger enough to hold him in place, for now at least.

"Sorry Matt, he's young, tends to get over excited. Take a seat, what can I offer you to drink?

"Whatever is open will be fine, thanks."

I glanced around as I waited for the drink. The smallness of the space was more than compensated for by an over-sized bay window overlooking the river. During the day, the view must be spectacular. Pictures of Andrew in various locations, uniforms, and grey ships - a common theme - adorned one wall. A low-set table in front of the large window supported flowers in a vase and silver framed photographs of Andrew and Anna. The backgrounds were mostly local and recognizable to me. It was unclear how this low island of homeliness survived the dog.

I sat in the floral-patterned sofa, Jess plonking herself down next to me. With her legs curled up beneath her, she gave the impression that the surroundings were comfortable and familiar to her.

"Did I see you on a *Honda Fire Blade* the other day?" she asked.

"More than likely. I think I have the only one in town. You know your bikes."

"My brothers used to be mad on them. Some of it rubbed off. And I had a boyfriend who took me on the back of one for a short tour in Northern France, many years ago."

She shuddered briefly and I found myself hoping it was at the memory of the boyfriend, not the bike trip.

"I still have the helmet somewhere. Not the boyfriend though, thankfully," Jess continued as Andrew thrust glasses of white wine at us. "You cruised the canals over in France a bit, I hear?"

"Yes, France, Holland, Belgium. I kind of got lost over there for a while."

She listened with interest as I recounted the slow pace of life, long stretches of pretty countryside, interspersed at regular intervals with a procession of small, idyllic towns; most with resident gangs of ducks and swans, not shy about pecking on the hull to demand snacks. And the locks, generally tight and sedate, a bucolic change in elevation, but the occasional few, whose concrete scale and immense flow would terrify the uninitiated.

I could see Jess imagining the scenes as I described them. But to be truthful, much of the beauty to be found drifting along, taking each day as it came, had been lost on me, wrapped up as I had been, in my own misery. It was time to switch the conversation back to her, but little was forthcoming before we were summoned to the kitchen table for dinner.

Over the main course, a surprisingly delicious vegetable concoction, I told Andrew of my planned trip tomorrow, with a man from *Natasha*, which brought a quizzical look to his brow, but no further enquiry. The conversation inevitably turned to the stupid antics of our youth. Tales of adventures which often probed at the known parameters of good sense and occasionally blew straight through the more defined line of the law.

We had a good laugh at the recollection of me climbing out through the sunroof of Andrew's car one night, the wind of sixty miles an hour buffeting me as I gripped the wipers and slid down the windscreen and across the bonnet. The careful approach, headlights off, to within inches of the back of the truck on a local, unlit section of dual carriageway had allowed me to clamber between the two vehicles, a gap of black tarmac howling along beneath me - opening and closing as Andrew concentrated on keeping pace with truck without touching it. The manoeuvre, repeated in reverse had me back inside the car a few moments later, the pair of us hysterical with laughter.

Anna and Jess listened in silence, before wondering aloud how two people who on the surface at least, had turned out alright, could have been so moronic. We had no answer.

Dessert over, my offer of assistance in washing up was declined - insisted upon - and finally accepted. I found myself stood alongside Jess, passing her dried crockery which she unerringly knew where to put.

"Have you known Anna and Andrew long?" I asked, carefully handing her a glass water jug.

"Only since I started working on the river. They helped me find accommodation when I arrived in town, and we became friends."

When the chores were done, Jess and Anna plucked a lead and a handful of small plastic bags from the side table near the door and announced their departure to give the dog his evening walk. The obviously pre-planned move left the way clear for Andrew to thrust a generous glass of port into my hand and bluntly ask once again, why I had left London. There was little prospect of stalling him anymore, so moving towards the bay window while holding down the emotions which were rising within me, I told him.

***

The call was to a fire in a derelict warehouse in the East end, a known haunt of the homeless on cold nights. Our brief was received while standing next to the breathing apparatus control board, that unchanging landmark of my trade.

'Search the upper mezzanine, the driest and most likely place to find anyone sheltering from the weather, to make sure it was clear before firefighting operations began from outside. No point putting crews at risk if no-one was inside.' I described to Andrew the conditions we had encountered; not intolerable, nothing that concerned us or hampered our search.

'We had climbed the rickety stairs, going up one at a time and were faced with two old offices overlooking the warehouse below. Once the home of management, presumably bustling with activity with staff balancing

inventory, income, and orders; perhaps casting occasional glances down to the worker bees. Now though, after time and vandalism had taken their toll, little more than plywood divisions remained. Here was the apparent seat of the fire and the last place for us to look before exiting. Then came the decision - my decision - given the acceptable visibility and tolerable heat, to split up and take an office each.'

Ignoring the tears welling up and threatening to drown my voice, I continued.

Conditions were worsening, but still within our tolerance. It was almost enjoyable, doing what we were trained to do in conditions that allowed us to do it. Two small rooms to be searched, a clear exit behind us, piece of cake. Then came the splintering crash from the office I had directed my partner into. No response on the radio. A few fast paces took me from my compartment to next door. There was no sign of Sophie. Just a gap in the floor where the joists had collapsed, leaving splintered floorboards pointing towards the ceiling.

I had to stop speaking. Standing, I stared out of the bay window with unseeing eyes, my mind fully back in the warehouse, every detail of that night remained crisp and clear inside my head - undiminished by the passage of time and the constant re-runs, trying to put me in that damned office instead. Andrew remained silent on the sofa as I cooled my forehead against the windowpane.

"She fell to the ground floor," I said, finally breaking the deafening silence. "I got there at the same time as the emergency team I had requested. She had fallen onto the remnants of some industrial machine. A steel bar had penetrated the back of her head and exited through her face mask." Tears involuntarily streamed down my face.

Andrew let out a long breath.

"Your partner was female."

I looked at him, struggling to get myself back under control.

"Any of that port left?"

He topped us both up with a heavy slug each.

"She wasn't supposed to be there that night," I continued. "We shouldn't have been working together. A crewing shortage meant Sophie was sent to us from a neighbouring station to make up the numbers."

Andrew could see from my face that I hadn't finished. He remained quiet until I blurted it out.

"She was my fiancé."

He didn't say much after that. No wise words, no panacea to send me on my way. But the talking to someone who knew me had lifted the weight a little more. I had tried. The fire service had tried, but until recently, I had made scant progress at putting the events of that night to rest.

It was eleven P.M. by the time I carefully climbed back on board *First Light*, a little worse for wear after the best part of a bottle of Port. I had managed to leave without running into Jess or Anna, glad not to have to explain my red puffy eyes. The rain had stopped, and I could see stars appearing through the broken cloud. *First Light* was gently rolling through a handful of degrees, hinting at the possibility of a more restful night. Even the wind had eased. The loudest sound on the river now was the squawking of a few gulls jostling for position, not yet ready to retire for the evening.

***

Five hours later, I conceded the port may have been a mistake. With coffee dripping far too slowly through the machine, I sluggishly began nudging the day into the required direction. Spoilt for choice with a myriad of apps, I checked the weather online, keeping the BBC radio shipping forecast on in the background for old time's sake. The wind of the last few days had dropped, veered, and was now little more than an offshore breeze. That meant conditions in the bay, at least, should be fine, with maybe just an underlying swell to contend with.

Happy about the weather, I tenderly stepped ashore and walked the dark deserted streets to the only remaining bakery in town. Unsurprisingly, the door was locked. It was too early for the morning rush on rustic loaves encrusted with sesame seeds; some clinging on for dear life while the remainder leapt to the relative freedom found in the bottom of a paper bag. Undeterred, I banged loudly on the glass.

"Hygiene inspection. Open up!" I demanded.

The door was finally opened by Harry. In his immaculate whites Harry was as dedicated to carrying on the family tradition, as the new supermarket on the edge of town was dedicated to trying to stop him. My money was on Harry.

"Would you knock it off Matt, that's not even funny." He led the way back through the darkened shop to the attached baking area. Similarly, attired staff, blue hair nets under their white caps, bustled about and I doubted a thorough search would turn up even a misplaced raisin. He was right. I should really find some other way of annoying him since cleanliness was never going to be an issue here. I resolved to give it some thought.

A couple of pasties and some doughnuts would see us through the day at sea I thought, although I was hopeful Vladimir would come with a hamper. Still hot from the ovens, I carried my purchases in a brown paper sack back through the shop where my thanks were drowned out by the monster dough mixer churning up the day's profits.

Back on board *First Light*, I dug out my limited fishing equipment. Two seldom used trolling rods with vicious looking lures still attached, and some tangled mackerel lines was the extent of my collection. Vladimir's reaction to this meagre arsenal would at least give some insight into his claim to like fishing.

As the sun was just beginning to show itself over the hills of Kingswear, I began to feel surprisingly upbeat about the day, comfortable in my skin now that the coffee was doing its thing, and happy to be on the water as the new day unfolded.

EIGHT

Carefully, I approached *Natasha's* starboard aft quarter at the appointed time. Huge inflatable fenders had been hung over the side, apparently no chances being taken with paintwork until my boat handling skills had been assessed. Lines thrown to smartly dressed deck crew were made fast fore and aft and a section of topsides was hinged back, allowing access to *Natasha's* teak side decks.

"Come aboard." The Captain, I guessed from the four golden bars on either shoulder, greeted me. "Vladimir will be here shortly."

He offered his hand to help me across the gap created by the over-sized fenders and up onto the pristine deck. Blue plastic shoe covers to protect the teak were handed to me, along with the inference that they were not optional. We walked aft a little way to the stern, where comfy looking chairs were grouped around an ornate mahogany table. To one side, a pile of bulging equipment bags looked out of place.

"Would you like a coffee while we wait?"

"Sure. Thanks."

'Drinks on a super yacht?' Hard to refuse, even if it was only coffee, and I was just the help. The arrival of Vladimir however, put paid to both the drink and my idea of sinking into one of the chairs and pretending my finances had taken a major turn for the better.

"Let's go. Have those bags lowered down to us," - this to the Captain, not to me.

Vladimir hurried up the side deck and jumped nimbly down onto *First Light*. To my annoyance, someone was already in the small aft open cockpit looking into lockers and generally making himself at home.

"This is Victor. He will be coming with us."

I joined the duo, suddenly feeling uncomfortable with the presence of these people in my space. Maybe I should have given this a little more thought. Looking at Victor, I saw the same latent strength and blank eyes which I had seen in Vladimir. It started to dawn on me that I was in over my head with this pair and whatever they had in mind.

Three equipment bags were lowered down to us, two of them clunking heavily on the deck. I had been around compressed air cylinders long enough for that clunk to tell me they almost certainly contained diving gear. My misgivings rose further. Why tell me they want to fish if what they really wanted was to dive?

Vladimir looked expectantly at me. I shrugged. It was a bit too late to back out of our arrangement now, and for a thousand pounds they could spend the day pretending to be *Jacques Cousteau* for all I cared, so I started the engines and called up to the waiting deckhands for the lines to be released. Vladimir joined me in the wheelhouse, leaving Victor in the aft cockpit to rummage through the black bags. We steadily headed down stream, towards the river mouth where Dartmouth castle slid gradually past our starboard side.

The open mouths of the castle's canons, capable of spitting death and confusion in a bygone age were now stuffed with empty drinks bottles and greasy food wrappings. Sullen looking seagulls perched along their length. Nelson would have despaired.

Not feeling the need to ask permission, Vladimir was clicking away at my electronic chart plotter, entering co-ordinates onto the large-scale chart on the screen.

"Take us here." He gestured to the mark he had placed, about five miles East of Start point. "When we arrive, set your heading to follow this track." He pointed at the thin blue line marked on the plotter.

I looked closer. From the starting position, he had entered a track which ran close inshore past Start Point, and continued in a south-westerly direction, keeping a mile or so offshore.

"That's not the best area to be if you want to fish." I threw this out like chum, interested to hear his response.

"We will see," was all I got. So much for my sleuthing.

We cleared the harbour limits, the Castle ledge buoy leaning away from the current and passed the jagged topped, cormorant covered Blackstone rock, which showed no inclination to lean for anything. *First Light* alternately lifted then dropped her bow to each on - coming swell, while the weak early morning sun set about trying to banish the chill of the December morning. I adjusted the autopilot to take us to

Vladimir's unexplained dot on the chart; and my VHF radio to switch between channel sixteen - the initial call up and distress channel - and zero-six; the inter-vessel frequency used by fishermen to hold long-winded conversations about not very much.

"You seem to know your way around boats," I proffered to Vladimir.

He gave a curt nod.

"It's twenty minutes until we get to where you want to be, so would you keep a look-out while I go below and put the kettle on?" I asked.

"No problem, black coffee for myself and Victor."

I gave a curt nod of my own before taking a quick glance at the instrument panel. Engine temperatures and pressures all as they should be, then out of the window - no boats close enough to be of any concern to us. Satisfied, I stepped down the four stairs leading into the warmth of *First Light's* accommodation.

When I returned to the wheelhouse bearing a tray of steaming mugs and sugar-coated doughnuts, I discovered Vladimir had been replaced at the helm by Victor and was now tinkering with a large Drone, complete with underslung camera, which occupied most of the chart table like a malevolent one-eyed bug. Doubting there would be any explanation offered, I pointedly ignored this bizarre addition to the day's proceedings and re-claimed my rightful position at the wheel from a cold-eyed Victor. Deciding to ignore him as well, I concentrated on stuffing one of Harry's award-winning doughnuts into my face.

Vladimir was impressed by the drone that had been commandeered from a reluctant deckhand. Few people realized the military had been making use of these devices long before they became an essential stocking filler. This machine in front of him though, was leaps and bounds ahead of what had been available to him for stealing birds eye glimpses into enemy positions not so many years ago. Highly stable and nearly invisible to the naked eye at a few hundred feet altitude, such devices had taken military surveillance operations to a level that had changed the game entirely. Vladimir was somewhat baffled by the fact that for a few thousand pounds, this capability was available to anyone with an interest.

"We are at your waypoint," I announced, disrupting his thoughts.

"Good. Slow down to five knots and follow the track I entered."

Vladimir's intonation left me in no doubt that he was used to giving commands and having them carried out without question. Though I was briefly tempted to upset this state of affairs, I nevertheless altered course and pulled back on the throttles to just above tick over. Pushing back at authority was a trait of mine which I was always trying to suppress.

First Light slowed to a crawl and with the underlying swell now on the beam, began to roll gently as the new heading took us towards Start Point. The shoreline of my youth could be seen out of the starboard windows. I recognized the small curve of gold at the foot of a green valley that was Blackpool Sands Beach, the longer stretch of golden pebbles which was Slapton Sands, bending along the coast to Torcross, Beesands and the derelict remains of Hallsands. Between us and the shore, a line of breaking waves appearing out of place in the relative calm of the bay. The Skerries Bank, a sand bar raising to within a few feet of the surface on low spring tides, the graveyard of many ships over the centuries before the arrival of the lighthouse on the point and the subsequent marvel of Global Positioning Systems.

Vladimir and Victor made their way out to the aft cockpit. On the chart table there remained two spare batteries for the drone, snug in their chargers, steady green lights signalling a lack of appetite. Abandoned coffee mugs were coping easily with the rolling motion.

Outside, Vladimir caressed the remote controller with its attached I-Pad, eliciting a high-pitched whining from the drone now squatting on the deck. Another control input and it lurched upwards, twitching into a head-high hover. A short period of assessment and stabilization followed before it was sent on its way, eager to observe and report.

Victor, turning away from this activity with a hint of scepticism on his face, rummaged around in one of the black bags and produced a small black cylindrical object, about a foot long, with an eye at one end and stubby fins protruding from two sides. Further rummaging resulted in a reel of line, with what appeared to be a thin electrical cable loosely fastened along its length. As I continued to watch, twisted around from my position at the helm, Victor connected one end of the line and electric cable to the cylinder and lowered it over the side. He took a turn around a cleat, controlling the drag as it paid out behind us. When only a few meters remained on the reel he fastened the line off to the cleat.

The bag now offered up a black box, about the size of a car battery and a set of high-quality headphones. Victor completed the set-up, plugging both the onboard end of the electrical cable and the headphones into the box. He then sat, headphones over his ears, and closed his eyes. I turned my attention forwards, somewhat bemused by all this technology and beginning to feel as if I was taking part in the making of a National Geographic documentary.

The next few hours passed with our steady progression along the coast, my ear half tuned into the intermittent banter on the VHF radio. The drone was seemingly programmed to follow us in a zigzag pattern and Vladimir's eyes rarely left the iPad screen. Occasionally I was required to alter course to remain clear of fishing vessels or their gear, which brought the ire of Vladimir back into my wheelhouse.

"Can't you keep it straight?"

The only break in this monotony occurred every half hour or so when the drone was summoned back for a change of battery. It was obvious they were searching for something and equally obvious from their demeanour that they were having no success. From my perch at the helm, I could see the chargers on the chart table were not keeping up with the quick turnarounds; flashing red was now the common theme.

I noticed the frustration growing in Vladimir, as each drone sortie became shorter and shorter. By midday, we were well past the entrance to Salcombe when at last, he threw open the door and proclaimed; "That's it for today, turn around and take us back."

Doing as he demanded, I asked, "What are you looking for?"

Vladimir looked at me, leaning against the door frame, frustration still showing on his face.

"That's no concern of yours. Just drive the boat."

"The thing is, Vladimir, I told you from the beginning that anything illegal would end our arrangement. I know flying a drone is not illegal, but you seem to be searching for something and I can't even begin to think what it could be, other than the obvious conclusion that its drugs, or drug related. So, how about you convince me that you are not looking for some wayward shipment, otherwise, we are done here."

Vladimir looked at me for a moment.

"I will not tell you what we seek, but it's not drugs." He turned away and began fussing with the drone. Victor had already hauled his contraption back on board and was busy re-stowing it into its bag.

We continued to make our way back towards Dartmouth, the atmosphere, previously frosty at best, was now tense. Vladimir was not forthcoming with any further information, and I was trying to decide how to proceed in this situation. I had no doubt whatever they were looking for, drugs or not, was going to be problematic for me if they found it. But, based on today's lack of success, there was a good chance that tomorrow would be similar, and I would pocket another day's fees without crossing any moral lines. During the remainder of the trip back to port, I worked on convincing myself that so long as payment was forthcoming this evening as agreed, I could go along with this nonsense for another day. I resolved however to pass on my misgivings to Andrew tonight and see if he had any pearls of wisdom which might guide me.

The same oversized fenders cushioned our arrival when we returned alongside *Natasha*. No invite for tea and biscuits though, just an envelope from Vladimir and a terse instruction. "Same time tomorrow."

The equipment bags were hauled aloft. 'A shame,' I thought. I had hoped they would leave them, so I could have a good rummage around in them. Back on my mooring, nautical housekeeping taken care of, I checked the envelope, half hoping its contents would give me an excuse not to turn up in the morning. Unfortunately, the fifty crisp twenty-pound notes gave me no way out.

NINE

Sunk into the comfortable sofa in Andrew's lounge later that same evening, I looked out through the window towards the *Natasha*. Her exterior deck lighting created a soft glow in the middle of the river rendering the lesser lights of humbler craft insignificant and almost comical in contrast. Andrew was thinking about what I had just told him of my day's events, crease lines of worry beginning to plough his forehead.

"Matt, I'm glad you made some money today, but you need to think about this. Something's not right about this situation."

I nodded my agreement with his assessment.

"You're right. These guys are something else. But we didn't break any laws out there, and another chunk or two of cash would get me out of a hole."

Andrew sighed heavily.

"You are dealing with people who operate on a different level to what most people are familiar with. From what you've told me, coupled with the visitor I had in my office this afternoon inquiring about *Natasha*, I think you should put some clear water between yourself and whatever they are up to. You're running the risk of getting tangled up in something that might well get out of hand."

I looked quizzically across at my friend. Andrew was not one to be melodramatic and I could see he was genuinely worried.

"So, who was your visitor today?"

He glanced down, one hand stroking Bailey who was sprawled across his lap and considered his words before answering.

"His name was Jake Mason. He is an officer in the National Crime Agency."

Andrew continued into my silence. "The thing is, I recognized him from somewhere else, and you can be sure that if the NCA is sending someone like him to our quiet backwater, then they have more than just a passing interest. Getting caught up with these players is definitely out of your league Matt."

I couldn't agree more, but, as he was well aware, I had always been willing to skirt with the edges of good sense. The truth, which Andrew remained unaware of, was that without this financial windfall from the Russians, I was probably going to lose *First Light* and end up sleeping on his sofa - something I was fairly certain neither of us wanted. I was happy to be back home, and I liked my life afloat, but for it to continue I had to survive the winter. A few more envelopes would allow that to happen.

"So, are you going to tell me how you know this policeman chap?"

Andrew thought for a moment while he stroked the dog, now fully asleep with a line of drool like a stalactite descending from the side of its mouth.

"You ever read any *George Orwell*?" he finally asked.

"Only *'Animal Farm'* at school, the same as you." I responded, wondering where this was going.

"There is a quotation attributed to him, something along the lines of, '*We sleep safe in our beds only because rough men are prepared to go out in the night and visit violence on those who would do us harm'-.*"

"And this 'Jake' is one of those 'rough men'," I concluded.

"Well he used to be, at least. Back in the 'Arab spring' of 2011 when Libya was falling apart, I was Captain of a Destroyer, part of the British fleet in the Mediterranean. We didn't do much. Spent a lot of time just cruising up and down in international waters working on our tans.

"Then we were ordered to Valetta in Malta where we resupplied and picked up some *guests*. We closed on the Libyan coast just South of Tripoli and our Lynx Helicopter dropped them ashore early one morning. About a week later we returned to pick them up."

Andrew stopped for a moment. "Obviously, what I just told you, didn't happen, right?" he asked.

"Of course," I nodded. "Illegally landing British Special Forces into foreign territories in order to nudge events in a certain direction would never be the policy of our government."

"Quite." He continued, "I have no idea what those teams got up to over there. I assume it was pretty grim, whatever it was. They weren't in great shape when they spilled back out onto the deck from the Lynx. And though I didn't have much interaction with these guys, no one did, I saw enough to be able to say our policeman friend was one of them."

We sat in silence for a while, both of us thinking things over, the stalactite of dog drool now a moderate sized stream.

"Here's the thing," I finally blurted, "I need to do tomorrow at least. The money's too good and I think I can keep myself out of trouble so long as they don't find whatever they are looking for. Up to that point I'm happy to keep taking their cash."

Andrew sighed - he must have known that would be my response - before slowly nodding.

"Well, your choice Matt, but I still recommend against it." He reached into his shirt pocket and produced a small business card. "Here is the policeman's number. I hope you don't mind but I told him of your day trip today. You should give him a call before he calls you."

"Thanks, I will. If things get out of hand." I stood up.

"Before then would be best, Matt."

Taking the card from his outstretched hand, I slipped it into my back pocket as I went into the small kitchen. I returned with a handful of paper towel. Looking down at the dog, I passed it to him.

"There you go."

"What's this for?"

"You'll see. Let's chat tomorrow when I'm back."

***

The following day was much the same as its predecessor, until it wasn't. This time the day's sedate steaming and aerial buzzing were cut short, not by flattened batteries, but by voices chattering on the VHF radio. The mid-morning coffee and doughnut frenzy had been cleared away and Vladimir had relinquished control of the *I-Pad* to Victor who was multi-tasking, headphones still clamped to his ears. Vladimir was back in my wheelhouse, pouring over the electronic chart, seeking, I presumed, some solution to their lack of success.

The skipper of a beam trawler going by the name of *Southern Cross* was calling Falmouth Coastguard on channel sixteen. Having nothing better to do, I idly followed their conversation over to the Coastguard's working channel sixty-seven.

"Falmouth, hello. We just trawled up something odd. Looks like an aircraft part. Propeller and gear box maybe, but I'm not sure. It is a bit battered but doesn't look like it's been underwater more than a day or two. What should I do about it? Over."

Vladimir stopped what he was doing and listened in keenly.

There was a long pause - fair enough, it wasn't your standard radio call. Some thought must be given as to the correct response.

Eventually it came; "*Southern Cross* from Falmouth Coastguard. Can you confirm there is no surface wreckage or anything like it? Over".

"No, nothing else, just this thing in our trawl. Over".

"*Southern Cross* from Falmouth Coastguard; okay, we have no reports of any missing aircraft, but we see your position from the AIS and will request an over-flight of the area to check for any other signs of wreckage. Keep whatever you found on-board. We will inform the police. They may want to see you when you're back in port. You're out of Brixham, correct? Over."

"That's right, Brixham. We are not planning on landing our catch back there until about midnight though. Over."

"*Southern Cross* from Falmouth Coastguard - okay then, you should expect a visit early tomorrow morning. Will you be on-board? Over"

"Aye, I tend to sleep here when we are back late. No point going home since she left. Over"

Another pause. The radio operator seemed unsure how to reply to the personal element in this response.

Finally; "*Southern Cross* from Falmouth Coastguard - copy that, thank you for the information. Falmouth Coastguard standing by channel sixteen." Some things even the Coastguard wasn't prepared to get involved in.

I noticed Vladimir had perked up considerably whilst listening to this conversation.

"Where is this *Southern Cross*?" he asked me.

"I have no idea, Vladimir. The beam trawlers tend to stay a little farther offshore to avoid trawling up static fishing gear. I don't have AIS fitted, so I can't see other vessels in that way."

He stared at me, processing this information. I decided to push a little.

"So, you're looking for an aircraft?"

Vladimir continued to stare, the coldness in his eyes was frightening.

"Do not question me, Matt.

I turned away from his gaze, unwilling to challenge further. I knew my limits and fronting up to the likes of Vladimir wasn't part of my skill set.

There were a few ways in which I could pin-point the trawler for him, including a direct call on the radio and just asking, but I had the distinct impression that I would be doing nobody other than Vladimir any favours if I located the vessel. I let him work it out on his own.

"So, these trawlers go up and down the channel, dragging a net across sea floor, correct?" he probed.

"Yes. They drag nets, usually two at a time, with chains leading the way, ploughing up the seabed for long periods - usually hours. Probably one of the most destructive processes we inflict on our seas," I added, in the unlikely event that he gave a shit.

He didn't.

"So, if something entered the net, it could be anytime from when the trawl touched the bottom to when it gets hauled up, would that be correct?" Vladimir continued to think it through.

I gave a small nod of agreement, unwilling to help him in his deliberations. I knew how sophisticated modern trawlers were. Some of them might give the impression of being rust buckets - barely able to keep the water out - but they were invariably packed with electronics, ensuring each drag of the trawl would be accurately recorded on a chart plotter, with its start and finish position noted to within a few meters. Pointless going over fishing grounds you had previously decimated, no money in that.

"Do they keep an accurate record of where they have been?"

Bingo! He got there quicker than I thought.

"I have no idea, I'm not a fisherman."

He dug into his jacket pocket and plucked out a mobile phone. The jacket bumped heavily back into place from something else in there. Looking at the screen he said, "Head back towards Dartmouth, but move closer inshore, I need a signal."

I guess he had reached the same conclusion that I had. The equipment on board *Natasha* would have no trouble in locating *Southern Cross*. Even a child with a laptop and internet connection would be able to find her. I set a course to take us back, hoping he wouldn't notice that we didn't close up on the shore. I had no intention of helping any further and something told me I was fast approaching the point where continued involvement in this caper, whatever it was, would start to have serious consequences.

Vladimir turned to re-join Victor outside, not bothering to close the wheelhouse door as he left. Their conversation was animated, as if new life had been breathed into their mission. He knew that the key to his search was now the *Southern Cross*, and he also now knew just how to go about finding her.

"We might need to be 'persuasive' Victor, but I think we are a big step closer to the gold."

Stepping to the back of my wheelhouse to shut the door on the pair of them, I saw the drone, discarded on the deck like a Christmas present on boxing day, no longer able to hold their attention.

Vladimir and Victor were facing away from me in the cockpit. But as I pulled the door towards me, I was fairly sure the indistinct group of words - part Russian - part English, which reached me, contained the word *Gold*.

As we cruised back to Dartmouth, that evocative word, not meant for my ears, had my brain working overtime. Despite common sense trying and failing to block the process, an idea began to form in my mind. I was surprised Vladimir had not come up with the same thought. Perhaps it was just a matter of time.

If looked at slightly askew and through squinted eyes, I could convince myself that what I was about to do was harmless. Not correct, or even legal, but I saw no immediate harm if it were to work.

Checking that Vladimir and Victor looked set to stay in the cockpit, where they were in deep conversation, I reached up and switched the transmission strength of my VHF radio to its lowest output of one Watt, the setting intended to limit the range of the call in order not to interfere with other users. If I were lucky, it might give me enough range to reach *Southern Cross,* whilst avoiding the ears of the Coastguard, who would undoubtedly take a dim view of me impersonating them.

I took a deep breath and a quick glance aft before pressing the transmit button.

"*Southern Cross* this is Falmouth Coastguard on channel six."

A long silence followed. Perhaps they were too far away after all.

Finally; "Falmouth Coastguard, *Southern Cross*, go ahead."

I had to be careful here, other boats in the vicinity could hear us and I also had to keep the skipper of *Southern Cross* from wondering why the Coastguard was not using the normal channels.

"*Southern Cross*, hello again. Please switch to channel seventy-seven."

This further change of channel would hopefully reduce the number of people listening in on our conversation.

"Falmouth Coastguard this is *Southern Cross*, switching to seventy-seven."

I let out a deep breath, so far so good. Vladimir showed no sign of coming back inside.

"*Southern Cross* from Falmouth Coastguard how are you receiving, over?"

"Weak, but readable Falmouth. Go ahead."

"*Southern Cross* from Falmouth Coastguard, sorry, there is interference on our normal channels. We have been informed the Navy are conducting manoeuvres out of Plymouth later today. They will be sweeping the area you found the propeller in, so can you please give me the start and finish co-ordinates for that particular tow?"

"Sure, standby a moment Falmouth."

"Who are you talking to?" The wheelhouse door had opened, Vladimir's frame filled the gap.

'*Shit.*'

"I'm trying to contact the harbour authority. They told me this morning that my normal berth might not be available later. Work on the ground tackle or something."

Vladimir stared at me, suspicion filling the space between us.

The door closed shut, just as the radio came back to life.

"Falmouth Coastguard, I have those numbers for you, over."

I wrote them down with the stub of pencil, awkward in my hand. My eyes were firmly fixed on the door as the voice from the trawler continued.

"We had a problem with one of the otter boards on that drag, it got fouled on the headline, the net was only on the bottom for a few hundred meters before we realized and hauled it."

"Thank you, *Southern Cross*, that's all we need. Remember, someone will come and see you tomorrow. Falmouth Coastguard switching back to channel sixteen."

I reset the VHF to its normal settings, more impressed than I should have been with my duplicity.

My phone gave a ping from the chart table. Vladimir would be pleased that we were back in range of a signal and I had a call of my own to make, another step down a path that perhaps should not be trod.

TEN

The message my mobile had received on the way back to port was a notification that a bailiff would be paying me a visit in two days' time to attend to the matter of missed loan repayments on my boat. 'Make sure you are available.'

'*Great.*'

With Vladimir and his toys dropped back on the *Natasha,* I tied *First Light* onto her deep-water moorings and headed to town in my dingy. I held off from making the call until I was up the slippery ladder and walking along the embankment.

"Southwark Debt Collection, how may I help you?"

My request led to a series of clicks, and the by a now familiar voice.

"Hello Mr. Curtis, you got my message I take it?"

"I can transfer fifteen hundred pounds to your account. Today."

I could hear the tapping of a keyboard in the silence which followed my words.

"That still leaves the amount of four thousand two hundred and fifty-six pounds, forty-four pence to clear your balance with us."

Numbers. Black and white.

"Yes. I know. But I am asking for a bit of slack here. Can you give me a couple of weeks to come up with the money?"

More tapping.

"Are you still using the vessel as your home?"

"Yes. Oh, and I'm fostering two orphaned children." Nothing ventured...

A shallow sigh reached my ear.

"Okay, Mr. Curtis. One month. *If* your fifteen hundred is transferred today."

The temporary reprieve failed to lighten my mood much. I still had the outstanding balance on the loan looming over my head as I headed for the inside of the café to a table set for two. The table was butted up against a wall on which scallop shells and plastic lobsters competed for space. The lobsters appeared to be winning.

Andrew was sat at the table, a plate of scampi and chips, as yet untouched in front of him.

"You alright?" he inquired.

Another envelope crackled in my pocket as I sat. It had been handed to me without a word about tomorrow and I suspected it would be the last, given the way events were unfolding.

"I'm fine. They are looking for an aircraft of some sort."

Andrew remained silent as I described the mornings activities, leaving out my Coastguard impersonation. I doubted he would have approved.

"Matt, from what you've told me, it seems likely that this Vladimir will try to obtain the co-ordinates of the tow from the crew of the *Southern Cross*. They need to be made aware that they might be getting a visit from the Russians."

"I agree. Can you get hold of their satellite phone number from somewhere?"

Andrew gave it some thought.

"I should think so, give me a moment," he finally said.

I addressed my fish and chips while he worked the phone. After a few minutes, he passed over the handset, saying, "His name is Paul."

Like I say, highly efficient these navy types. A series of clicks and buzzes, and the by now familiar voice of Southern Cross's skipper was once again in my ear.

"Hello?"

"Paul, good afternoon. My name is Matt, this is going to sound strange but hear me out."

A short silence whilst my words were considered.

"Aye, go on."

"There is a good chance you will be approached, either at sea or when you get back, by someone trying to find out where you dragged up the piece of wreckage today." I paused while more clicks and buzzes filled the gap.

"I have already given the Coastguard that info. Who are you?"

I ignored his question. "These people are not from the Coastguard. You should do your best to avoid them if possible, but if not, then just tell them what they want to know."

"Aye, maybe," he answered, sounding sceptical. "Who are you?" he asked again.

"Be careful with these guys. If they show up, they may not be too friendly. Just humour them."

He responded with a grunt.

I hit the end button before he had the chance to press me further and passed the phone back to Andrew who was looking at me thoughtfully. A waitress fussed around us, inquiring if all was well with the food. Nods of affirmation sent her happily away. I waited until she was out of earshot.

"Do you still have our old diving equipment?"

"Yes, it's all in my lock up, haven't used it for a few years though. Why?

"Because I know where the aircraft is, more or less, and I want us to take a look."

Andrew leaned back in his chair, placing his knife and fork on the side of his plate. His words weren't long in coming.

"No way, Matt. How the hell do you know where it is anyway? And why would I want to go diving in the middle of the winter in the freezing English Channel, more than likely in the dark, and possibly in the company of at least one corpse?" He took a swig of his water, then went on. "Not to mention the very real possibility of having a couple of hostile Russians breathing down our necks."

I knew Andrew would take some convincing and when he put it like that, I could see his point.

"Because it will be fun?"

He stared at me incredulously so, I pushed harder.

"I overheard the word 'gold' today, when they were on my boat."

Andrew raised an eyebrow at that.

"Look, I know, it's risky. And, I am more on edge about the chance of coming across corpses than you are, I can assure you. But, aren't you at least slightly intrigued by this?"

He was still looking at me as though I was certifiable.

"Forget the dark and the cold and the corpses," I pressed on. "Let's just go and take a quick squint. The depth in the area were the wreckage should be is only about seventy feet, we can get down, take a peek and be home in time for tea."

I could tell he was wavering. We had both loved diving in the bay as teenagers and the mystery of this situation made it appealing to his nature. The risk taking of our youth had been subdued and tempered by our training in disciplined services, but I knew it still existed within him, or I wouldn't have come this far with my proposition.

"A few hours of your time. I can't do it without you."

Finally, he capitulated, "Okay, let's do it. But it will need to be today since Anna and I are leaving tomorrow afternoon for my Royal Navy Reunion this weekend. And we only go so long as we remain ahead of your new *friends*, got it?" Not waiting for a response, he continued, "The moment *Natasha* slips her moorings, we back well off, agreed?"

As I nodded my agreement, he came up with another condition.

"One more thing, you have to tell the policeman, Jake, everything about today before we do anything else, got it?"

"I'll call him as soon as we're done here," I acquiesced, surprised and relieved that Andrew didn't pursue the question of how I thought I knew where to find the wreckage. The seaman in him kicked into gear.

"How much chain do you carry?" he enquired. "Enough for us to anchor safely in that depth?"

"I have one hundred and fifty feet. That should be fine if this settled weather continues, especially if we use the anchor as the tie off point for our guidelines. We will soon know if it starts to drag. I'll check the tides. If we can dive at slack water, so much the better.

He thought about it for a moment, visualizing the set-up and overlaying it with possible complications and their solutions. Something else occurred to him.

"What about your agreement with Vladimir? Isn't he expecting you to be available to take him out again?"

I shook my head. "I think he will take one of *Natasha's* fast tenders to locate *Southern Cross*, probably already has. If he finds her, which he will, and convinces them to pass over the co-ordinates, it makes more sense for him to use *Natasha* to carry out the search. They are better equipped and wouldn't need to hang around too long drawing attention to themselves... No, he doesn't need me anymore."

I stood, sliding a crisp new twenty out of its nest to cover the bill.

"I've got to go to the bank, and then shop for a few things. Can you go check over the dive gear and bring it down to the town dock?

"Sure, but I'll need a bit of time for that."

"Okay, then I'll get *First Light* over to load up this afternoon when you're ready. Oh, and, if you get a chance, can you log on to *marine traffic.com* and see were *Southern Cross* is now?"

Andrew nodded. On that note, I crammed the last of my chips into my mouth and hurried out to begin my errands before he changed his mind.

ELEVEN

While Andrew and I where making our plans, Vladimir and Victor were slamming their way out into the English Channel. The sea remained relatively calm, but at thirty knots, the underlying swell caused the Riva speedboat to intermittently break free from the grip of water and lurch optimistically skywards, before sinking back into the only element it could realistically excel in.

Southern Cross's position of half an hour ago, found by *Natasha's* AIS, was entered into the small chart plotter at the helm in front of Victor. The mobile satellite phone in his pocket would enable an exact location to be passed to them when they were closer. Behind them, the green and grey coastline dwindled from view until no more than a suggestion remained.

Braced in the seat next to him, his head down below the short windscreen in an effort to remain clear of the spray slicing out and upwards with each crash of the bow, Vladimir slid the magazine out of a Glock 9 mm semi-automatic pistol.

Satisfied with the glint of brass which peeked out from the holes lining the length of its trailing edge, he inserted it back into place with a click, cycled the top slide to feed a round into the chamber and replaced the weapon in his pocket.

***

Paul Weir, Captain of *Southern Cross*, leaned against the transom, ignoring the seagulls circling and screaming at him from aloft. They had been a part of his life for so long that their racket barely registered. Another long-term fixture was the cigarette wedged between two fingers of a huge gnarled hand.

His other hand was raised over his forehead creating a visor against the low winter sun, as his eyes tracked the speck of black rapidly closing on the stern of *Southern Cross*.

Being approached at sea by another vessel would always put a Captain on edge. It usually preceded trouble or inconvenience of some description. After the mystery call of earlier, Paul was disinclined to receive uninvited visitors with open arms. Flicking the half-smoked cigarette over the gunwale into the sea, he picked his way between fish boxes, coils of line, and other assorted paraphernalia to be found on the trawlers deck. Making his way back towards his bridge, he pondered how to deal with the approaching boat. Had he but known that he had less than fifteen minutes to live, he might have been inclined to linger a while longer on his cigarette.

***

Vladimir stood, left-hand holding the upper edge of the windshield for balance, his right hand enveloping the butt of the Glock.

"Put me alongside, midship, where the gunwale is lowest and don't worry about our varnish."

Fifty feet away on the trawler, a crew member was vigorously waving them away. A loosely aimed deck-washing hosepipe reinforced his demand with a white jet of aerated sea water arcing towards the speedboat but falling short in its quest.

The shot from Vladimir had no chance of finding its target at that range from a moving platform. Nevertheless, it had the desired effect of making the crewman and deck-wash drop out of sight behind the high sided gunwale. Victor crunched the port side of the Riva hard against the *Southern Cross* and held it there as Vladimir vaulted up and across to the larger vessel.

The next two shots, delivered almost as one, were never going to miss. Both bullets tore through the flesh and bones of the cowering crewman's hand, which had been raised in a futile attempt at defence. Barely hesitating at the hand, they smashed through his skull before exiting, energy mostly spent, onto the steel deck. The abandoned deck wash continued to do what it did best - diluting and flushing the evidence of violence into the sea.

Vladimir moved quickly across the cluttered deck. He thought a boat this size would require three or four crew members to operate; and three expressions, ranging from anger to horror were staring down at him from behind the wheelhouse windows. There didn't appear to be anyone else outside. Two more rounds loosely directed at the sloping windows failed to penetrate the toughened glass-which was designed to counter the might of Atlantic rollers - but the faces disappeared from view.

Moving rapidly down the side of the bridge to get to the weather tight door before it could be barricaded against him, Vladimir's eyes briefly registered the crumpled red and white tail rotor blades, complete with transmission and a short section of tail boom which had been securely lashed to a stanchion on the deck. Confirmation that he was on the right track. As he reached the door, his brain automatically updated him on his shot count. Twelve rounds left.

Once in his grip, the door opened heavily outwards towards him as he squatted down on his haunches. In front of him, a flight of stairs led up to the wheelhouse. The air was suddenly filled with blinding red light and acrid smoke as the flare tore through the space where his head should have been. Vladimir had a fleeting moment of respect for the remaining crew. The projectile, a distress rocket tipped with flaming magnesium and capable of reaching an altitude of one thousand feet would undoubtedly have changed the outcome of today's events for them if they had only aimed it lower.

Confronted with the gun and with no further defensive options open to them, the three men in the wheelhouse had retreated as far away from the door as possible. These where hardened seafarers, tough men in many regards, but in no way equipped to understand or counter the malevolence that had entered their world.

"Captain?" demanded Vladimir, the Glock trained towards the group. A wary nod from Paul, the gun pointing in his direction causing a feeling of abject terror to well up inside him. Knowing a few pounds of pressure on this intruder's finger would spit eternity at him, drained any remaining resistance and rendered him powerless and mute.

"Give me the location where you found the tail rotor."

***

Vladimir left the wheelhouse, leaving the door open behind him. Six rounds now remained in the Glock. He returned to the deck and dragged the first casualty of today's activities back to join the carnage in the bridge. *Southern Cross* was still steaming sedately in a South-Westerly direction, the auto helm making small corrections to hold her course true as Vladimir left the wheelhouse, closing the door tightly behind him.

He climbed the rusty ladder to the wheelhouse roof. Casting around, he quickly found the bright yellow automatic distress transmitter and removed it from its water-pressure activated, float-free bracket. His shoes were now slippery with the grey and white seagull droppings that covered the roof, and he carefully retraced his steps back down to deck level, the transmitter tucked under one arm.

A second watertight door squeaked open as he pulled, emitting the rumble of an engine mixed with the higher pitched whine of a generator. Ear mufflers, still in their packaging hung from a hook on the bulkhead. To his left, a short corridor led to an odorous crew area with curtained bunks around a central table and a tight galley along one side. Dirty plates and pans were piled in a sink, destined never to be tackled. To the right of the door was a ladder, treacherous with years of accumulated grease and oil and offering precarious access down to a filthy, noisy engine room. Stepping onto it, with the distress beacon still tucked under his arm, Vladimir descended into the cacophony of the engine room. To one side, crammed between various pumps and machinery, a chaotic bench offered up a variety of mismatched tools. He made short work of smashing the transmitter beyond any hope of functioning.

A few more deafening minutes were spent tinkering with unfamiliar valves and pipework before making his way carefully back up the grimy ladder to the deck. His ears still ringing, Vladimir made a final check around the vessel, wedging open all the hatches and watertight doors - except the one to the wheelhouse. Satisfied with his work, he returned to the trawler's side, gesturing for Victor to close in and pick him up.

As the Riva traded more varnish in return for Vladimir, *Southern Cross* continued on her way, becoming steadily lower in the water and increasingly sluggish in her action. In time, the rising water level would snuff out the engine, and the *Southern Cross* would drift to stop before starting her final voyage to the seabed. The gulls, still circling overhead, were yet to realize that a new caterer would soon need to be found.

***

True to my word, as I hurried from the café, I pulled the policeman's card out of my pocket and dialled the number, standing in the narrow doorway of the café.

"Yes?" Briefly thinking I had called Kemp by mistake, I asked, "Jake Malone?"

"Yes. You are?"

"Matt Curtis. I believe we have a common interest in a chap called Vladimir. If you're still in Dartmouth, can we meet?"

"Yes, that would be good. Where are you?"

I told him the name of the café.

"Ten minutes," Jake responded, and hung up.

"Still here?" enquired Andrew, holding the door open for an elderly lady on her way out with a small poodle cradled in one of her arms. A tartan shopping trolley trailed from the other.

"The policeman is coming for a chat. Let's wait for him together," I suggested, lowering the phone. We headed back inside, to the same table at the back, seemingly no ground lost or gained by the lobsters.

Ordering coffee to justify our seats Andrew pointed out, "You know we are running short of daylight Matt. It will be getting dark in about four hours."

"I know, hopefully this won't take long, but I agree with you, this is a conversation we should have even if it makes us run a bit late."

I knew Andrew wasn't as familiar as me in operating at odd times of the day and night, but I had the beginnings of an idea that would possibly give us a head start on the Russians, if this meeting didn't take too long.

A man entered the café, his eyes casting around methodically before settling on us. Dressed in trainers and jeans topped with a loose-fitting brown sporting jacket he didn't look like any policeman I'd ever seen, but something about his appearance was familiar to me. He made his way over to us, certain in his selection.

Looking at Jake, I saw few outward signs of the abilities inferred by Andrew. Just a steady gaze, not lingering longer than necessary, before gliding elsewhere. If I had to describe him in a word, it would be '*aware*'. Given the luxury of two words for the task, the other would be 'assured'.

"Thanks for meeting with me, Matt." Easing his wiry form into a plastic chair whilst shaking his head at the approaching waitress, Jake got straight to the point.

"Firstly, can you confirm this is the man you know as *Vladimir* from the Motor Yacht *Natasha*?" He held his phone out towards me, a picture on its screen.

I looked at the photograph, seeing Vladimir, dressed unfamiliarly in a suit and tie, walking alone along a tree lined street. The angle of the shot made me think it had been taken from inside a car.

"Yes, that's him," I confirmed.

"Tell me again how you met and what he has been doing with you and your boat."

Beginning with the introduction in the pub and the subsequent charter of *First Light*, I explained all that had happened in the last few days. I told him, as unlikely as it seemed, I thought they were looking for a downed aircraft of some description.

Jake sat back, his face giving away nothing, while I went on to tell him about the *Southern Cross* and Vladimir's interest in their unexpected by-catch. When I'd finished, he remained silent for a while longer, busy with his own thoughts as he pieced things together.

"From what you have said, and what I know of Vladimir, I think the crew of that trawler may be in some significant danger," he finally concluded.

"I agree, and we already called them to warn them they could be approached. A warning from you though, would be taken more seriously," I replied, somewhat relieved that my worries about *Southern Cross* and her crew had now been shared with officialdom.

"You still have the number?" he asked, mobile poised for action. Andrew messaged it across to him somehow, and Jake tapped his screen a couple of times before holding the phone up to his ear. After a few moments he lowered it and asked, "Are you sure that's right? The call's not going through."

Andrew redialled from his phone's history, with the same lack of success.

"Well," he said thoughtfully, "I suppose there could be any number of reasons why we can't get through. I will keep trying, but there is a more official way to reach them. You could ask the Coastguard to get in touch with them by radio, and that request might be best coming from you, Jake," proffered Andrew.

I kept quiet, anxious to stay well clear of the subject of coastguards and radio calls.

"Yes, I'll do that right now. In the meantime, I suggest you avoid any further contact with Vladimir. He can be extremely dangerous. And call me again if they get contact you."

Jake was pushing his chair back when I asked, "Have you any idea what they are looking for?"

He looked at me thoughtfully for a moment, sinking slowly back into place as he decided how much he wanted to tell me.

"I'll tell you this because you are tangled up in this situation but keep it to yourself," he eventually said.

He looked at me, then Andrew. His slate grey eyes were presumably seeking some outward sign that we weren't blabber mouth's. Apparently, he found it, as he continued.

"It seems likely he is trying to find his boss's helicopter. It has gone missing. His boss was not onboard, unfortunately, and we don't know who or what was, but we are certainly interested in finding out."

TWELVE

The automatic counting machine in the last remaining bank in town rattled through my twenties with a disappointingly short burst before they were squashed into a tantalizingly open drawer of cash. A few quick taps on a keyboard by the bored teller and I had bought myself another few weeks with a deck under my feet. As I headed out of the bank towards my motorbike, I tried hard not to think about the final payment due in two weeks' time.

It was past three o'clock by the time I returned from my trip out of town, sliding the bike backwards into its usual slot close to the dingy landing pontoon. Its exhaust pipe immediately began pinging its way back down to a more sensible temperature. My backpack rattled with the purchases made in several places as I swung my leg back down onto *terra-firma*. The idea I had for slowing down the Russians may or may not work, but if it did, there would be a mightily pissed off yacht Captain baying for someone's head. Various shops, combined with choosing the most disinterested cashiers to handle my transactions, might help prevent that head from being mine.

Ten pulls on the starting cord of my outboard failed to produce any result other than heavy breathing. The eleventh pull was followed by a mismatched sequence of bangs and a cloud of smoke. The water around the stern of my dingy turned into rainbow colours as fuel leaked from somewhere. I unscrewed the motor from the transom and lifted it awkwardly inboard to stop more petrol from running into the harbour. It was obvious the engine was beyond the stage where tinkering with a spark plug spanner would produce results. Resigning myself to a long row, I reached for the oars before remembering that I had Jess's phone number in my pocket.

"You know, you could ask me out for a drink without going through this rigmarole every time," Jess teased, when I explained my predicament. Thankfully, she continued with; "Sure, Matt. Just give me ten minutes to finish what I'm doing, and I'll be there."

Waiting for her to arrive, I was surprised at how much I was looking forward to seeing her again.

"Time for a new outboard methinks," Jess quipped once I was on-board the now familiar harbour launch. She was right of course, not that it was an option for the time being. As we headed out across the river, the only other movement was that of *Natasha*'s tender coming from the direction of the river mouth and heading towards her mother ship.

"Can you head over to them, for a closer look?"

As Jess altered our course to close the distance between our two boats, I could see deep scratches and damaged trim along the speed boat's port side. Streaks of dark blue paint were at odds with the tenders varnished wood finish. The two figures slunk behind the Perspex windshield were undoubtedly Vladimir and Victor. And they didn't seem too interested in stopping to chat. No harm in trying though.

"Hello Vladimir," I hollered across the gap between us. "Do you need me again?"

He ignored me as he manipulated the tender controls, intent on coming alongside *Natasha*. The same over-sized fenders were waiting in anticipation - perhaps it wasn't just my boat handling skills which were doubted. Victor stood. His cold gaze shifted between me and Jess, before he waved us away, shaking his head. I got the message.

"Are those the men you have been taking out in the bay?" Jess obviously remembered the conversation at Andrew's dinner table.

"Yes, a couple of times now. But I think that gig is over."

"They don't strike me as being nice people. What on earth did they need you and your boat for when they have all that?" She was looking across at the vastness of the *Natasha*.

"It's a long story. I will tell you all about it, but for now I am a bit pushed for time."

Jess didn't speak as she re-aimed the boat's bow towards *First Light*. I stared over at *Natasha,* where flurries of activity could be seen on the bow and stern. If my idea was going to work, I would have to get a move on.

"Going to put the kettle on?" she inquired as we came alongside *First Light*.

"I would like nothing more right now, but there is something I've got to do which can't wait."

I could see the hurt under the surface of her green eyes as she pushed the launch away from my boat.

"Don't worry about it, Matt. Give me a call if your schedule opens up any time soon."

With a flash of what may have been anger, she turned away, the stern of her boat squatting low with the abundance of revs. Jess was the first person who had managed to get through to me since Sophie's death, and I was busily destroying that friendship before it had even begun. *Idiot.* I was going to have to work hard to rebuild that bridge.

***

I had a small diving set on board consisting of a dive cylinder with about a twenty-minute duration, connected to a cheap buoyancy compensator jacket. Not for serious use, it had only ever been used once to clear an entangled line from my propeller somewhere in France. It should still contain enough stale air for my purposes.

By the time I had kitted up, wetsuit, weight belt, and buoyancy jacket snugly adjusted, the radars on *Natasha* had begun to rotate, a sure sign she was getting ready to proceed to sea. I had to find a way to slow things down a bit. Shrugging the cylinder off my back I reached into the wheelhouse and grabbed my phone.

"Go ahead, Matt," said Andrew.

"*Natasha's* leaving, can you delay their departure by half an hour or so? Tell them there are no line handlers available to disconnect them from the buoys or something."

"I might be able to do that, but I'm not sure how long it will hold them. What are you planning?"

"Best you don't ask Andrew, I'll tell you later." I hung up, anxious to be done with this before common sense got the better of me.

I sat on *First Light*'s stern, out of sight of anyone on *Natasha*. Next to me was a net bag crammed full of aerosol cans complete with plastic tubes affixed to the top. Hoping I had got my weights correct to counter any buoyancy issues, I inflated BC jacket and slowly slid into the freezing water. 'Christ, I hope Andrew still has our dry suits,' was the thought running through my mind as the cold, grey green water closed over my head.

***

On the bridge of the *Natasha*, the Captain and his First Officer were going over departure checklists. Vladimir and Victor sat behind them, unspeaking, but the impatience to be underway displayed clearly on their faces.

"Call down to the engineer and have him start the main engines," the Captain instructed his First Officer, as he reached for the VHF radio and requested departure assistance from the harbour.

A faint vibration started under their feet, as the two huge marine Caterpillar diesels rumbled into life, three decks below them. The Captain cast a perfunctory glance across the instruments coming to life in front of him as he waited for a reply from the harbour authorities.

"*Natasha*, we don't have anyone available to assist you at the moment. We can get a tender to you in about an hour."

"Damn, really? Can't you send someone to release our lines sooner?"

"Sorry, we'll be there as soon as we can," came the reply.

Vladimir was on his feet and turned to the Captain.

"Why can't we go without their assistance?" he demanded, a frown etched across his forehead.

"Because there are four lines, two forward and two aft, shackled to the moorings. They have to be released before we can haul them onboard," replied the Captain. "We could launch one of our tenders and have a crew member unshackle us from the buoys, but that process wouldn't be much quicker than waiting for the harbour to send someone out in their boat."

Vladimir digested this information.

"Well keep on them. We need to get going as soon as possible. And, if they don't show up within the hour, do it yourself."

The Captain nodded, not overly enamoured by being given orders on his own bridge by Vladimir. Avoiding Vladimir's gaze in case annoyance was showing in his eyes, he picked up the intercom and instructed the engineer to shut down the engines, no point burning fuel needlessly while they waited.

***

Underneath *Natasha,* I was trying to bring my heart rate back under control. The noise of the main engines starting up was terrifying. If she started manoeuvring whilst I was here, I had little chance of avoiding the two large bronze propellers which would most likely cut me into pieces - which wasn't in the plan. As soon as I heard the engines start, the noise and vibrations jolting fear into me, I began to swim rapidly out from under her, thinking I had left it too late to attempt my delaying tactic.

But, as I swam away from her oppressive black hull, the noise stopped abruptly. Only the more strident note of a generator remained. I hesitated before heading back underneath. 'This really isn't sensible,' I thought. Poised to turn tail again at the first rumble, I tentatively made my way back-not completely sure what was motivating me to take this risk - and began searching for the grills that would be covering the engine cooling water intakes.

The needle on my air pressure gauge wasn't pointing anywhere good by the time I found what I was looking for. Two openings, each about two feet in diameter, covered by steel grids, with holes an inch square allowing ample volumes of seawater through but keeping plastic bags and the larger forms sea life out. They were situated opposite each other, one on either side of the keel. I wasted no time in emptying the contents of my net bag into these openings; six aerosols squirted into each. Cramming the last of the empty cans back into the bag, I was trying to see what effect they might be having, when my air ran out.

I wasn't worried about drowning. It was a short swim to the surface. Even with nearly empty lungs I could manage that. What concerned me more, was being spotted in the water by the crew of the *Natasha*. Surfacing alongside a super yacht, gasping for air would take some explaining. Nothing to be done about it though, I would have to take my chances.

Sucking the last gasp out of the begrudging cylinder, I finned myself away from the keel. The black above my head was replaced by the light grey of the sky, and I gradually ascended, attempting to break the surface as close to the side of *Natasha* as possible. The only way I would be spotted would be if someone were looking directly over the side into the water. Luck was with me and I bobbed up unobserved. I swam towards the stern, too low in the water to see into the portholes and with a slight current pushing me along. My luck held; no one appeared gesticulating and shouting on the aft deck and I drifted unchallenged back to my boat, wondering how effective my delaying tactic might be.

The day was slipping away from us as I clambered back onboard *First Light* via the rickety plastic swim ladder and shed the diving gear. I forgo a shower, even though the idea of ten minutes in hot water held a huge appeal right now and concentrated on getting across to the town quay to rendezvous with Andrew and our equipment.

THIRTEEN

Alone now on *Natasha*'s bridge with departure delayed, the Captain's mind began to wander. Earlier, he had stood at the back of the garage watching the recovery of the primary tender. His presence instilled an anxiety to impress, as deckhands and engineers carefully craned and manoeuvred the damaged Riva into its leather covered chocks. The damage he had seen, crushed wood and trim discoloured with dark blue paint, could only have been inflicted by contact with another vessel. When asked, Vladimir had been dismissive, making it clear that information on the subject would not be forthcoming.

The Captain knew better than to press. He was well aware that he was a pawn in a larger game and understood he had crossed a line when following his employer's instruction not to report the missing helicopter to the authorities. And whatever had happened at sea with the Riva, he was in some way responsible. He did not know how much longer the kudos and salary of his position would stifle his qualms and hold him in place. Perhaps the time was drawing closer to find another job, if it was not already too late to escape with some vestige of integrity. He was snapped out of this train of thought by the voice from the VHF radio.

"*Natasha,* we are sending someone to assist you now."

"Great, thanks," he answered. Swapping the radio handset for the telephone intercom, he hit the button to call the engineers control room. It was answered immediately as he knew it would be, one of the pictures on the bridge security camera screen showed the Chief engineer attending to his Candy Crush addiction on the computer.

"Fire them up again Danny, we are about to leave."

On the monitor he could see his engineer reluctantly pull away from the colourful images and reach towards the engine controls.

The reassuring rumble once again reached the bridge. Pulling free the hand-held radio clipped to his belt, the Captain continued, absorbed now in the familiar tasks required to transition the yacht from a tethered, port bound hotel, into a self-sufficient sea-going entity, requiring of no outside help. At least until the next time they needed food, fuel, or shelter from the weather.

Over the personal radio he instructed his First Officer; "Confirm that all hatches remain secure and be ready to release our lines, please Ben. And two crew in the bow, two on the stern."

"All done, Sir. We are standing by, waiting your instructions," came the crisp reply.

"Good, the harbour assistance will be here shortly."

As the Captain lowered the handheld radio and looked across at the approaching launch, the vibrations under his feet faded away to nothing. Strident alarms sounded, and red lights beckoned for his attention. He was confused by the information on the screens. What they were telling him was highly improbable. To lose both engines at the same time had never happened to him during a quarter of a century afloat. One, sure, although even that was a rare event, given the amount of money available for maintenance and servicing. Running through various possibilities in his head, and coming up blank, he headed down to the engine room, hoping to avoid Vladimir until he knew what was going on.

Similar alarms and flashing red lights greeted him in the control room, a small office to the rear of the machinery space. Grabbing a set of ear defenders from the hook on the bulkhead, he joined his engineer who was crouched at the forward end of the starboard *Caterpillar*. Danny was using his hand to test the temperature of various bits of convoluted pipework.

A tap on the shoulder and Danny turned and straightened, acknowledging the Captain's presence with a perplexed raise of the eyebrows. Intimating with a jerk of the head that they should retreat to the relative quiet of the control room, Danny led the way back between the gleaming but recalcitrant engines. They passed the complex looking desalination plant with its huge internal pressures, and the towering red tool cabinet, mostly organized, but with an open drawer of jumbled and mixed up spanners which made the Captain's skin itch every time he saw it.

Once in the quieter space of his office, the engineer closed the door behind them and removed his ear defenders. Muting the alarms with a couple of quick taps on his control panel, he turned to the Captain.

"The sea water impellers on both engines are red-hot," Danny explained. "No water is getting to them. It can only be a blockage in the sea water cooling intake."

"But they have separate intake's, don't they? How can they both be blocked?" enquired the Captain, frowning as he conjured up a mental image of the pipework.

"You're right. There are two intakes, one on each side of the hull, but they are connected by a manifold. If one intake gets blocked, the other can still supply enough cooling water to keep both engines cool, at low RPM at least. They must both be blocked. That's happened to me once before, on a previous boat." A faraway look crossed Danny's eyes as he recalled the incident.

"We were anchored somewhere in Greece, can't remember where. During the night, a huge number of jellyfish ended up in the bay. They were small but there were thousands of them. When we started the engines, they were sucked into the intakes, and we had a hell of a job getting rid of them-"

"So, it might be jellyfish?" the Captain interrupted impatiently, bringing Danny back into the present.

"No, it's unlikely to be jellyfish here, too cold," Danny firmly concluded.

"Well, how soon can you check what it is and sort it out?" The Captain, silently wondered, not for the first time, why his engineer went off on such weird tangents sometimes.

"I can close the through-hull valves and pull the strainers from the manifold which will show us what's blocking them, but then I will need to take out the impellers on both engines as well. They've got hot enough to melt the rubber blades and will need replacing. Then, I will have to bleed any air out of the pipework. I suspect the whole job is going to take two or three hours, or more. Meanwhile, could we maybe send a deckhand underneath just to check the grills are clear?"

"Good, get on with it," the Captain said matter-of-factly. "Grab anyone from the deck crew to help if it will speed things up. And I will put someone in the water to see if they can find anything."

He leaned across and pulled the keys from the engine ignitions, placing them in the desk drawer. From the same drawer he lifted a laminated sign, declaring: 'DIVER DOWN, DO NOT START ENGINES OR THRUSTERS' and placed it over the control panel.

"Quick as you can, please Danny, I have Vladimir pushing me to be out of here as soon as possible."

Danny shrugged as he reached again for his ear defenders. It would take however long it took, regardless of what Vladimir or anyone else wanted. He was reminded how grateful he was that his role isolated him from the pressures of command. The extra salary just wasn't worth the hassle it came with as far as he could make out.

***

Vladimir was pacing up and down on the bridge when the Captain returned. Silently fuming, he listened as he was informed of the reason for the further delay. As frustrated as he was, he knew there was no point in berating the Captain. This was to be just another misfortune on his road to recovering the boxes. Once again, he wondered what else could go wrong.

"So, it will take at least two hours to sort this? How much longer is this settled weather going to stay?" Vladimir had stopped pacing and was sat now in the helmsman chair with his feet up on the dash, eyes staring straight ahead through the glass into the fading evening light. His mind briefly jumped to another bridge, less plush than this one, the smell of fear and cordite probably washed away by now.

The Captain clicked away in the background, rechecking various online weather information services before replying. Vladimir remained staring ahead, lost in his thoughts.

"Another twenty-four hours or so, according to most of these sites. Then a gradual decline of conditions until another cold front pushes through the day after tomorrow."

Vladimir contemplated this information. He thought it was still possible to find the helicopter and recover the boxes in the time available before the weather turned. Momentarily he considered turning to Matt and *First Light,* thinking a couple of hours could be saved, eventually deciding against it. For one, he didn't know for sure if Matt could be found or easily convinced to go to sea at this time of day, with darkness rapidly approaching. And loading all the required gear would also take some time.

As far as he knew, other than the Coastguard, no-one else had the co-ordinates. And, as long as another trawler didn't decide to operate in that area, the site should remain undisturbed for the moment at least. No, nothing else for it but to soak up the delay and stick to his original plan. In the meantime, he would take Victor and check over the diving equipment. As he came to this conclusion, simultaneously swinging his feet down off the dash, the radio on the Captains belt came to life.

"Sir, this is Danny, you had better come down and see this."

FOURTEEN

Despite our best efforts, it was dark when *First Light* finally slipped out between the castles guarding the river entrance. The moon was showing us the way, a road of silver laying on the surface of the black sea. I was sat at the helm with Andrew stood next to me, silent and thoughtful. The diving kit had needed some attention after so long in storage. I had waited in frustration on the dock until he had finally appeared, pushing a loaded trolley with both hands, mobile phone jammed between his shoulder and ear. He had looked at me quizzically as he finished the call and helped load the equipment onboard but remained silent until we had cleared the harbour limits.

"So just what did you do to *Natasha*?" he finally asked. "Because I have had the Captain on the phone claiming some sort of sabotage has been carried out, and he is furious."

I thought a while before responding.

"I squirted twelve tubes of expanding builders' foam into their engine's sea water intakes."

Andrew turned his head slightly towards me. "Did you know what it would do?"

"Well, to be honest, no," I replied. "I had hoped it would block the filters to some extent and slow down their departure for a few hours until they were able to clean it out. I assume from your phone call that I was at least partially successful?"

"You could say that. The Captain says the entire intake pipe on both sides is blocked, and they're struggling to dig it out. I imagine they are going nowhere until tomorrow at the earliest." He paused before continuing into my silence. "Oddly, as angry as he is, he didn't want the police to be informed. He said they would sort it out themselves, which kind of reinforces our view that they are up to no good, don't you think?"

I thought about their reaction for a moment. For the Captain not to inform the authorities when a thirty-million pound super yacht is deliberately sabotaged by persons unknown certainly suggests they do not want the eyes of officialdom casting their way. It made me think, not for the first time, that we were out of our depth in this situation, whatever it was.

"Do you want to stop this and turn back?" I finally proffered. "We could just step aside and let Jake and his crowd take it from here."

To my surprise, Andrew didn't respond right away. After a moment of reflection, he answered.

"Realistically, we *should* leave this to Jake and the authorities. He probably already has the position given to the Coastguard by *Southern Cross* and I'm sure he'll push the information up his chain of command. In due course a Navy dive team is likely to investigate, but from what I know about how fast organizations move, that won't happen for a day or two, at best. With *Natasha* out of action, we have a window of opportunity to take a look - *if* we can find the wreckage."

He paused looking at me enquiringly, then continued."That raises the question, of how you know where to look? You're going to have to explain that to me at some point." Andrew left the words hanging in the air as he alternately scanned the instruments and horizon, old habits returning unbidden.

Thinking I might as well come clean, I told him the details of my radio call, including that I may have slightly pretended to be the Coastguard. Disapproval clouded his features momentarily, but we kicked my actions around from every angle and concluded that no harm could come from my it, illegal as it was. The Coastguard already had the information required to mount a search for any potential wreckage and survivors from a possible aircraft ditching. Given that, we thought that no damage was likely done by me also obtaining this information, albeit in a duplicitous manner.

I was relieved though, when the conversation moved back towards what we should do from this point forward. Our deliberations were interrupted by the buzzing of my phone, for once fully charged and in my pocket. *Number withheld* was emblazoned across the screen.

"Yes?" I answered curtly, trying on a newly discovered telephone manner, and finding it surprisingly satisfying.

"Matt, it's Jake. I want to let you know no one has been able to get in contact with the *Southern Cross*. There has been no response to radio or satellite phone calls and her AIS system is no longer sending a position. I'm told it's unusual for an ocean-going fishing vessel to be unreachable, so a search will start for them at daybreak."

'*Shit.*' I recalled seeing the damage on the port side of *Natasha*'s tender, the crumpled woodwork, and streaks of blue paint. The conclusion was obvious, and I passed on my misgivings to Jake. The telephone was quiet for a while, long enough for me to wonder if we had lost connection, but a moment later Jake's voice came back.

"Okay. I'm going to push this up to my superiors and aim to get a warrant to go onboard the *Natasha*. I'll need you to write up a statement with everything you have told me so far. And everything you haven't. First thing in the morning, Matt."

***

It took us three hours of painstaking searching, Andrew's eyes fixated on the bright screen of the depth sounder, shades of red and yellow slowly scrolling from right to left, depicting the sea floor beneath us. All sorts of weird shapes and colourful speckles filled the centre of the display, their identity only to be guessed at; but the line showing the seabed remained resolutely flat, with only an occasional undulation to break the monotony. My attention was focused on the chart plotter where the boat symbol in the middle of the screen trailed a line recording our track as we criss-crossed over the position given by the skipper of the *Southern Cross*.

"What's that?"

Andrew's finger pointed at an irregularity on the otherwise flat red linen the depth sounder. I pushed a button on the plotter marking our current position, before turning to stare at the screen. The scale on the right-hand side showed a small red blob rising about two and a half meters from the bottom, much higher than any other irregularities we had so far seen.

"Maybe," I said. "I'll come around and drive over that spot again to see what it looks like from a different angle."

Andrew, happy to take a break from staring at the screen, scrunched up and rubbed his eyes, as I swung the helm around and tried to put us back exactly in our reciprocal track. We both held our breath as the boat symbol on the chart plotter covered the mark I had placed, our eyes alternating now between the plotter and depth sounder. Right on cue, the red blob slowly, incrementally, made an encore from stage right. It could still have been just about anything, from a rock to a shoal of fish, but it was certainly the most likely target we had seen since we began.

I continued steaming into the ebbing tide, until the intriguing blob departed the left side of the screen. Having taken up a position on deck, Andrew stood hunched over the small anchor windlass on the bow, awaiting my signal. A few seconds of astern on my engines stopped our headway and the short blip on the horn told him all he needed to know. Using both hands, he turned the windlass brake carefully anti-clockwise. With a sudden rush of chain clanking though the gypsy wheel, the anchor came free of its housing and started its decent into the darkness. As more chain was pulled from the locker under his feet, Andrew gradually tightened the brake to control the speed of the deployment. I allowed the tide to carry us back, my eyes once again glued to the depth sounder, waiting for the shape's reappearance.

And finally, interminably, it reappeared on the screen, seventy feet below us. Now, no longer scrolling across the display, but static. *First Light* held her position as the anchor bit into the sea floor, arresting our backwards movement with a creaking as the chain came tight and stretched out at a sharp angle from the bow. The forces in play balanced out, and we sat there comfortably, rolling in the underlying swell. Above us, a sliver of moon cast a disinterested glance in our direction.

"So... you still up for this?"

"Let's do it before we come to our senses," came the reply from the cockpit. Andrew, already in the process of donning his dry suit, was using action to mask his nerves, a hint of trepidation still evident in his voice. "We got lucky with the tide, no way we would be able to do this if it was springs."

Our buddy checks completed, and with a couple of chemical glow sticks securely fastened to our cylinders, so we could see each other, we stepped off from the modest platform on the stern. The last of the flood tide made for a stiff swim to the anchor chain where we began our descent. We had decided that swimming down the chain and using it as a tie off point to search from would be the safest course of action.

Without our torches, the dive would have been impossible. The absence of daylight in the plankton filled water meant anything not illuminated within the two-meter cone of light stabbing out from our torches ceased to exist. Even the seabed, when it loomed up at me out of the green-black darkness, came as a surprise. My sudden back peddling resulting in a swirl of silty sand erupting from the surface before being cleaned away with the current. I realized it was going to take a good element of luck to find our 'blob'. We could be within touching distance and have no idea.

Stabilizing myself and adjusting my buoyancy to remain just above the seabed, I made off the end of the guideline to the anchor chain with an overkill of knots, a task not made easier by the thick gloves of my suit. It struck me how similar the environment down here was to some of the situations I had found myself in the fire service. Perhaps a few more fish, but still plenty of things that could kill if you didn't pay attention. Or sometimes even if you did.

Staying close together, we allowed ourselves to slowly drift with the weakening current, now on the cusp of slack water. It gave us a window of less than an hour before the invisible, immense pull of the moon and sun continued its endless cycle, bending countless billions of tons of water to their unknowable will and sweeping us away in the process. It was with this existential thought in my head that I was carried headfirst into the shattered remains of a Perspex canopy. Thankfully enough of the broken canopy remained to prevent me from being pushed into the cockpit and into the lap of the horror which was to be found still tightly strapped in the pilot's seat.

An involuntary noise rose unbidden in my throat as my torch picked out the gruesome detail. The helicopter was lying on its side as if it were a toy, broken and abandoned. The corpse of the pilot was bloated unevenly, held in its seat by the harness. Its arms where buoyant, waving gently in the current to whatever creatures of the deep happened to pass by. I saw the rough outline of a head, slumped sideways on its shoulder; but that's where the similarity ended, as legions of tiny crabs and even tinier sea lice simmered on its surface and entered into the caverns where presumably the good bits were. Panic and revulsion overwhelmed me.

Desperate in my need to put distance between me and the contents of that cockpit, I flailed backwards. As my arm struck something, *someone*, in the darkness, the remaining strands of whatever held me together threatened to let go before the wide, alarmed eyes of Andrew, wreathed in a cloud of bubbles, came into focus. With immense effort, I controlled my breathing with deep, sucking breaths and slowly, I was able to squeeze my panic into a more manageable size.

When I had myself more or less back under control, I gestured for Andrew to close up on me, and we again approached the crashed helicopter. This time, I avoided looking in the cockpit, doubting that the image would ever leave my head. Andrew, forewarned by my histrionics, took a tentative look while I tied the guideline off to the twisted tube of metal, which I assumed was probably one of the landing skids. When it was secure, I turned and concentrated on checking out the rest of the wreckage.

The overall picture was hard to piece together given the visibility, but it looked as if the helicopter had settled on its starboard side on the seabed, mostly intact. Most of the damage appeared to be to the front of the machine, presumably where it had impacted the sea. Its rotor blades were gone, ripped off, leaving only ineffectual stubs protruding from the hub. Some fuselage panels were missing, giving a view of the surprisingly small engine. As I moved along the tail-boom, it ended abruptly, the aluminium tube cleanly severed about six feet from the main body. A short distance from the end of the foreshortened tail boom - at the limit of the beam of torchlight - was a rocky outcrop only a meter or so high, but a relative mountain on the flatness of the sea floor. A lobster was looking at me out of its crevasse home. I wondered what he made of the new addition to his front garden.

Andrew reappeared at my shoulder, shaking his head in disbelief. The small part of his face that was showing through his mask was looking, to my imagination anyway, noticeably paler. I motioned for him to follow me as I ascended the fuselage and located the side door to the back seats of the helicopter. Shining my torch down through the Perspex window, I forced myself to look inside, one small section at a time. If the back of this wreckage held similar horrors as the front, I reasoned that having smaller snapshots to haunt me would be preferable.

The rear compartment appeared free of further unpleasantness. Instead, most of the space appeared to be filled with a jumble of solidly constructed storage boxes, more military grade than *Ikea*. Broken tie-down straps undulating gently in the water, suggested the boxes had at some point been strapped down, and had ripped free on impact. I tried the door, getting only two of my gloved fingers into the recessed lever which operated the opening mechanism.

To my surprise, the door moved. A gap of about two inches appeared before it stopped. Presumably, the frame was bent by the impact, but the opening was big enough for us both to get a hand inside and wrestle it fully open, accompanied by the muffled sound of tortured metal as we pulled. There was only room for one of us to enter the confined space, and Andrew didn't seem too keen, so I moved around him and dropped cautiously down into the cabin.

The uppermost box was white and held closed with small clamps built into the top edge. It was almost too heavy for me to move, but after a struggle, I managed to pick it up and pass it overhead to the hands reaching down to take it. I was looking down at the boxes which remained, wondering how to go about getting them out, when, with no warning, my torch went out.

It was a matter of seconds before the reassuring beam of light from Andrew's torch cut down in the cabin where I stood on top of the remaining boxes, but those moments were not pleasant in any way. I was trained in moving around in the dark, but the disturbing scene in the front cockpit had rattled me. My imagination began to run out of control, and I wanted, once again, to be as far away from this tomb as possible. I swam upwards towards Andrew's light as soon as it appeared and signalled to him it was time to go. A check on our gauges confirmed this. We still had to make a safety decompression stop on our way up and could not afford to loiter much longer.

Andrew had dropped the first box down onto the seabed next to the wreckage of the helicopter. It sat there, to my mind, inviting further inspection. In my eagerness to get it out of the cabin, I had not really considered what we would do with the box at this point. We lacked the equipment to float it to the surface and it was far too heavy to try to carry with us. We could easily find ourselves in difficulties on the way up if we attempted it. Calmer, now that I was out of the confines of the helicopter, I indicated I was going to look inside the box. Andrew tried to dissuade me, concerned at our limited air supply and the very real possibility that opening it underwater would damage its contents. But I hadn't come this far to leave without at least seeing what was inside.

Deflating my buoyancy jacket a little, I sank to my knees on the seabed alongside the box. Once the disturbed silt settled around me, I started to lever open the catches that held the top in place. Andrew's curiosity took over and after a quick examination of both our air gauges, he too dropped to his knees and began to address the remaining clasps.

The lid lifted off without any bubbles following it, so either the box was never watertight, or it had lost its integrity upon the impact with the sea. Whatever the case may be, I felt better that my impatience to open it now seemed like the right decision. Jamming the lid under my knee to stop it floating away I peered inside.

The contents were covered with a thick layer of black felt, tucked tidily down both sides. Pulling it aside, we were presented with orderly rows of oblong plastic packets, measuring about an inch by an inch and a half. With the protective felt fully removed, the light from Andrew's torch resulted in a golden glow which had us looking at each other in wide-eyed excitement. Andrew pointedly looked at his gauge and made the 'ascend to the surface' signal with his thumb.

Ignoring him, I reached into the box and pulled out a handful of the plastic packets. They each contained a slim ingot of what appeared to be gold. The weight in my hand was surprisingly satisfying, as I began stuffing them into the pockets sewn into my buoyancy compensator jacket. I began to get a sense of the power gold can exert on the human psyche. Rational thoughts relating to our situation were pushed aside. No matter that we were seventy feet down on the floor of the English Channel, our life span in this environment measured only by the ever-decreasing distance of an impartial red needle from an equally disinterested 'zero.' No matter also, the dead pilot being slowly devoured, not three meters from us, and the cold-eyed Russian who undoubtedly had his own views about the ownership of these boxes. Everything became, for a brief, avaricious moment, irrelevant as I stuffed as many of the small plastic wrapped ingots as possible into my jacket. When the pockets could take no more, I discarded the removable weights, their purpose to negate the natural buoyancy of myself and my equipment and filled these spaces with yet more of the packets.

Across from me, I observed Andrew doing the same, hunched over and oblivious to anything other than the riches in front of us. Somehow, this reflection of my own greed seeped through my gold fever and brought me to my senses. *'Okay that, and the fact that I couldn't cram any more packets in anywhere.'* Brushing aside Andrew's hands, still reaching into the box, I placed the lid back on top and began refastening the clamps.

It was past time to go, but the idea of leaving this box, *our box*, sitting out in the open, couldn't be contemplated. Between us, we dragged it back towards the wreckage, Andrew's eyes quizzical behind his mask. Passing under the broken tail boom, we left the box behind the rocky outcrop with its lobster still in residence, before finning our way back to the landmark of the helicopter.

Studiously avoiding looking into the cockpit, Andrew untied the guideline from the twisted skid. Coiling it as he went, we followed it uneventfully back to our anchor chain to begin our ascent. Cutting our decompression stop five meters from the surface as short as we dared, we clambered back on board *First Light.* Little in the way of life sustaining air remained in our cylinders, but wide stupid grins were plastered across our faces.

***

We were both largely lost in our own thoughts for the first part of the trip back to port. If we had had more dive cylinders, or a compressor to fill our empty ones, there was no doubt we would have remained over the wreck, suppressing any thoughts as to what the *correct* course of action might be. We would have ignored the dead pilot, shoved aside any underlying uncertainty of the fate of the *Southern Cross,* and focused solely on recovering as many of those boxes as we could. To have to motor away from what appeared at first glance to be an immense fortune was not made in any way easier by the fact that it was our only possible course of action.

Discarded on the chart table was one of the hastily ripped open plastic packets, lying next to the slim gold ingot which it had contained. The bar was stamped with the characters; '*FINGOLD 1oz*' and had been poured over by us in great detail. It even had our teeth marks on it, as final confirmation of its authenticity to our minds.

"We have to tell Jake. The authorities. Whoever. It is not ours to take." Andrew finally broke the silence from his seat on a stool behind the chart table. Dim red light illuminated his worried features.

"Probably," I conceded. The entrance to the harbour was beginning to define itself through the windscreen.

"There is no 'probably', Matt," he stated. "People have more than likely been hurt or killed for those boxes. And they don't belong to us," he reiterated. "It remains to be seen who *does* own them."

He was right of course, but the sight of them, filled with who knew what manner of riches, was a hard one to push aside.

"Alright. So, we tell Jake we found the helicopter. And we tell him about the dead pilot." I paused. "But we don't necessarily need to tell him about the boxes in the back"?

"I think they come as a package, Matt."

I emitted a heavy sigh, only a fraction of which was theatrics. "I'll call him now."

Picking up my phone I saw that I had received a message from Kemp: *'Need you to provide cover at the station tomorrow from 07:00 - or the pump will be off the run. You are the only OIC in town tomorrow'.*

Swiping it away for the time being, I dialled Jake.

FIFTEEN

The wheelhouse clock was showing ten minutes to midnight when we docked in an empty berth on the town quay. The excitement of the last few hours was still coursing through our veins, the tantalizing memory of the boxes imprinted on our minds. Jake was waiting on the dock, leaning against a railing designed to stop tourists from falling in the river and something about his stance made me suddenly recall where I had seen him before. As unlikely as it was, I was certain he was the man I had seen talking with another stranger, at the house-fire a few nights ago.

In the absence of a police station, long since closed by budget cuts, and keen not to have officialdom any closer to our dive kit than necessary, we settled on going to Andrew's office to write our statements. I still wondered what possible reason Jake may have had to be at the scene of that fire at four o'clock on that morning. As we walked, I texted Kemp.

'Could really use a couple more days leave if possible'.

My phone rang back almost immediately. I excused myself and answered.

"You're the only one left in town with command qualifications, Matt," Kemp said. “Dennis has gone off long term sick with his back and Steve is away on business. If you really can't cover the station for the day, we will have to take the pump of the run, and you know the implications of that."

I was still coming to terms with the way these smaller, rural stations were run. It was getting harder and harder to find suitable people and expect them to spend most of their working day within five minutes of the station, ready to drop everything and respond to emergencies at a moment’s notice. With more and more people working out of town, or in jobs which would not allow them to leave, the frequency in which some provincial stations were unable to adequately crew an appliance was increasing. It had become a matter of honour among some of us, to not be *that* person; the one who had to make themselves unavailable and in so doing, take a fire engine out of service. Usually, this selfless stance came with consequences. Missed birthdays, annoyed wives, cancelled plans to dive on crashed helicopters stuffed with gold - that kind of thing.

"Okay, Boss, I will be on call from seven in the morning."

With a coffee maker spluttering away in the corner and a couple of extra chairs sequestered from a side office, we sat, loosely grouped, around Andrew's desk. It was an expansive oak affair, battered and seemingly unloved, jammed into a bay window overlooking the harbour with tidy stacks of paperwork at either end. Random nautical items were abandoned elsewhere on its stained surface. Small shackles, various bits of broken VHF radios, and odd lengths of line - their purpose only to be guessed at - made up most of the detritus; although tide tables, old and new, contributed to the overall impression that this was exactly how a harbour master's desk should, indeed, *must,* look.

Andrew had taken the opportunity while I was on the phone to bring up the subject of Destroyers, Libya, and the coincidence of over-lapping careers; and when I returned, the two of them were busy reminiscing about the good old days in the service of queen and country.

Two cups of mediocre coffee later and with our statements recorded, Jake sat back in his chair.

"What on earth made you go to the lengths you did to get the position of the wreckage from the *Southern Cross*? And then go and dive on it, at night, I might add."

I had to think a little about my answer before replying. At last, I concluded it was because I didn't really like Vladimir and his cohort Victor, and the chance of getting some information they desperately wanted, before them, appealed to me on some primal level. *I omitted to mention that I had sensed some sort of financial gain from having this knowledge, not that I'd had any idea how it could have manifested into something concrete until a few hours ago.* Jake nodded at my explanation, seemingly amused at my actions. I got the impression that it was exactly what he would have done.

That said, he was very clear in his order for us to cease and desist in any further involvement with this situation, echoing Andrew's earlier thoughts that we were in way over our heads and ill-equipped to deal with sunken helicopters and the likes of Vladimir. Given the uncertainty over the whereabouts of the *Southern Cross*, I had to agree with him on that.

In our statements however, we hadn't come completely clean either. Neither myself nor, to my surprise, Andrew, had made any mention of us opening and relocating a box down there.

I also reasoned, no matter how I slanted it, bringing to light my involvement in criminally damaging a super yacht was probably not in my best interest.

"Well, thank you for these," Jake said, gathering up his recording device and closing the laptop on which he had been taking notes.

"What do you think will happen now?" asked Andrew.

"I will speak with my boss first thing in the morning," he said. “I think they will put together a team from Plymouth police to board the *Natasha* so we can examine their damaged tender. I've spoken with the Captain, who was not forthcoming, but I imagine he will be more accommodating if we impound the vessel and refuse them permission to leave until this is all cleared up."

As he made to go, Jake turned back to us with a stern expression. He reiterated his earlier advice, this time making it sound more like an order.

"Stay away from them. These are dangerous individuals who will not hesitate to ruin your day."

I walked with him to the front door. Outside, an insolent looking seagull was pecking holes into a rubbish sack, the pure white of its feathers contrasting sharply with the black plastic. Glancing sideways at us in the doorway, we were dismissed as irrelevant, our presence apparently not imposing enough to sway it from its task. Rubbish day in Dartmouth.

"Goodnight," I proffered. "By the way, I hope you don't mind me asking, but didn't I see you in the early hours of Tuesday morning in Church Road, at the house fire? Was that connected to this business in some way?"

Jake looked at me carefully before responding.

"I must be slipping, I used to be much better at going around unnoticed."

I waited. After a pause where he seemed to consider his reply, he continued. "Yes, it was me. It was a totally unconnected case, one which has now died, along with the chap you dragged out of the house."

There was a note of finality in his voice, an intonation forestalling any more questions on the subject. With that, Jake made his way down the road, avoiding the pools of orange light cast by the streetlights and was soon enveloped by the shadows.

***

At about the same time as Jake had been greeting us on the town quay, merely seven hundred meters away, the bridge of the *Natasha* was once again the scene of heated debate. At least, one side of the debate was heated while the other sat in cool silence, until the Captain finished his rant.

"You know I am loyal to Dimitri, as are the remaining crew, and you know we have never questioned the activities on board."

Vladimir waited for the inevitable '*but.*' He was not disappointed.

"But the yacht has been immobilized to the point where the crew are working all night to try to fix it. And there is no guarantee they will be able to, without lifting the boat out of the water. On top of that, an official claiming to be from the British National Crime Agency has been in contact asking me for an explanation on our tender's movements. An explanation that I am unable to give him. Whatever game you are playing, it appears to be getting out of control."

"What's this about an official?" Vladimir asked, suddenly interested. "Which agency did you say?"

"He said he was from the National Crime Agency-"

Vladimir was on his feet, pacing the bridge at the same time as digging his mobile phone from his pocket and tapping the screen.

The Captain continued. "Had some 'routine questions' regarding the vessel's movements for me-"

Vladimir held up a finger, demanding silence, as his call went through.

"I assume you have something important to tell me, calling at this hour?" Dimitri's voice contained traces of sleep and irritation in equal measure.

"Sir, I believe I know the location of the helicopter. By tomorrow I may have some better news for you."

The line from Cypress remained silent for a moment.

"I don't want hopes and maybes, I want my fucking boxes!"

Vladimir stifled his exasperation at having to deal with this man, who, if all had gone to plan, would have been in the early stages of decomposition by now, instead of giving him grief on the phone.

"I understand your frustration, Sir, but I am working on getting them back. The reason I'm calling is that there is something you might be able do from your end to help."

"Which is what, exactly?"

"We are receiving some attention from the National Crime Agency." He left the statement hanging with more silence waiting to be filled.

Dimitri pushed himself up on an elbow, looking over at the woman sleeping next to him, her brunette hair splayed across the pillow, features sagged by sleep. It didn't bother him that he couldn't recall her name.

"Wait a moment, I'm going to my desk." Eventually he asked, "What sort of attention?"

"I'm not sure of the extent, but at least one officer in this area is sniffing around and asking questions."

Vladimir pictured Dimitri sat in his office at the villa. *A Kimono robe around his corpulent frame. Russian religious icons looking down at him from the walls, the judgment and oversight they contained, skilfully imbued by long dead artists, presumably lost on him.*

"I can try to shut that down, although my influence there is waning. Anything else?"

"Perhaps you can have a quick word with your Captain. He seems to be getting cold feet." Vladimir didn't wait for a reply. He passed the phone over to *Natasha's* Captain who reluctantly took the proffered handset, a shadow of fear in his eyes.

***

The next call originating from the icon festooned room in Cypress was to an unregistered, pre-paid mobile, no identity required for its purchase, no record of who owned it. It rang five times, on the cluttered bedside table of a discreet town house located in a quiet mews just off Kensington high street. A reluctant hand slid out from under the goose down duvet, fumbling around before finding, and clicking on the ornate lamp. The line of light escaping from the gap in the curtains was noticed and dismissed as irrelevant by the guard detail standing in the small security post at the entrance of the mews.

The call was answered with a note of irritation.

"Yes?"

"Call off your dogs, right now."

***

With Jake gone, I re-joined Andrew, and we headed up the stairs to his apartment.

"No Matt, we are not going back down there."

One floor up from the office, ensconced in his comfy sofa with a chunky glass of whisky in his hand, Andrew sounded adamant. Anna, busying herself with pouring drinks, trailed Andrew's statement with one of her own.

"It's simply too dangerous."

She passed me my drink, the amber liquid sloshing against the sides, no ice to baffle the free surface effect of the large glass. Sitting down next to Andrew on the sofa, a splash of wine her choice, she continued.

"You boys have had your adventure." Anna turned to me. "And by the way, don't think we aren't going to have a conversation about the risks you took with my husband's life. But enough is enough. In any case, with us going away tomorrow and you on call for the fire station all day, leaving things to your new policeman friend is the obvious course of action."

Not to be deterred just yet, I said, "I want to show you something."

I pulled out my phone and opened my search bar to where *Google* confidently told me today's spot price of gold. (*A term I was familiar with, thanks to a disastrous foray into the roller-coaster world of financial spread betting a few years ago. Dreams of beating the markets, quickly and inevitably turning into the nightmare of chasing losses and margin calls. Fun while it lasted, but unsustainable on a firefighter's salary).*

Currently the gold price stood at eight hundred and forty pounds an ounce. By my reckoning we had about one hundred of the small packets crammed into each buoyancy jacket, approximating a total value of one hundred sixty-eight thousand pounds.

That information, when I told them, resulted in the levels of their glasses falling to an unacceptable level. I made the rounds, replenishing the drinks in near silence. The only sounds to be heard was the splash of liquid and the sound of squabbling seagulls through the bay window. A sense of paranoia crept over me, an illogical dread, that even now, someone was finding our stash, taking it from us. The feeling left me stifling the urge to run back to *First Light* and check on our haul. I wondered if this is what being rich felt like.

"Just the one box has probably got another two thousand bars in it." I let them to do the mental arithmetic, wondering if their viewpoint may now change.

"One point six million!?" Anna got there first. "And how many boxes did you see?"

"It was hard to tell, but I think there were about five or six which looked similar to the one we got out."

Andrew nodded in confirmation, and I continued.

"There was also a black one at the bottom of the jumble, but it's possible they don't all have gold in though..."

My last sentence was lost on them as they were already working on the additional maths, as was I. This time it was me who got there first, thanks to my phone's calculator.

"Another six boxes, assuming the same contents, would bring the total to about ten million, give or take."

We kicked it around for a while longer, thinking through how we would get the rest of the boxes to the surface and where we would hide them. And, taking the inevitable flight of imagination, deciding what we would spend it on. Eventually, though, the voice of reason seeped into our conversation as we recalled Jake's direct order to 'stay away'. His warning about Vladimir's ruthlessness, coupled with the lengths Vladimir might be prepared to go to in recovering his boxes, made the risks seem too great. It also didn't sit well with us that we were almost certainly pilfering a crime scene.

So, it was with considerable reluctance that we decided to do nothing more for the moment, other than go about our usual lives, trying to quash the thoughts of the untold riches within our grasp. Riches lying guarded only by the ghostly, and gradually diminishing remains of the pilot.

I wondered how long we would keep that up.

SIXTEEN

Dressed for a run around the local park, Deborah Hance was on the way out of her front door by seven A.M. which was usually the best time of the day to accomplish this undisturbed. Not today though. The mobile phone strapped to her upper arm squeezing motivational power ballads to her ears through thin white wires, rang before she had even reached the street.

"Good morning, Sir."

Surprise crept unbidden into her voice. She could not recall ever being called by her boss this early on a Saturday morning. The Director General was well-known as a late riser, an inevitable consequence of long evenings spent socializing with the movers and shakers in his world. A seemingly endless stream of dinners and functions, any one of which might and often did, lead to a connection, a snippet of information - the inside line in his quest to rise higher.

Straight to the point, he asked, "Are we still running an investigation into Dimitri Petrovich?"

Deborah stopped, her free hand on the latch to the low gate which gave access to the deserted pavement.

"Yes, albeit in a limited form. Dimitri is no longer in the country, and we will refuse him leave to return, so I have redirected resources, for the most part, to other cases."

"So, what exactly *are* we doing and where is it leading?"

She paused before answering, glancing wistfully down the empty street, and wondering how the remnants of this investigation had piqued his interest. And why had he felt the need to inquire in person at this hour, rather than remaining true to his more usual approach of waiting for the weekly updates to ping into his inbox. Sensing her morning run was fading away into the distance without her, she quickly and concisely filled him in on the events, as far they knew them, surrounding the departure of Vladimir, the disappearance of the helicopter and their ongoing limited surveillance of the Motor Yacht *Natasha*.

"So, you just have one officer down there?"

"Yes sir, Jake Hadley. I'm expecting an update from him this morning when I get to the office."

"Isn't Jake Hadley the new guy, over from MI6?"

Debora was impressed. The Director General's job, whilst requiring a level of involvement and oversight in the day to day operations of the NCA, was more a strategic and political role. She hadn't credited her boss with keeping track of his staff, certainly not the officers all the way down at the sharp end. Her respect for him clicked up a notch.

"Well, Officer Hadley isn't all that new to us. He came over from MI6 about two years ago and before that, some secret squirrel branch of the Military. He was in the same area as the yacht, which as I mentioned, we believe to be owned, somewhat circuitously, by Dimitri. We tasked Hadley with nosing around and shaking a few trees. He's keeping an eye on the boat and seeing what Dimitri's enforcer, Vladimir gets up to. I'm expecting a report from him today, but to be honest, running surveillance with only one officer is rather pointless. Depending on what his report contains, I was probably going to stand him down and put him on something else."

The DG reflected on what Debora had told him.

"Bring him back today. As you say, surveillance with only one set of eyes is not effective or productive."

"You don't want to wait until I receive his report, Sir? I know it's a long shot, but he may have come across something we can pursue."

"No Debora, we haven't got the budget for wild goose chases," he answered bluntly. "I'm sure we can find a better use for him elsewhere. There is a budget meeting coming up next week and I don't want to have to explain to the bean counters why we are wasting resources on an operation that we are not fully committed to. He needs to come back. Today."

"Okay then, sir, I will recall him this morning."

No longer in the mood for running, Debora turned and headed back towards her front door, thoroughly bemused by her boss's early morning directive. Jake's call, coming not five minutes after hanging up from the DG, didn't make her ruminations any easier.

***

"So, we have a missing trawler, the disappearance of which is possibly connected to Vladimir, and two locals claiming to have found a helicopter with a dead pilot in it at the bottom of the English Channel."

Despite being mostly desk-bound at this stage in her career, Deborah was a detective at heart with skills learned the hard way during the early years in uniform, the same skills tempered into effectiveness by repeated investigations as a detective sergeant in the Met. She had first-hand experience of having her work and her conclusions dismissed as not reaching the required threshold of proof for prosecution or further action, despite knowing she was right. It was through this filter of experience that she looked at the information Jake was relaying to her.

Given the standing of the two locals intertwined in this investigation, locals who Jake had assessed as '*reliable members of the public, not prone to flights of fantasy*', it was reasonable to accept they had indeed found Dimitri's missing helicopter. How they managed that - and she had listened with a frown of disapproval to Jake's explanation of Matt's radio deception - she was still not completely sure. But, if one was to accept *that* as believable, then the suspicion that the *Natasha's* tender had been damaged in an incident with a fishing vessel must also be given some weight. Or at a minimum, not dismissed before consideration of the possibility.

Jake had been convinced by them, and Debora knew there was enough to go on to at least get a warrant to examine the damaged tender and ask some other agency, probably the Navy, to go and investigate the helicopter wreckage.

"You did make it clear to them not to be go back to the helicopter?" she asked. "And to stay well away from Vladimir?"

"Yes Ma'am, and I think they will do just that. What's not making sense to me, is why the *Natasha* is still in port. If Vladimir had managed to get hold of the co-ordinates of the wreckage from the *Southern Cross*, you'd think they would have set sail immediately to try to find it. I'm told the good weather will only remain for another twenty-four hours or so down here."

"I don't know why that might be either, but it gives us some time to get on board and ask some questions," Debora said. "I was supposed to close down this investigation today and reassign you, but given what you have told me, I need you down there. I will set things in motion with regard to examining the *Natasha's* tender and organizing the Navy to carry out a dive. You stay in place and liaise with the local force. I want you on that yacht today."

Without waiting for a response, Debora hung up, then immediately rang her superior to relay Jake's findings. Given the new information from Jake, Deborah, had not expected to meet much resistance to her not following her boss's directive of this morning. She was mistaken.

"Damn it all, Debora, I told you to close it down, not start chasing half-baked leads!"

"But, Sir, we can't ignore this," Debora insisted, "surely there is enough here to warrant further action. We may be dealing with multiple homicides here."

"Based on what?" came the reply. "You only have anecdotal evidence that the yacht's tender was damaged, and even if it is, it could be totally unconnected. Boats are always bumping into things, goes with the territory. Did this pair of locals bring up anything to prove there is a helicopter down there? Anything at all?"

"No, but Sir, don't you think it is too coincidental that at the same time as we are aware of a helicopter going missing - *Dimitri's helicopter,* I might add - his yacht and henchman turn up in the same place where two upstanding members of the public, unconnected to any of this, claim to have stumbled across it?"

The Director General of the NCA stifled a sigh with some difficulty. He was not happy with the position he now found himself in. Debora was not a fool, but she was also not the only recipient of an early morning phone call today.

His had come from the rarefied air of Whitehall. The words had been spoken with hushed confident undertones, latent power infused in every calculated word and sentence. A seemingly harmless enquiry into a case all but closed and forgotten. An unspoken inference to 'let sleeping dogs lie, no good to come of it old chap, cast your inquisitive mind elsewhere, this is old news'.

He was not unfamiliar with the currency of favours. A quid pro quo here and there was the oil that eased the doors on the upward-sloping corridors of power. He was not even averse to it, keen to be treading those very same corridors himself in the not too distant future. But he knew it would not be possible to pull the wool over Deborah's eyes. She was too good a police officer, and he recognized that he had already pushed things with her to the point where alarm bells would be ringing.

So, surprising himself slightly when the revelation hit him, he discovered that despite the insatiable desire for his professional upward trajectory to continue, he was not inclined to step too much further beyond what could be considered the normal give and take of political expediency. It was becoming clear that something was going on down in the West Country, and he, like Deborah, was a policeman first and foremost, and getting to the bottom of things is what they did. Another sigh, this time not stifled, but the Katabatic out flowing of a decision reached.

"Fine. Put together a team to investigate the *Natasha* and her tender. And start the ball rolling with the Navy. I'm sure they will be more than happy to have something to do. Actually, now that I think of it, get the police dive section to handle the diving with the Navy. If there has been foul play, better that there are trained officers down there rather than some *Jack Tar* in heavy boots. Keep me updated." He hung up the phone, wondering what he would say to the Home Secretary if he called again.

***

After his conversation with Deborah, Jake left his hotel room and made his way down the hotel's narrow stairs, each wooden step squeaking with age. Over a hurried breakfast in the communal dining room, he made a call to the Duty Sergeant at Crown hill police station in Plymouth and identified himself.

"Can you rustle up some spare bodies for a search and some interviews? I know its short notice, but I need them today."

"You know its Saturday, right?"

"I know, sorry. Use your overtime budget if you must. I'll need at least four officers. Anyone with some knowledge of boats would be an advantage. I will be there in an hour to brief them. Oh, and you'll need to provide the transport."

A sigh reached him through the handset. "I will have to check with my inspector, but I'll see what I can do."

Apparently, it had not proved too difficult to find four officers willing to poke around on a super yacht, weekend or not. By mid-morning, Jake was stood to one side of the group on the small landing stage in front of the Harbour office. A battered looking work launch approached and docked neatly alongside.

"Step aboard gentlemen."

Andrew joined them just as they had all clambered into the launch with varying degrees of inelegance. Taking a seat up in the bow, he was more than happy to let Jess take care of the boat handling. She was something of an enigma, Andrew reflected as they chugged out across the river towards the *Natasha*. One of his most hard-working and trusted workers, despite having joined the team only a few years ago, Jess's persona hinted at an intelligence and depth which was at odds with the minimum wage, mostly manual work which she seemed to like so much, irrespective of the weather. Andrew's secretary had told him of the time Jess, on one her infrequent forays into the office, had solved an issue with the recalcitrant and outdated computer system, with an ease hinting at knowledge unlisted on her resume. A woman of well-hidden depths, but she could certainly handle a boat as if to the manner born.

'Yes," he concluded, 'if anyone could help Matt get over Sophie, it would be Jess.'

His musings were cut short as they came alongside the Natasha. A frowning Captain reluctantly opened the side gate to allow the police officers, led by Jake to step onboard. Andrew and Jess remained in the launch. When the last of the policemen had clambered up onto the yacht, Andrew turned to Jess.

"They will be awhile here, and I have a long drive ahead of me today. Drop me back ashore would you, then come back here and wait for these guys to finish."

"Sure thing, Boss. I hope you enjoy your reunion, how long has it been?"

He answered as they chugged back across the river.

"It's been twenty-five years since we all passed out of the Naval College." Andrew's shaking head intimated disbelief that such a period of time could have elapsed. "It would have been a lot easier for me if they had organized the reunion here, instead of four hundred miles away. Thanks again for dog sitting while we are away." He stood as they approached the dock.

"My pleasure. I'm just sorry I can't keep him at my place, but the landlord is adamant about no pets. One of those allergy types." Jess rolled her eyes in mock exasperation.

Andrew smiled as he stepped out of the launch on the town quay. He pushed the bow of the boat out with his foot, sending her on her way.

"Call me straight away if anything crops up work wise."

She flung a loose salute at him before chugging away across the river. As he watched her progress back towards the *Natasha*, he couldn't help but think once again, she and Matt were made for each other, if only he could be persuaded to let go of the past.

***

"I'm letting you on as a courtesy," the Captain said, matter-of-factly. "This is a Cayman Island flagged vessel and you have no evidence of any wrongdoing, so you don't have any authority to board us," As an afterthought he added, "And, we don't have anything to hide."

"It's appreciated, thank you," replied Jake as the group of police officers followed the Captain down the side, before spilling out onto the expanse of the aft deck. A crew member standing optimistically with a box of blue plastic shoe covers was ignored. The Captain didn't push the point, the look in Jake's eyes told him it was never going to happen.

Jurisdiction issues on foreign flagged vessels were complex, as Jake had found out when applying for permission today. The best the police lawyer was able to come up with over the phone at short notice was, 'I'm not sure'. Jake got straight down to business.

"Do you carry any firearms on board?"

The Captain paused briefly before replying, wondering what Vladimir and Victor could have been up to, to prompt the question.

"Well, we keep a couple of sporting shotguns for clay shooting off the stern when the owner has guests onboard. When we are in open water, of course. But that's it. They are in a safe in my cabin."

"Show me. In the meantime, these officers can start talking to the crew."

The Captain's quarters were located at the back of the bridge. They consisted of a small office with an uncluttered desk, an en suite marble bathroom and a sizable bed. With the door open, Jake thought it would be possible to see most of the important *Navionics* screens on the bridge from the duvet covered bed; had the Captain felt like taking a sick day.

Opening a wardrobe door, an armful of neatly pressed clothes was slid to one side, revealing the grey gun safe bolted to the bulkhead behind.

"Who has access to this?" Jake asked, as a code was tapped into the safe's keypad.

"Only me. And It hasn't been opened since we arrived in UK waters."

The safe door swung open to reveal two shotguns snugly held in velvet covered clamps. Other than the two shotguns, the safe was empty. The *'couple of sporting shotguns'* looked to Jake like *Purdeys* and were undoubtedly worth as much as a small house. He lifted them out of their rack one at a time. He broke the highly engraved action open and looked along the smooth bore of the twin barrels. If they had been fired recently, it didn't show. The barrels were spotless, with a thin film of oil protecting them, inside and out, from the salty marine environment.

Wiping the oil from his hands onto his jeans as the Captain relocked the safe, Jake made his way out of the cabin, back onto the bridge. If there were weapons on board other than what he had just been shown, he knew finding them would be next to impossible. There were just too many places on a vessel this size where they could be hidden. He decided to take a different tack.

"Why is your tender damaged?"

Before the Captain had a chance to respond, they were interrupted by the arrival of a third person at the top of the bridge stairs.

"I can answer your question."

Jake recognized Vladimir from the briefing notes which had been sent to him. They eyed each other warily, both seeing something in the other which demanded a degree of caution.

"I'm listening." Jake waited.

"I will answer your question, not that I am obliged to. And then you and your policemen will leave. You have no cause or authority to come aboard this vessel, and *he*" -Vladimir pointed at the Captain- "should have refused to let you onboard."

Next to Jake, the Captain visibly slumped. He may be the one wearing the stripes, but there was no doubt as to who was actually in charge here. Jake continued to stare at the newcomer on the bridge.

"And yet here I am. So, tell me what happened to the tender, and we can be on our way."

Vladimir returned Jake's stare, the silence stretching out, until at last, he said, "The *Riva* received some damage due to my carelessness. That is all. I was taking a trip up the river, practising my boat handling for want of something to do. Coming alongside a wharf, I misjudged the tide, and we crunched into the stone wall. Unfortunate, and I will need to have an awkward conversation with my boss, but these things happen."

"And was this stone wall painted blue?" Jake asked.

Vladimir stiffened almost imperceptibly as he processed Jake's statement. The information that the damage to the tender had included streaks of blue paint could only have been passed to this policeman by Matt, or his girlfriend, after they had seen Vladimir and Victor return from the *Southern Cross*.

"I see we have mutual friends. But they are mistaken, there is no blue paint on the damaged tender. Come, we can look together. And then you will leave." With that, Vladimir turned and descended the spiral staircase.

Jake followed him down, unwilling to lose sight of the person that his well-developed senses were telling him to be extremely careful of. But considering Vladimir's offer to inspect the damage, he was in no doubt that any trace of blue paint would be long gone. Unless the interviews with the crew members had thrown up anything, Jake realized they were probably wasting their time here.

And, so it turned out. Settled on its chocks, the tender was in the final stages of repair, damaged woodwork already cut out and skilfully replaced, bare wood awaiting varnish. If there had been any blue paint, it was no longer evident. Speaking to the crew had proved equally unforthcoming, with them remaining tight-lipped and monosyllabic in their answers.

Having climbed back down the side of *Natasha* into the launch, Jake pulled his mobile phone free of his pocket and called Deborah. Nothing tangible had come out of the visit, in fact, it had been mostly a waste of time. But now Vladimir knew he was on the radar, it was possible his hand would be forced, which was when mistakes were made.

SEVENTEEN

Four hours before Jake and his ensemble where stepping onto the Natasha, my alarm woke me, if awake is what it could be called, after a restless, dream filled sleep. Upon my return last night, the first thing I did was to check on the gold with the growing feeling that this was going to be a reoccurring theme.

At some point during the previous evening, Andrew and I had decided the best place for it - for the time being at least - was exactly where it was, masquerading as dive weights. Marvelling at how such a small sliver of metal could be worth so much, I had replaced the ingot we had opened back into its torn packet before sliding it with some difficulty back into my B.C. Then, after double, *triple,* checking the pockets were all secure and the dive gear locker was fastened with a padlock, I had finally crashed onto my bed.

I knew there would be a list of routine testing of equipment and cleaning duties to be carried out at the fire station, and I hadn't exactly been pulling my weight in that department over the last few days, so I resolved to make up for it by actually going in for the day, rather than just clipping the pager to my belt. Hopefully keeping busy would stop my mind from wandering back to the events of yesterday. After a shower, coffee and a stale, leftover doughnut, I jumped down onto the dock and headed towards my motorbike, proud of myself that I only went back once to double check the padlock.

***

My heart wasn't really in it, but after another cup of coffee, I put my mobile phone in my locker for safekeeping and unhooked the fire trucks from their charging leads. The concertina doors to the appliance bay rattled open, and I drove the trucks out onto the forecourt. Other than for the two oil drip trays, the red tiled floor space was now empty. I began to lackadaisically sweep the floor with an oversized broom whose head was about to fall off.

Kemp was right, the tally board showed only five people available, including me, to man the pumps today. Fingers crossed we didn't get a big working job as it would be a long thirty minutes or more waiting for support appliances from neighbouring towns to show up.

Time dragged. Tasks I usually enjoyed became frustrating and mundane. It was impossible to keep the images of yesterday's dive from running through my head and it was all I could do to stop myself from returning to *First Light* to check on the gold ingots. I also wasn't completely sure that I would be able to resist going back to the wreckage. Even though we had agreed the risks were too great, the lure of those boxes was seeping through the barrier of good sense and beckoning me like the siren call of a mermaid.

No calls to action came to break the monotony of the morning. Not even a seagull stuck in the anti-bird netting which was slowly proliferating the town. Beans on some dubious toasted bread was all I was able to rustle up for lunch in the small kitchen. It was a measure of my boredom that even the idea of getting pecked by the vicious beak of an ungrateful seagull whilst at the top of a thirteen-meter high ladder held some appeal.

After lunch, more out of boredom than a need for cleanliness, I lifted my fire kit off its peg and shook the boots free of the leggings. Going through the numerous pockets on my way to the station's battered and leaking washing machine produced a handful of items, the like of which I knew could be found in most fire fighters' kit. A spring-loaded centre punch, *nothing better for turning the side windows of most cars into a white haze of small crystals, free to rain down harmlessly onto the tarmac.* Laminated aid-memoirs for more complex incidents, a whistle, stubs of chinagraph pencils and a knife completed the inventory. But coming up enclosed in my fingers on the final dig, along with the never used penknife, was a small hard rectangle of plastic. The metal tongue sticking out of one end identified it - even to me - as a memory stick.

I recalled for the first time since that incident, picking the object up from underneath the house fire casualty, not three days ago. Intrigued, and not just a little concerned about introducing a virus to the station computer, I nevertheless slid it, at the second attempt, into the slot on the elderly desktop unit, which seemed most willing to accept it. Opening the files it contained was simply a matter of a few clicks. Which was good because even this relatively simple task had taken me to the border of the wasteland that was my computer literacy.

The screen showed two lines of file icons, a total of ten separate documents. Clicking on the first one revealed a type of spreadsheet, names and numbers meticulously ordered. Most of the remaining documents were similar, some contained address, hundreds of them, spread all over the counties of Devon and Cornwall. The last two were written in what appeared to be code. Lines of gibberish interspersed with what may have been dates, defied translation. By me, anyway.

My sleuthing was interrupted by the sudden cacophony of the stations call-out system. The air filled with the sound of a siren and the lights flickered on automatically. It never got old, being at a station when the 'bells went down'. Ejecting the memory stick from the computer I took it to my locker. Leaving it on the top shelf, I reached in and pulled out my spare fire kit, getting dressed before hurrying back to the office to read the printout chattering out of the teleprinter. Outside, the first of a handful of cars screeched into the yard.

It was a different perspective, to be sat in the front left seat of the appliance, and not in the back. A mindset more focused on how to manage your resources towards a safe and efficient outcome, rather than just running through the narrower requirements of your role, as the guys in the back would be doing. This job though, was bread and butter to me. I had turned out to plenty of car fires during my career and the procedures came as naturally as breathing.

I twisted round to brief the crew as we headed out of the station.

"If it's actually something, two B.A.s with hose reels, and Dave, find us a hydrant as soon as possible, got it?"

"Yep, got it, Matt."

A plume of thick, black smoke could be seen towering skywards as we arrived at the car, parked on the opposite side of the road to a boutique hotel. A small crowd had gathered, standing a respectful distance up-wind. Two small, red fire extinguishers had been discharged and were now lying discarded to one side, their meagre contents proving no match for the ferocity of the fire in the engine compartment.

With the appliance parked diagonally in the 'fend off' position, providing a degree of protection to the crew from the traffic, hose reels were run out. My two colleagues, in full breathing apparatus approached the car, checking that it was empty. Their arrival coincided with the scream of the pump, as it was clutched in, feeding high pressure water from the onboard tank to the nozzles in their hands. My last remaining crew member ran out a couple of lengths of red hose. Plugging it into a hydrant was a priority as our tank would last for no more than a few minutes.

Happy that all was as it should be, I took care of the radio messages to Control and watched as the copious amounts of water turned the black smoke white, before finally diminishing it to nothing more dramatic than the odd wisp. Even they gave up in the end.

"You're going to have to call it in as arson," Simon said as he pulled his face mask off. I looked in surprise at his sweaty face.

"Really?"

"There is a blow torch, on the road under the engine compartment. Looks like that's what started it off."

"Haven't seen that before. Thanks, Simon."

With the police in attendance and a recovery truck on its way, I noted the ping pong ball in the appliances sight glass jiggle its way back up to the top as the hydrant replenished our tank. Free of anything to do, my thoughts returned inevitably to the helicopter and its boxes of gold. The frustration of not being able to go back down there required constant suppression. My mind was brought back to the present by the arrival of Jake, an unreadable expression his face.

"What happened to my car?"

"That was your car?" I couldn't keep the surprise out of my voice.

"Well, not exactly mine, but I do have to account for it."

I sympathized with him, knowing only too well the paperwork he would face. I had scratched and dented more than my fair share of fire service vehicles in my career. Never had one set alight though.

"It looks like you have pissed someone off," I said before going on to explain the blow torch under the engine.

"We took a look around the *Natasha* today. I would guess that this was Vladimir's way of expressing his displeasure."

"Did you find anything?"

Jake shook his head.

"No, nothing useful. But looking at that" -he pointed at his car- "we touched a nerve."

***

Shortly after five P.M., the fire station's availability board began to look healthier. Out-of-town workers, home from their day jobs were once again able to answer the beepers clipped to their belts. By six o'clock, enough people had put themselves back on call for me to contemplate throwing a leg over my motorcycle and heading down the hill to my floating home. But try as I might, I could not get the idea of going back for those boxes out of my head. And I didn't know if my resolve to stay away would be up to the job if I went back on board right now. If I was going to remain true to our word, a distraction would be required.

Seeing a clear starlit sky and dry road outside, my mind was made up. A decent meal wouldn't go amiss since the cupboards on First Light contained only pasta and pesto. It occurred to me that this might be a good opportunity to make amends with Jess for my apparent reluctance to have a drink with her. Rescuing my phone from the locker I saw there was a message from Andrew.

'Need to tell you something, give me a call when you get this.'

I called him back, getting only his voice mail. Resolving to try again later, I dialled Jess, with a degree of trepidation.

"Hello, Matt. If you need another lift, I'm sorry, but I'm not working."

'Ouch'.

"No. No lift required. I wondered if you would like to take a bike ride along the coast, make good on that drink I owe you, or maybe even some dinner? Unless you have other plans?"

The chill had disappeared from her voice when she answered.

"On the bike? Yes, that would be great."

"You said you might have a helmet lying about somewhere?"

Without it I was going to look like a bit of an unprepared buffoon, an image I didn't want her to have of me.

Thankfully, she replied, "I last saw it on top of my wardrobe, so definitely, it's around here some place."

"I will pick you up in twenty minutes. Where do you live?"

"Oh, I'm staying at Andrew and Anna's place to watch their dog, while they are away for a few days. But I'll run back to my place for the helmet before you get here."

"Great, see you then."

I finished the remainder of my chores with a spring in my step, the images of box's full of gold not completely eradicated but at least dimmed by the thought of seeing Jess again.

***

After running the bike's engine until the temperature gauge began to show signs of life, I clambered onboard and turned right out of the yard towards the town centre. The front door of the harbour office opened at the sound of my arrival and with a squeeze of my arm, she threw her leg over the seat and hopped on. Adjusting to the addition of a passenger on the back, I failed to notice Victor, sat hunched in a car parked down the street as we pulled away.

The coast road out to Torcross village was a joy of twists and turns, little traffic at this time of the evening and the motorcycle beneath me came alive. It was in its element, as I braked hard into corners and powered out of them, the sensation of precision and control more the result of *Honda* engineering than any skill on my part, but the exhilaration was not to be denied. Jess was a natural, leaning with me into the bends, the only clue I had to her presence were the arms wrapped around me. A not altogether unpleasant sensation.

EIGHTEEN

The Start Bay Inn used to be the only place to consider if a decent plate of fish and chips was required. Hopefully, that proved to be still the case. The pub was tucked behind the concrete sea wall, with its wave deflecting curved upper edge seeing plenty of action when the winter storms blew through. I recalled it was standing room only inside during the summer months. Tonight though, lots of empty tables were to be had. Only a few locals lined up along bar, giving the usual unwelcoming vibe, which was overridden by the bar tender, keen to welcome a couple of new customers. Not much passing trade this far down the coast at this time of year.

"Good evening, what will it be?"

"Jess?"

I waited while she mulled over her choice.

"A glass of dry white wine please."

"And I'll have a half of whatever bitter you sell the most of."

"Coming up." The bar tender reached under the bar, bringing out a glass and examining it critically in the light for any blemishes. "Are you having food this evening?"

As he spoke, the bartender pulled my drink by means of a well-worn wooden lever. Clamped to the lever was the brewer's emblem - the face of a wizened old seafarer - recoiling away from me with each pull.

"Yes, please."

He lifted his gaze to the near empty dining room and said, "Take your pick. Menus are on the tables. I will bring your drinks over and take you order."

Jess and I unanimously chose the table nearest the log fire, settling into the comfy chairs across from each other.

"You grew up in a beautiful part of the world," she said.

"I know. There is something special about this area isn't there? Where are you from? Your accent is hard to place."

Jess smiled, giving the fire a run for its money in terms of wattage.

"I was born up near the Scottish border. Berwick, to be precise. My mother was from Kent and my father from Birmingham. Add to that mix, my years at university in Oxford, and you begin to get an idea why my accent is difficult to figure out."

I nodded, before prompting her further.

"So what path, convoluted or otherwise, brought you to Dartmouth?"

We were interrupted before she could answer.

"Are you ready to order?" the barman asked hovering, pad and pencil poised, eager to get stuck in.

"Ah. We didn't look yet, but do you still do fish and chips?"

"Yes." Came the reply, the tone suggesting a certain sympathy for the neglected items on the menu. I guessed even ten years on, fish and chips were still the predominant reason people came here.

"Jess, more time to look at the menu?"

"Um... do you have anything vegan?"

"Yes, we could rustle you up one of those new *Beyond Burgers* which seem all the rage right now if you like?"

"Yes please, with some chips would be great. Thanks."

The barman made a suitable notation on his pad before turning to me.

"And the fish and chips for you?"

It was my turn for an *um*..."Well, I came for that, but have been meaning to try one of those burgers for a while, so, I'll have the same please. With an abundance of chips, just in case."

"Two veg burgers coming up."

I looked expectantly at Jess as the barman receded.

"So...back to how you ended up in Dartmouth?"

Jess replied after taking a sip of wine.

"After university, I worked at various firms around the country," she continued. "Even a short spell in America."

I was a bit surprised someone with a degree from Oxford could be found making what must be a modest living pottering around in boats.

"What did you study?"

"I've got a Bachelor's in Information Technology and Information Systems." Jess appeared a little embarrassed by her answer. "And you are now wondering why I am working on the river?"

"Well, yes, to be honest."

She smiled ruefully. "Just the usual clichés, nothing out of the ordinary. I woke up one morning with the realization that I did nothing but sit and stare at a screen all day. Couple that with a fiancée who turned out to be a monumental asshole. The idea of walking away from it all and doing something a bit more practical had overwhelming appeal. I knew boats a little," she shrugged. "We had a small river boat and then Dad bought a sailing yacht. Most weekends were spent either sailing or fixing it." She was smiling at the memories when our plates arrived.

The food didn't disappoint, and between mouthfuls Jess deflected further questions about her, with a few of her own.

"Isn't it unusual for a fireman to live on a boat?"

"A little, I guess, but it works for me. I've got used to the impracticalities, such as dodgy outboards and banging my head a lot. I can't imagine living ashore again."

As I spoke, I was reminded that that was exactly what I might be doing in a couple of weeks, if I couldn't come up with the final payment for *First Light*. A thought which kind of took the wind out of my sails.

"What's the matter?" Jess asked, noting the change in me.

"Absolutely nothing, Jess."

I forced the gloominess which had settled on me to one side. Dealing with my troubles would have to wait a bit longer. Right now, I was sat in a cosy pub with a pretty girl and in this moment, all was well in my world. After all, I *had* spent the last two years deluding myself, another evening should be a walk in the park.

Then the door opened, and a couple walked in. The cool air of the night followed them through the door, momentarily reaching us, until the door was closed and the warmth from the fire valiantly retook its lost ground. The couple approached the bar, going through a similar routine to ours, before turning, drinks in hand to pin down their seating options.

As their eyes passed over us, I was struck by the girl's similarity to Sophie. She was close in age, with the same frank, open gaze and a curve of the lips suggesting it wouldn't be too hard to induce a smile. Her hair was of a colour and style that brought a heated tingle to the back of my eyes. Even her clothes would have found Sophie's wardrobe full of kindred spirits. The suppressed memories came back in an uncontrollable torrent and I caught myself struggling to keep the sadness from crushing me.

Jess was looking at me, concern etched on to her face.

"You look like you've seen a ghost. Do you know her?"

"I'm sorry. No, I don't know her. She reminds me of someone I used to know. I wrenched my attention fully back to Jess, who had reached across the table and was clasping one of my hands between hers.

"Your fiancé?"

I was surprised I didn't feel annoyed at Andrew. Maybe it would come later.

"What did he tell you?"

"Just that you were engaged. And that she died. Nothing else."

Well at least he had only given the edited version.

"It's all right Matt, we don't need to talk about it." Jess squeezed my hand in hers, a prelude to releasing her grip.

"Would you like to know?" I asked, strangely feeling that I owed her some sort of explanation.

"I really would, if you don't mind telling me." Her hands remained around mine.

Taking a large swallow of my drink, for the second time since Sophie's death I recounted the events of that night.

Jess released my hands, sat back, and looked at me reflectively when I had finished telling her. Most of it anyway.

"I'm really sorry. I can see how difficult it would be to move on from that." She paused. "But maybe one day you'll be able to let go and make room for someone new in your life?"

The hint of anticipation in her voice was not lost on me.

"I'm working on that, Jess."

I glanced across to the newcomers and forced myself not to see Sophie. She was gone and not coming back. And I was going to need to start accepting that fact, if I wanted to stop the downward trajectory my life was taking. I resolved to begin the process, as hard as it might be, by ordering another drink for us, in the hope that Jess would keep hold of my hand for a good while longer.

***

Outside, the late evening was still speckled with stars, but thin strands of high-level cloud were streaming in from the west. An old man from the bar followed us out, his tattered jacket zipped up to the neck. He watched us as we went through the dressing rituals required prior to winter motorcycling. His woollen hat and massive scarred hands shielding an equally scarred pipe could only have belonged to a fisherman. Glancing at the sky he offered, “Change in the air."

"Aye," I replied into my helmet. No other response seemed to fit.

The effects of my two halves of bitter had been nullified by time, food, and the double shot of espresso which Jess had insisted upon before consenting to climb back on the bike. The thrill of the ride and the pleasing sensation of Jess's arms around me, meant I barely registered the headlights following us out of the car park, remaining a respectful distance behind us as we sped back to Dartmouth.

Stopped outside the harbour office, my crash helmet balanced on the tank in front of me, I said goodnight to Jess.

"I had a nice evening, Jess. Thanks for lending me your ear."

She had the keys to Andrew's flat in one hand, her crash helmet tucked into the crook of the other arm.

"You're welcome, Matt. I had a nice time too." She hesitated before stretching up on tiptoes and planting a quick kiss on my lips. "Since your boat is on the town quay, maybe I can swing by in the morning for a pre-work coffee?"

"Of course, that would be great." I quickly put my helmet back on to hide the soppy grin on my face, watching as she let herself into the side door of the harbour office. It was hard to see in the dim glow of the streetlight, but I was fairly certain she threw a wink in my direction as I trod on the gear lever and pulled away.

***

Jess was smiling as she closed the front door and turned towards the stairs. There was something very appealing about Matt, and she found herself wishing the night away so that morning coffee could bring him close again. Opening the door into Andrew's apartment at the top of the stairs, she was greeted by the frantic attention seeking antics of the young dog. Twisting sideways to foil its bouncy attempts to plant a lick on her face, she kicked the door closed behind her and fought her way to the sofa. After a while and with aid of a belly rub, Bailey had calmed down enough for Jess's thoughts to turn inwards, a feeling of contentment settling over her as she recalled the evening with Matt.

***

Victor waited for the rear light of Matt's bike to disappear around the corner before easing himself out from behind the wheel of the cramped hire car. The simple *Yale* lock securing the Harbour Office door succumbed to the torsion wrench and rake pick in only slightly more time than if he had had the actual key. He grinned at the ease of it at as he slipped the thin tools back into a small pouch containing an assortment of his favourite picks. Stepping through the open door, he couldn't help but recall times when he had had to work much harder for his fun.

The knock at the door drew Jess's gaze as well as a puzzled look. She was sure she had shut the door at the bottom of the stairs and there was no other access to the apartment's front door. At her feet, Bailey stopped being playful, and was also staring at the door, a deep growl rumbling from his throat.

Maybe she hadn't shut the door properly and Matt, or someone else had come up to tell her. The growl from Bailey turned into a bark, the hackles on his neck standing up as the knocking repeated.

"Matt?" Jess levered herself from the sofa and walked towards the door, a sense of unease growing stronger with each step. "Matt, is that you?"

With the security chain in place, she cautiously opened the door. Behind her, Bailey's barking had become more frantic. The security chain, fixed as it was with two short screws into the soft wood of the door frame, might just as well not have been there. Victors momentum ripped it free and the door flew open, hitting Jess hard in the shoulder as she tried to process what was happening.

Bailey knew the ancient instincts which had generated his initial growl were not mistaken and hurled herself at the intruder, his jaw latching down hard on an arm. Unfortunately, it was not the arm holding the suppressed pistol, and without the slightest hesitation Victor fired a round into the dog's head. The lifeless body collapsed onto the carpet as Victor brought the pistol back up and jammed it into Jess's uncomprehending face.

"Not one sound."

NINETEEN

After parking the bike and making sure the rain cover was securely in place, I began the short walk along the embankment, towards where *First Light* was moored. Thoughts of gold had all but disappeared, to be replaced with another colour, this one the green of Jess's eyes. Not many people were about this late on this cold winter evening, but those who were, would not have failed to notice the spring in my step as I made my way along the river front and down the ramp to the floating pontoon that was the town Quay. The improvement in my spirits proved short-lived.

Stepping up over the gunwale and into *First Light's* cockpit revealed a figure sat motionless in the dim yellow glow cast by the streetlamps on the road above. I couldn't make out any features, but there was no mistaking the pistol held loosely in one hand and the empty can of builder's foam in the other.

"I didn't think you had it in you, to be honest," Vladimir spoke softly, recognizable at first by only by his voice. Then he stood, and the wan yellow street lighting defined the contours of his face. He gestured with the gun for me to move towards the front of the cockpit. I had never had a gun pointed at me before and the effect was chilling. My limbs grew leaden and the feeling coming from the pit of my stomach could only be described as terror. I had had no idea the debilitating effect that fear of being shot would have, nor given much thought to the fact that by means of having a weapon, someone was able to totally control you.

Looking at the gap between the dock and the side of the boat, I calculated whether it would be possible to turn and jump, and have the cold waters close over my head before a bullet might thump into me. I thought it unlikely and Vladimir seemed to agree. His voice pierced through the shroud of fear enveloping me.

"Make no mistake, I *will* shoot you. Open the door and sit in the helm seat. Now."

"The key is in my pocket," I told him, keen for my fumbling not to tighten his finger on the trigger.

Vladimir gave a short snort of derision. "You have been watching too much television. Just take out the key and get inside."

I turned away from him and slid the key into the lock, opening the door. Every fibre of my being did not want to go inside with this guy. At least whilst still outside there was the possibility of our drama being seen by someone, and the open air gave a small illusion of freedom. Once inside, my already limited options would become even more threadbare.

Seeing no choice, I pushed open the door and entered the warmth of my wheelhouse. Vladimir followed me in, the gun continuing to usher me to the seat behind the helm. He shut the door behind him, locked it, and closed the curtains lining the side windows. All the while, the muzzle of the ugly little pistol never wavered from pointing at my heart, or near enough to make no difference. The only windows without curtains were the main windscreens, but we were facing down the river towards the sea, so it was unlikely we could be observed from that direction.

"What you did with this foam has caused me a great deal of trouble. I'm inclined to shoot you now, but you may have some usefulness left in you. Firstly, you're going to tell me why you did it." Vladimir sat on the wooden bench running along the starboard side of the wheelhouse, the old leather creaking a little as he lowered himself. Behind me on the bulkhead, the VHF radio which I had forgotten to switch off when we returned to meet Jake earlier, hissed loudly with static.

"Do you know what I have been looking for?" he continued.

I figured he knew the answer to that, just about, so I nodded cautiously in affirmation. "I know you are looking for an aircraft, but I don't know why."

Vladimir digested this. "I don't know how you did it, but you must have found out where it is, or why go to the trouble of sabotaging the *Natasha*?"

"Can I switch that off?" I asked, turning my head in the direction of the hissing radio.

"Yes, turn the damn thing off."

Trying to block his view as my hand reached up towards the VHF radio's control buttons, I fumbled for the small red flap.

"Tell me what you hoped to gain by immobilizing the yacht," he commanded.

Hoping he couldn't see, my index finger flicked open the plastic hatch located on the front of the unit and pressed the button found underneath. This was not a function I had ever used, so I had no idea if one press was enough, so I pushed it again and then again, holding the last press down as long as I dared, before turning the volume knob fully anti-clockwise. I turned back towards Vladimir.

He looked at me thoughtfully, raising the gun to point at my head.

"You really shouldn't have stuck your nose into my business."

Desperation crept unbidden into my voice as I contemplated the fact that I was about to get shot in the face.

"You're right, Vladimir, but you still want to get to whatever it is that's down there, and with the *Natasha* out of action, you're going to need another boat," I ventured. I didn't bring up the question of a charter fee, it probably wasn't the right time.

"I need a boat," came the response. "But I don't necessarily need you. And you still have not told me how you know the position of the wreckage?"

The gun showed no sign of wanting to point anywhere other than my head, and I was desperate to keep him talking, in the hope that all my button pushing would yield some result.

"I called up the *Southern Cross* on the radio by pretending to be the Coastguard and asked them."

At the mention of the trawler, an expression crossed his face, too fast to be tied to any particular emotion, just an underlying disturbance, such as sometimes found on the surface of river running over submerged rocks, an interruption to the normal, laminar flow.

"You've got balls, I'll give you that."

"What happened to the *Southern Cross*?" I was stalling for time, hoping I had not chosen the wrong subject, but desperate for the seconds, minutes, to grind away, still not sure if I had in any way altered the eventual outcome of this interaction.

"Like you, they got in my way. Unlike you, they are no longer a problem."

I had nothing to say in response to that. Wondering just what had taken place out at sea between Vladimir and the trawler, I was unable to come up with a comforting scenario. A phone rang, the sound emanating from Vladimir's pocket. The gun remained steadfast as, one handed, he reached for the handset, accepted the call, and brought it to his ear. He listened briefly.

"Good, take her to the yacht." Vladimir pocketed the phone and lowered the gun slightly before continuing. "But you are correct. I do need a boat, since your actions look like they have made *Natasha* unavailable for the moment. But more importantly, you are going to help me recover what is mine."

Behind him, through a crack in the not quite closed curtains, the flicker of headlights on the road above grew steadily stronger. Hope crept through me, one cell at a time, like the passage of water into a dry sponge.

"Tomorrow morning, at six, you will take me out to find the wreckage."

A bit more time was needed, so I reluctantly nodded my agreement. "Sure, I can do that. But can we continue this conversation without the gun pointing at me?"

Vladimir looked blankly at me. The gun began to descend into his lap. A loud knocking on the hull brought it back up again.

"Matt Curtis, you in there?" The knocking continued and was joined by a slight rocking of the boat as someone climbed on board. The voice was now at the door.

"Matt, a bunch of people are about to show up here, who - incidentally, would rather be in bed - wondering why your VHF is transmitting a distress call. Could you open up, so we can all go home?"

I triumphantly glanced over at Vladimir's face. He didn't seem as worried as I had hoped he would be at this sudden influx of guests. He remained seated.

"Tell them to go away, nothing is wrong."

"So, are you going to shoot me in front of all these witnesses? There must be three or four people out there."

Vladimir didn't look as if he shared my point of view. The beginnings of a smile reaching his mouth.

"You wouldn't get away with it," I persisted.

"You are proving to be quite resourceful for a local fireman. First the foam and now this," he gestured to the commotion in my cockpit. "Well done. But do not take me for a fool. Whilst we have been sitting here having our, how would you say, 'cosy little chat,' an insurance policy has been put in place, by way of your girlfriend."

Dread squeezed down on the hope that hadn't lived up to its promise. Over the renewed banging at the door I clutched at straws.

"Prove it."

Vladimir ignored me.

"Get rid of them." He inclined his head towards the door.

I hesitated, not yet ready to give up on the hope of getting away from this chilling character. The banging on the door intensified.

"You have met Victor. If we had more time, I would enjoy telling you some of the things he has done to people that will chill your bones. Things that I also did, but in my case through necessity, a means to an end, if you will. With him, there is a larger element of fun in his actions, and he gets a bit carried away. Don't take the chance that I am bluffing, not even I can hold him back when he is given the opportunity to, let us say, express himself. Now, *Get rid of them."*

I unlocked the cabin door, opening it just enough to squeeze through into my cockpit. I held up a hand in apology.

"Sorry, I'm really sorry! That radio has been playing up recently, I've been meaning to have it looked at. I can't apologize enough." I recognized the young man standing in front of me as one of Andrew's employees, but couldn't recall his name.

"Okay, no worries," he said. "These things happen, but make sure you turn the darn thing off, would you? I don't want to be called out here again. *They*" -he pointed at the small inshore lifeboat fast approaching the quay- "will be of the same mind, I'm sure. I will speak to them, but maybe you should put something into their donation box tomorrow morning."

"I will, for sure. And again, I'm sorry for dragging you out here."

"I'm not even supposed to be on call tonight," he grumbled, climbing back over the side onto the dock. "Jess is meant to do this sort of thing when Andrew's away, but apparently, she doesn't feel like answering her phone."

Watching him leave reiterated the reality of the situation I was now faced with. I wanted desperately to get off the boat and find Jess safe in Andrew's apartment, rather than considering how my inquisitiveness had put her in such danger.

Pushing my way reluctantly back into the wheelhouse, I found Vladimir standing with his back to the chart table and no sign of the gun. Its absence was a definite improvement to the general ambiance.

"I want to speak to Jess," I insisted.

"Later, but first, you caused me enough trouble with this thing." He walked over to the port bulkhead and undid the two plastic knobs holding the VHF set in its bracket. A good tug separated it from the various cables feeding into it and I watched in silence as he strode to the door, stepped outside, and threw it into the river. I guess, from his perspective, he had a point.

Vladimir glanced down at his watch.

"It is midnight. Bring your boat along the port side of the *Natasha*, out of sight of the town, at six o'clock. If you talk with anyone between now and then, or do not show up, you will be looking for a new girlfriend."

"Let me speak to her. I won't take you out to your helicopter until you let me speak with Jess."

"No! Just do as I have told you. Don't be late." He turned to leave, paused, then turned back to me with a frown. "How did you know it is a helicopter?"

'*Shit*'.

"Just a guess."

He did not like my answer judging by the blur as his fist slammed into the side of my head, collapsing me to the floor with shards of agony radiating through my head. The gun made another unwelcome appearance; its single malevolent eye staring at me a couple of insignificant inches away from my head.

"You can be useful to me, but I *can* do this without you. So, think carefully before you answer. *How did you know it was a helicopter?"* he demanded.

I was in no doubt he would pull the trigger if he doubted my answer, so I told him, leaving out as much as I dared.

"I found it eventually, on the depth sounder, and took a dive on it. I didn't have enough air to do more than take a quick look. The pilot says hello, by the way."

Vladimir answered my witticism with a sharp kick to my gut before turning to my chart plotter and zooming in on the marks I had entered the night before.

"Are these the exact co-ordinates?" he demanded, allowing me to push myself upright to view the screen.

"Yes."

Vladimir took is phone out and snapped a picture of the numbers on the screen.

"Tell me what you saw down there."

The gun was once again inches from my head. Not seeing any alternative, I told him how I had found the helicopter settled on the bottom. How it was on its starboard side, with a jumble of boxes in the rear. I didn't mention the pilot again, one kick in the stomach was enough.

"Did you touch anything?"

"No, I told you, there was only enough air in my tank for a quick look."

Vladimir stared at me in silence for a moment.

"You continue to surprise me. But you have had your final warning. Do exactly as I tell you from now on or both you and your girlfriend will die." He reinforced his words by slamming the side of his pistol against my already pounding head. "Six A.M. Don't be late!" With that, he turned and left through the wheelhouse door, the boat rocking again as he jumped down to the dock.

A wave of nausea swept over me as I hauled myself across to the low bench to catch my breath. The pain in my head was incredible and I had a ringing in my ears which wouldn't quit. Given he had taken Jess, it was now easy to imagine Vladimir had been responsible for the disappearance of the *Southern Cross* crew. Now I had an idea of what was down in the wreckage, I began to understand the lengths he was prepared to go to in order to retrieve it. I also reasoned that once he had whatever it was, there would be little chance of him just letting me walk away.

Five minutes later, clutching a bag of frozen peas to my face, I approached the door to the harbour office. The door swung open with a gentle push from my toe. *Shit. Shit. Shit.* I contemplated calling Jake, but the impression I had that Vladimir was way out on a limb with nothing to lose, stayed my hand from reaching for the phone. I had no doubt he would be true to his word if I didn't do as he had instructed.

Inside the small entrance hall to the left, a door led off to the offices and to the right, the stairs that gave access to Andrew and Anna's flat. A framed photograph, once mounted in the stair well, which dramatically captured a trio of Navy warships - line abreast, with long slashes of white wake boiling from their blunt sterns - had fallen onto the stairs. The glass was cracked into crescent shaped slivers as if it had been trodden on. I stepped over it, reluctantly reaching the landing and stepping towards the open doorway of the apartment.

My eyes were drawn to a sliver of splintered wood stuck out at a jaunty angle from the door jamb.

"Jess?" I called, surprised how hard it was to get the sound out. I didn't expect a reply. Moving forward slowly, with dread in every footstep, I stepped into the apartment. Bailey lay on the floor, blood staining the carpet beneath him.

A quick search told me Jess was gone. Back at the entrance, I took a moment to bend down and stroke Bailey's fur. Seeing him like that, lifeless and discarded, hammered home Jake's warning. I was seriously out of my depth getting involved with these people. As if a gun in my face and a split skull weren't enough to convince me.

Despite Vladimir's instruction not to talk with anyone, the dead dog convinced me that I was going to need some help. I pulled out my phone and called Jake. *Voicemail. Please leave a message.*

'Just great,' I thought, waiting for the *beep*.

"Jake, it's Matt. Vladimir has taken a friend of mine hostage. Jess Harper, she works on the river with Andrew. I think she is on the *Natasha*. Vladimir is armed and wants me to take him diving on the helicopter tomorrow. I need help, call me back as soon as you get this."

I would try calling again, but for now, saw no other option other than to do as Vladimir asked. In the meantime, I saw no reason why Vladimir should be the only one with a weapon, so stepping over the dog, I reached into the pewter bowl on the side table, and rifled around among the small denomination coins and other pocket detritus for the keys to his lock-up which I knew resided there.

It was past one A.M. when I got back on board *First Light*, and nearer to two by the time I had finished experimenting with various bits of string and tape. After several attempts a combination of masking tape and *Velcro* seemed to fit the bill for what I was planning. Time would tell.

TWENTY

Jake's number continued to go unanswered, as did my attempt at sleep until, at four A.M. tired of watching the minutes tick by on wall clock, I got up off my bed. Checking the tide tables for the local area before casting off, I made my way slowly across the river to the *Natasha*. If I couldn't sleep, then I was more than happy to share the tiredness with Vladimir.

There was no one on deck as I approached the port side as instructed but, holding down the button on my ship's horn for twenty seconds did the trick, bringing a flurry of activity. Fenders where dropped into place and a worried looking Captain took the lines I threw and made them fast. By the time they were secured, Vladimir and Victor had appeared alongside the Captain. None of them looked pleased at all the noise I had made.

"Six A.M. I said. You're early."

"Yes Vladimir, the pain in my head interrupted my sleep. Sorry about that," I shrugged. "That and the fact that we need to get going soon if we are to have any chance of making a dive at slack water. The tides are too strong for diving at any time other than an hour either side of the tide turning."

He seemed to see the sense in that.

"You stay on your boat."

"I want to see Jess."

"You will."

"Now, Vladimir. I'm doing what you ask and will continue to do so, but I want to see her before I do anything else."

Before Vladimir could reply, a rumbling was heard, followed by the steady muted vibrations of *Natasha*'s engines coming alive.

"Finally!" the Captain said. He turned and headed towards the engine room, a look of relief at hearing the sound of his engines again, etched across his face.

Ignoring my demand to see Jess, Vladimir pointed at me and commanded Victor to join me on *First Light*. Victor jumped nimbly down onto my deck, raw scratch marks showing on his cheek. Pulling out a depressingly familiar looking pistol, he motioned for me to go back into the wheelhouse.

"Follow us out of harbour. When the *Natasha* is anchored, come alongside," Vladimir continued. "Then you and I will dive to recover my boxes. You can have your girlfriend and your boat back after that."

Victor, still ushering me inside, appeared to find Vladimir's words somewhat amusing. His grin suggested that he had had a rather different conversation with Vladimir regarding our collective futures.

Before Vladimir was out of earshot I said, "Why don't you take your *pal* here diving instead of me? I promise not to drive away and leave you both down there, honest." Once again, my misplaced wit fell on deaf ears, quite literally as it turned out.

Vladimir leaned over the side of the yacht as he answered, "Unfortunately, Victor has a perforated eardrum. Courtesy of an overlooked Chechen booby trap. In any case, he is much more useful in, shall we say, 'supervising' *my guest.*"

"If you have hurt her, I will do my very best to kill you."

Vladimir looked as if the prospect gave him some amusement as he ignored me, straightening up and disappearing from view. With no other course of action left other than do what they wanted, I took up my position at the helm as *First Light's* lines were undone and thrown back on board. My brain was trying to desperately come up with some scenario which resulted in getting Jess and myself out of this mess unharmed. But as far as I could see, our only hope lay with Jake checking his voice messages soon, and taking them seriously.

Once we were clear of her side, *Natasha* slipped away from her moorings, the deck crew seemingly just abandoning their lines, which remained shackled to the yellow mooring buoys, fore and aft. The ropes floated in the current and I hoped the Captain would drive over them and entangle them in his props, but no such luck. With grudging admiration, I watched as he skilfully allowed a combination of tide and engine inputs to carry the vessel away from the risk of entanglement, before heading towards the harbour entrance. The sedate pace gave no clue as to the unfolding drama of the day. To me, the abandoned mooring lines did little to suggest that coming back to Dartmouth was part of their plan.

"Stop pointing that thing at me," I ordered Victor. "You can't shoot me, your chum needs me today. Go and make yourself useful. You know where the coffee machine is." For a moment I thought I had pushed it too far. The squat little pistol stared straight into my eyes, a game of blink which I was never going to win. Then the gun dropped as Victor glared at me.

"Your usefulness will run out soon. Then we will see where your smart mouth gets you."

I guess I would have to make my own coffee.

Once clear of the castles guarding the river entrance, it was obvious the old fisherman from the pub last night knew what he was talking about. The wind was freshening from the south-west, introducing a sense of purpose and direction in the small waves. The cloud base was lowering and a tap on the brass barometer mounted on the bulkhead behind me caused the needle to let go of its optimistic hold on 'Fair' and lurch to a point midway between 'Rain' and 'Stormy' - hedging its bets in the way that barometers seem to do.

I held a position two hundred meters off the port side of the *Natasha* as we headed out across Start Bay. We had this part of the sea to ourselves, overseen only by the ever-present gulls encountering moderate turbulence by the look of it. The yacht's bow gently rose and fell in the swell, occasionally throwing out a low curtain of spray as a larger wave challenged her presence. It was clear we wouldn't have much of a time window to dive before the weather drove us off. I wasn't sure if that was a good thing or not.

Natasha slowed as she approached the co-ordinates of the wreck site. She rounded up into the wind, dropped her starboard anchor and drifted sluggishly backwards until the chain arrested her drift. There was enough movement in the sea now to make being tied alongside only possible with the protection of the large inflatable fenders hung over to receive us. Victor, his gun put away for now, served as deckhand and passed up our lines to the crew on *Natasha*. Once moored alongside, the difference in the two vessels' relative movements made for a lot of squeaking, as lines were stretched and fenders squashed. It would be lucky if no damage were done, but that appeared to be the least of my troubles for the moment.

I stepped across to the *Natasha* and was led by Vladimir through the sliding glass doors opening into the plush main saloon from the aft deck. There was no one to challenge me on my footwear today as I ploughed a trail through the thick carpet. At the far end of the saloon a lobby, panelled in a rich dark wood, gave the traveller a choice of routes. More carpet led forward, presumably to a dining room or other essential space. A marble stairway, the treads inset with discreet lighting and with a handrail looking more gold than polished brass, offered access to the lower levels. The final option was a spiral staircase, leading as I was about to find out, up to the bridge.

On the port side, the Captain was leaning over his chart table as we entered, and I could see he was working on a passage planning chart depicting the approaches to the Mediterranean. Sharp grey lines recently dragged across the clean paper terminating at what looked like the island of Cypress. To the front of the bridge, beneath the expanse of windows, an array of electronics was laid out before me, touch screens with all manner of information displayed. And yet more screens with the rotating green sweep of the radar showing a dearth of other vessels, only the familiar curving line of the coast pulsating with brightness every few seconds.

"Is this it?" Vladimir stood sideways to allow me to see what he was pointing to. Behind him through the bridge window the horizon had become indistinct, as if drawn with a thick marker pen. I looked, inevitably at another screen, this one showing the bump that I knew to be the wreckage of the helicopter.

"Looks like it."

To the Captain, who was studiously avoiding eye contact with us, he said, "Drop the second anchor directly under our bow. Make sure it's done by the time we are kitted up."

The Captain nodded as he repeated Vladimir's order into his personal radio. Not a happy man was the impression I got from his demeanour, making me wonder what hold Vladimir had on him.

'Let's go."

Vladimir was already stepping down the spiral staircase. We retraced our steps back through the interior and made our way down from the main deck to the swim platform at the stern. The huge transom door was open and laying nearly flat just above the surface of the grey sea. Every few seconds a wave slapped up into it from beneath, producing mechanical groans from the hydraulic rams holding it, and a wince from a crew member whom I presumed, from the stylized propeller printed on the shoulders of his overalls, to be the engineer. It was obvious the platform was designed to be opened only in calmer, flat water to allow swimming in secluded bays. The engineer reached back inside to a panel of buttons and the hydraulic rams hissed the platform up into a steeper angle. The slapping stopped, for now at least. I wondered what effect the waves were having on the item hastily strapped to my own, more modest swim platform, just a few hours ago.

Revealed by the opening of the transom, was the immaculate garage space, all stainless steel and neon lighting. Racks of water skis, wake boards and windsurfers lined the walls and a duo of futuristic looking *Sea Bobs* were fastened to leather covered cradles. The lockers and cupboards lining the sides no doubt held all manner of other water sports equipment to amuse and entertain owner and guests when they had got bored with drinking champagne.

The space remaining in the centre of this Aladdin's cave, was filled with a selection of diving equipment including an empty, voluminous white bag, the sort found in builder merchants to hold a ton of sand, or chippings. Next to this were two heavy-duty air bags, tightly rolled up for their journey down to the wreckage. Once there, they could then be attached to the white bag, presumably by now containing the boxes, and inflated with the air from our dive sets. Physics would do the rest. It was clear that with the right equipment, of which there was no shortage here, recovering Vladimir's boxes could be a relatively simple process. Which was a shame, since I figured it was in my best interests to find a way to complicate it as much as possible.

"Tell me again how the helicopter is lying and where the boxes are." Vladimir was all business, sat on a cushioned bench, donning a dry suit.

"The machine is on its starboard side. The boxes are a jumble in the back compartment." Nothing was to be gained by not telling him - he would see for himself very shortly.

"The second anchor should be close to the wreckage," he said. "We will descend the chain and search in a circle outward until we find it. Since you were so keen to get your hands on my boxes, you can go back inside and pass them out to me. When they are all in this bag" -he gestured towards the white builder's bag- "we will attach the air bags and float them to the surface."

I could see him thinking the process through, checking it for weaknesses, the same as me.

"What's to stop them from drifting away down current as it ascends?" I asked, already knowing the answer, and not liking it much.

"Once they are inflated, but not enough to lift off of the bottom, I will tie a line, that one," -once again he gestured at the pile of equipment and a spool of light but strong looking braided line- "to the bag containing the boxes. Then I will go back up to *Natasha* paying out the line. Once aboard, I will signal you to finish inflating and follow them up. A few good taps with a hammer on the propeller shaft will make enough noise as a signal. This line will stop them drifting away and when they are at the surface, the jet ski crane will lift the load onto the deck."

It was a good plan from Vladimir's point of view. Not so good from mine. Once Vladimir was back on board with his precious boxes, there would be little point in him letting me back onboard. He wouldn't even have to shoot me. All he had to do was pull up the swimming ladder that gave access to the sea from the platform and I would be consigned to a miserable death from exposure or drowning.

"And then you will give me Jess, and we go merrily on our way, whilst you set sail for whatever sun-baked tax haven your boss lives in for your pat on the back?"

A hint of a grin touched his face.

"No, that's not the plan at all."

"Then, fuck you. You're not exactly giving me much motivation to help you. How about you get your own boxes."

My defiance was born out of desperation. I couldn't see any realistic way of getting out of this unscathed or even alive.

"You want some motivation?"

Vladimir walked stiffly in his drysuit over to the bulkhead and picked up the intercom handset. A button pushed, then; "Bring the girl."

Fear rose in my throat, threatening to choke me.

"No, don't. I will do it."

"Alas Matt, you have been a thorn in my side for too long. Perhaps a demonstration of how insignificant you and your friend are to me will instil some cooperation in you.

"I'm sorry. I'll do whatever you need to get the boxes up, but please don't hurt her," I pleaded with him.

Vladimir wasn't listening. He turned and walked out onto the swim platform where Victor appeared with Jess held in front of him. Her hands were zip-tied behind her back, and he controlled her at arm's length by means of a handful of hair. She had bruising around one eye, but was nonetheless fiercely kicking backwards, trying in vain to break free of his grip. Her struggles, however, served only to amuse him. Victor looked at Vladimir, who nodded.

Jess was forced to her knees at the edge of the platform, facing towards the distant horizon. She calmed down, as if her fear was finally shutting down her ability to resist.

"Don't do this, Vladimir."

He looked at me, eyes telling a story I was incapable of reading.

"Do it," he commanded Victor.

Victor reached behind him and pulled his pistol out of a holster in the small of his back. Pointing it down towards Jess's head, the knuckle on his index finger steadily whitened as it curled around the trigger.

"Enough! This stops now!" The Captain yelled as he hurled himself down the steps and crashed into Victor, pushing him aside.

A shot rang out, the bullet ploughing harmlessly into the sea. Victor whirled around and, in an instant, had his arm in a chokehold around the Captains throat, the muzzle of the gun firmly pressed against the back of his skull. Jess shuffled back away from the edge and began to vomit. Victor turned and looked at Vladimir, looking for direction. Two strides carried Vladimir to the entwined pair. As part of the same movement, he took the pistol from Victor's hand.

Another shot, a bullet once again finding its way into the sea, but this time taking a route through Captain's skull. The body crumpled. Victor shoved it away from him as it fell, splashing into the water, where it floated, minus the front of its head. It drifted away from the stern, keeping pace with the cloud of red water that was beginning to surround it.

Victor reclaimed his pistol once again pointing it in Jess's direction.

"That won't be needed Victor, he gets the message," Vladimir interceded.

I was close to puking myself, not wanting to believe in the existence of such cold violence or accept the chilling reality of what had just happened.

"Take her back down below. Then round up the crew and make sure they don't give any trouble. Keep them away from the bridge. Lock them in their quarters for now."

Turning back to me, Vladimir spoke quietly, "Enough of your shit. Finish getting rigged up."

TWENTY-ONE

For the second time in as many days, the cold water of the English Channel closed over my head. Visibility was not much better this time around, despite it being daylight. We descended slowly down the vertical anchor chain, the links rising and falling rhythmically as *Natasha* gently nodded her head in the increasing swell.

Vladimir ensured that I went first, keeping himself a safe distance away as we progressed into the murky green waters. He had made sure to remove the obligatory diving knife from my equipment before we entered the water, a smart move on his part as I had been contemplating the best way of burying it into the back of his neck at the first opportunity.

Bereft of a weapon and hampered with armfuls of bags as I was, I couldn't see how me turning and trying to attack him somehow would end well. I hadn't had to physically fight anyone since secondary school, and I was sure Vladimir's skills in combat, even underwater, would be in a different league to the teenage fisticuffs of the school playground. I would have to wait and hope for a better opportunity to present itself.

Reaching the bottom, I tied off a guideline to the anchor, and we began our search. Vladimir remained behind me as we slowly circled outwards. Keeping an eye on the compass strapped to my wrist, I increased the length of line by a handful of meters each time the compass told me we had completed a full circle. Imperceptibly, the shape of the mangled helicopter began to define itself before me, halfway through the third rotation.

It appeared unchanged from the last time I had laid eyes on it. Having no inclination to look into the cockpit again, I made my way down the side of the helicopter, loosely lashing the guideline and bundle of lifting bags to the bent landing skid which extended out from the helicopter at head height. Vladimir indicated for me to stay where I was, while he quickly finned his way around the wreckage. Pausing briefly in front of the smashed canopy, he finished his circumnavigation and re-appeared from the direction of the broken tail section. Once again, he gestured to me, this time indicating we should ascend to the side door, still sticking up at a jaunty angle from my previous visit.

Vladimir peered down into the rear cabin at the jumble of boxes. Forestalling another gesture, I brushed past him, descending for the second time into the passenger cabin, and began to manhandle the boxes upwards to his waiting hands. I was breathing heavily and sucking down hard on my air supply by the time all five boxes had been removed from the cramped compartment. The final one had, thankfully, proved much lighter than the others and looked like a larger version of the kind of waterproof cases commonly used by photographers to carry their equipment. I was surprised to be no longer interested in what it or the rest of them, may contain. As far as I was concerned, Vladimir could have his damn boxes and sail away, so long as I could get Jess out of the predicament which my curiosity had put her in. An outcome that was looking increasing unlikely.

As I followed my bubbles up out of the compartment, Vladimir looked across at me from where he was loading the boxes into the big white bag on the sea floor. A cloud of sediment, kicked up from all the movement, was slowly dispersing in the weak tidal flow. He made his way towards me, holding up six fingers as he came. I shrugged and shook my head, holding up five fingers of my own and indicating that he could look for himself.

He did and judging from the steel grip he put around my throat with one hand when he returned, was not best pleased. I tried to pry his hand free, reaching out with my other arm to attempt to rip the breathing regulator out of his mouth, but he kept me at arm's length and all I could do was flail helplessly in his grip. My vision became blurred and darkness crept stealthily forward from my brain into my eyes. My movements were becoming weaker and less co-ordinated before the pressure around my throat weakened as his rage receded.

Presumably, the practicalities of what still needed to be achieved with my help reasserted themselves into his consciousness. He released me, and gasping for air, I worked hard to make good the deficit that my lungs were screaming for me to address. Breathing with some difficulty, I backed awkwardly away from Vladimir, his anger visible through the small window of his mask. I had no doubt that he wanted to kill me and probably would, the minute I was no longer useful.

Turning away, he kicked his way closer to the helicopter, as he tried to work out what I could have done with the sixth box. It didn't take him long. Vladimir disappeared out of sight as he circumnavigated the wreckage, eventually reappearing, dragging the box awkwardly behind him. I guess like me, the lobster hadn't put up too much of a fight.

Keeping a wary distance from him in case the urge to crush my windpipe came over him again, I watched him turn away, bending to the task of loading the final box into the builder's bag and attaching the floatation bags to the sturdy nylon handles. A couple of long bursts of air from his regulator into the narrow mouths of the yellow lifting bags had them standing to attention above the load of boxes, albeit in a saggy, half-hearted way. They waved lazily to and fro in the current like flames hunting for oxygen.

Not wanting to risk lifting the boxes off the seabed just yet, he stopped inflating and replaced the regulator into his mouth. Tying the end of the spool of line to the same nylon handles as the airbags, Vladimir gave me a final look, then faded from sight as he swam back to the anchor where he began to make his way to the surface - paying out the line as he went.

I had absolutely no idea what to do. Even if I were able to follow and somehow overpower Vladimir on the way up, unlikely at best, there still remained the problem of Victor waiting for me on board the *Natasha*. I couldn't stay down here indefinitely. At some point I would have to surface, whether I wanted to or not. I could leave the bag of boxes down here and surface without them but doing so would only put Jess in more danger. Perhaps if the boxes came up, they would provide enough of a distraction for me to do something, although it was still unclear to me what that might be. What *was* crystal clear to me, however, was that Vladimir had no intention of allowing me or Jess to survive. The shooting of the Captain had firmly shut that door in my mind if it had even ever been a possibility.

As the reality of my situation sank in, a growing fear crushed down on me with more pressure than the seventy feet of water above. Through my despair, as I struggled to come up with any sort of plan, the far-off metallic banging of steel against steel reached me, sounding like a distant blacksmith pounding on an anvil. There was nothing else for it. I was going to have to inflate the lifting bags and one way or another take my chances at the surface.

Taking a deep breath first, I removed the demand valve from my mouth and offered it up to the openings at the bottom of the yellow bags. The steady air gushing into the open mouths stiffened them up and breathed purpose into their apparent indecision. As they began to strain upwards, I gave myself another breath before pushing shorter bursts into them. As they ascended, and the external pressure around them decreased, the volume of air inside the bags would increase, which in turn would increase the buoyancy and the rate of ascent. Too much air at the initial inflation stage could result in the bags breaching the surface at high speed, potentially collapsing them, and spilling enough air out of them to initiate a return journey to the seabed.

Seconds later, the white builders bag stretched upwards as far as it could, breaking free of the sea floor in a cloud of sediment that was whisked away in an instant. The current was picking up, reminding me it would not be long before remaining in place would become a strenuous fight against the tide. I watched as the builder's bag strained its way up and out of sight, its movement eager, as if it knew it didn't really belong down here. When the bag's whiteness was absorbed by the murky green above, I reluctantly finned my way back to the guideline, untied it, and steadily made my way back to the anchor chain to begin my return to whatever awaited me at the surface.

The electronic dive computer was telling me I had not spent enough time at this depth to require more than the usual five-minute safety stop at five meters. But I lingered, holding onto the chain which was rising and falling with an urgency that matched my growing fear. A glimmer of an idea was forming in my mind. I thought that If I managed to remain unseen and climb aboard *First Light*, rather than the *Natasha*, then maybe I could get to the portable VHF stowed in the cluttered drawer under the chart table. Kept as a backup and rarely used, it might not even hold enough charge in its battery to function, but if it did, it represented the only way I could think of to get help. It was a long shot, but it was either that or a probable bullet in the face if I surfaced anywhere near *Natasha's* swim platform.

***

"There they are!"

The satisfaction was evident in Vladimir's voice as the yellow bags broke the surface, twenty meters from *Natasha*'s port side, drifting in the tide towards where he stood with

Victor on the stern. Above them, the jet ski crane, fully extended, had its shiny hook lowered to the waterline in anticipation.

Side by side, Victor and Vladimir slowly pulled on the braided line tied to the load. When the yellow lifting bags were alongside, Vladimir, still in his dry suit, but now equipped only with a mask and snorkel in place of the air tank, climbed back down into the water and attached the crane's hook to the handles of the white bag before clambering back on board.

"Up," he directed Victor, who was manipulating the buttons on the cranes bright yellow portable control unit.

A thick curly wire ran from the unit and disappeared into the garage. High pitched beeping irritatingly insisted that attention was paid. Seawater streamed from the bag as it was raised to the height of the swimming platform and slowly swung inboard. Water trickled onto the deck, and the yellow lifting bags, devoid of purpose, hung limply upside down, as if exhausted by their task.

"Down... down...Stop!"

The crane lowered the bag until it contacted the deck and stopped swinging around. Vladimir slid a wicked looking diving knife from its scabbard strapped to his leg and sliced open the white bag, revealing the boxes stacked inside.

"Good. Lift the swim ladder so Matt can't get back onboard. We can deal with him later if the sea doesn't beat us to it. Help me bring these up and get them onto *First Light*."

"Why not put them in the garage?" Victor looked confused as he jerked his chin towards the open space.

"Change of plan. This boat is now too much of a liability. We are going to take Matt's boat instead."

Victor thought it through for a moment before nodding in agreement. He had long thought the yacht was far too high profile for this operation, not that he would ever question Vladimir's decisions. Now that an alternative was tied conveniently alongside, the plan made a lot of sense.

Vladimir continued, "Once we have these boxes loaded, set fire to this thing."

"What about the crew and the girl?" Victor left the question hanging.

"They can all stay."

Vladimir reached down, taking one side of the nearest box, waiting for Victor to take the other.

"Hurry up, let's get this done before the weather gets any worse."

Victor bent to the task of transferring the boxes to *First Light*. The instruction to lift the swim ladder was forgotten, as he focused on lifting the heavy boxes from the heaving deck.

TWENTY-TWO

Figuring enough time had elapsed for Vladimir and Victor to now be busy with their treasures of the deep, I completed my ascent, breaking the surface under the wide flared bow. No one had their head over the side looking for me, but conditions up here had deteriorated considerably. The waves were now sporting white caps and the *Natasha* was pitching heavily beneath the grey sky, like a tethered thoroughbred, denied easy movement by the anchors snatching at her bow and holding her in place.

Fearing *First Light* would break loose with all this motion, if she hadn't already, I reluctantly let go of the plunging anchor chain and allowed the current to take me down the port side of *Natasha*. As I cleared the curve of the bow, *First Light* came rapidly into view. She was tossing up and down, each downward movement violently arrested by the tortured lines holding her to the yacht. I was surprised the deck cleats had not yet ripped free, or the mooring ropes parted. It was clearly just a matter of time before they did.

Even with my fins, I was struggling to slow down my progress along the gleaming white hull, such was the increasing strength of the tide. It was obvious I would have just the one chance to grab hold of my own swim platform before being swept along and into full view of anyone on the aft deck of *Natasha*. Not that it would matter much, I thought. They would only have a limited window of opportunity to shoot at me before I was carried out of range and into the realms of a much slower, but still certain, death.

As the bow of *First Light* filled my vision, I kicked hard away from the side of *Natasha*, to avoid being ground to a pulp between the two hulls. With my hands scraping along the wooden side of my boat and my legs kicking madly to counter the drift and keep me up close, the low swim platform appeared. I made a desperate grab for one of the steel struts holding it in place. My grip held, and the current swung my body around into what seemed to be slightly less tide, almost a back eddy created by the transom.

With an arm hooked around the centre strut of the platform, I could now shrug off the buoyancy jacket and its attached cylinder. Holding the discharge valve underwater to mute the hiss of air being discharged, I purged the jacket of its remaining air and let it sink slowly away from me. The fins were next, followed by the mask, until unencumbered I could contemplate pulling myself up out of the water. Before that though, it remained to be seen if my lashings of the previous night had help up.

"So, you tried to steal one of my boxes."

'Fuck! This guy had a real knack of turning up when not expected.' I worked frantically on the tape and *Velcro* as Vladimir peered over the back of the cockpit, gun in hand, to where I floundered in the water below him.

Vladimir continued, "You really shouldn't have interfered, but, no matter." He flicked a gold coin into the sea next to me. "This is yours. For services rendered shall we say. Perhaps the ancient Egyptian's were right in believing worldly riches smoothed the way for them in the afterlife. I hope, for your sake they were, although personally, I think it unlikely."

Once again, I looked at the eternity being offered by the mouth of a pistol. The feelings it produced didn't improve with repetition. The super-heated bullet left its snug barrel at a speed of around seven hundred meters per second, which was far quicker than the spear from Andrew's gas powered speargun could ever hope to attain.

As soon as the bullet began its journey, circular grooves inside the barrel induced it to spin, ensuring a truer trajectory towards its target. But the now violent motion of *First Light* served to cancel any engineered accuracy. The failure to kill me was measured in not more than a few centimetres. Grazing along the side of my skull, the heat of its passing scorched a path through the wet hair plastered to my head. The sea absorbed the bullet with indifference - one more made no difference.

At about the same time that the nine-millimetre wide slug of lead was dragged to a relative standstill and began its more vertical descent, the lightly corroded spear which had spent the last few years languishing in a damp lock-up, embedded itself in Vladimir's upper torso. Exactly where on his torso was unclear to me as Vladimir disappeared backwards into the cockpit as it struck. But having used both hands to aim and fire the speargun, I was now drifting rapidly away from the stern of *First Light*, unable to make headway in the choppy tidal conditions.

Turning on my back, I kicked hard and attempted a desperate backstroke. Waves slapped into the back of my head, streaming salty water over my face, forcing me to hold my breath whilst my muscles screamed at me to do the opposite. Risking a glance over my shoulder in between the dunkings, I saw I had drifted sideways behind the *Natasha*; but the distance to the still open transom door was steadily increasing despite my best efforts. Once again, my head was submerged by a breaking wave, bringing with it the cold realization that a continued fight against these elements was pointless.

I had come to the end of the road in a way that I couldn't have imagined only a handful of days ago. The desperation of my frantic swimming turned almost seamlessly into lethargy and resignation. Tears of frustration and anger flowed down my face, their saltiness a pale imitation of the salinity which was about to claim me. Feebly treading water, my energy mostly spent, I brought my arms into my sides, hugging myself against the cold and exhaustion creeping rapidly into my bones. Trapped inside the circle of my folded arms, something pressed against me. Grabbing at it with numbing fingers, I raised my hand in front of my face to see a length of line; the same line I had last seen tied to the white bag of boxes on the sea floor. It now stretched out as a sliver of hope, between me and the no longer receding stern of the *Natasha*.

With this tenuous improvement in my situation came renewed strength. I pulled myself hand over hand along the line, praying it would remain attached. The gap closed inexorably, as I plunged my head through the steady onslaught of waves, gasping for breath after each one. I began to make out details on the swim platform as I dragged myself painfully closer. The line that I held so tightly was still attached to the nylon handles of the white builders bag which in turn, were held in the hook of a boat crane. Deflated yellow lifting bags hung limply down, draping themselves around the white bag which flapped emptily in the stiffening breeze, the bottom neatly sliced open, contents removed by caesarean.

In their haste to get at the boxes, the line, attached by Vladimir, which had stopped the entire ensemble from drifting away on the way up, had been disregarded and allowed to trail in the water once the bag had been hooked to the crane. *Poor seamanship*, but to be fair, understandable, knowing Vladimir's eagerness to be reunited with his gold. And probably not in the same league of bad seamanship as shooting your Captain in the head.

Apart from the abandoned mess of bags, the platform was deserted. A few more muscle sapping pulls, and I was within reach of the stainless-steel swimming ladder, surprisingly still in place. With my arms and legs trembling from the exertion, I climbed heavily up onto the heaving platform, wondering how much more pounding from the sea it could cope with before snapping off.

Exhausted, I sat on the deck. Concealed from view as much as possible by the swinging bags, I thought about my next move. On the plus side, I was still alive, but despite that positive, I didn't know if Vladimir was dead, nor did I have any idea as to the whereabouts of Victor. Finding and escaping with Jess was still going to be a daunting task.

***

At the sound of Vladimir's gunshot, Victor dropped the last of the boxes on the main deck and rushed to look down over the side into the cockpit of *First Light*. Vladimir lay, sprawled on top of the first four boxes, a shaft of metal sticking up out of his shoulder. Heaving himself upright, Vladimir grimaced in pain as the end of the spear protruding from his back jarred against the side of the cockpit.

"Get down here!"

First Light was now snatching violently at the lines which held her as each wave passed under her hull, the twisting, corkscrew motion making it hard for Victor to judge his step as he dropped down into the cramped space. Vladimir leaned sideways over the cockpit coaming, doing his best to keep the protruding spear from touching anything. His breathing became ragged and laboured.

"That fucking Matt. I should have killed him down there."

"Where is he?" Victor asked, pistol in hand as he scanned the scene. He thought he saw a blob in the water, a darker patch in the confusion of grey and white behind the boat, but when his eyes returned to interrogate the image, nothing separated itself from the turmoil of the seas surface.

"He's probably gone. The current is too strong to swim against," Vladimir groaned in pain.

Not convinced, Victor peered cautiously over the stern to confirm Matt was not tucked under the swim platform, before slipping the pistol into its holster and turning back to help Vladimir.

"Let me see."

The spear had gone through the upper right side of Vladimir's chest. Protruding out of his back were six inches of the shaft terminating at the barbed tip. From the front of his chest, about two foot of shaft terminated in a sleek eye, similar to that of a needle, to which a line would usually be attached, joining the spear to the gun.

"It's got to come out," Victor said matter-of-factly.

"Go get the medical kit from the bridge of *Natasha*."

Vladimir sat patiently as Victor scrambled back across to *Natasha*, thinking about the process of removing the spear. He had been injured numerous times on the violent path he had trodden and was in no doubt the pain he was currently feeling was going to increase significantly when the spear was pulled out. If he'd had the luxury of going to a hospital, he knew leaving it in place would be the smart thing to do. The very presence of the steel shaft would stop, or at least slow, any bleeding from torn blood vessels, and the shaft could be cut and withdrawn with the use of anaesthesia. Without the option of professional medical care and equipment, he was left with a more brutal solution that was going to hurt like hell.

The red bag of the first aid kit thumped down next to him, followed by Victor.

"We are dragging anchor."

"It doesn't matter, we are just about done here," Vladimir said. "Now, get this thing out of me."

Victor opened the bag and produced a bottle of hydrogen peroxide, two thick wound dressings and a roll of tape. He splashed some of the liquid onto the shaft protruding from the front of Vladimir's chest, and even as it continued to fizz and foam, moved behind Vladimir and steadily pulled the remainder of the shaft through his body. Vladimir screamed in agony as the spear finished its journey and was tossed in the same movement over the side. Ignoring the gasps of pain which followed the scream, Victor poured yet more hydrogen peroxide into the entry and exit wounds which were both trickling with blood.

"You're going to have to get out of this dry suit before I can apply the dressings."

Vladimir was pale, his teeth were clenched and sweat beaded on his forehead. "I'll be fine now. Just undo the shoulder zip and help me get my arms free."

Vladimir stood up facing aft and balanced precariously as the boat bucked beneath him. While Victor helped him peel down the top half of the dry suit, he focused his eyes on the distance where a black speck was smashing out regular bursts of spray. Each white impact brought the speck closer and Vladimir knew the time for him to go had arrived.

"Go and set her alight, Victor. Make sure you do a good job of it. When it's done, we can get the hell out of here."

Vladimir watched as his loyal lieutenant, unaware of the approaching trouble, or the fact that the person to whom he had shown so much loyalty and devotion to over the years, was about to throw him to the wolves, climbed back aboard the *Natasha* and disappeared from sight.

Hoping the distraction Victor was about to create would allow him to slip away unnoticed, Vladimir steeled himself against the pain and stepped awkwardly around the boxes, the inside out arms of the dry suit flapping at his waist. Each movement radiated pain across his chest causing him to wince sharply, as he carefully eased himself into the warmth of the wheelhouse. With *First Light's* engines burbling reassuringly under his feet, Vladimir made his way, step by painful step to the deck. Every twisting, pitching movement of the boat under him brought a fresh agony, but the increasing flow of warm blood flowing down his body and the distant sound of a hull slapping through the waves, spurred him on. Once all the mooring lines were cut free, Vladimir staggered back to the wheelhouse as the distance between the two vessels slowly opened. Water churned out from the stern of *First Light* as he pushed the gear levers forward, spun the helm to starboard and headed away from *Natasha,* in the general direction of France.

He didn't look back.

TWENTY-THREE

Fatigue was seeping into me as I crouched, still hidden from view behind the bags on the swim platform. I knew I had to move from here and work my way into the bowels of the yacht in search of Jess. What I didn't know was how I was going to manage that. The rusty spear had, hopefully at least, slowed Vladimir down, if not killed him. Presumably, Victor was still roaming around like a murderous bear and an encounter with him was unlikely to end in any good way for me.

I was snapped out of my indecision as the platform beneath me was once again shoved upwards by a wave. The hydraulic arms groaned and creaked in protest at the immense force testing them. Remaining in place was no longer an option if I didn't want to end up dumped unceremoniously back in the sea. Keeping my head down, I headed cautiously up the teak steps to the main deck as the platform continued to creak and groan behind me.

The aft deck was empty, other than the last box that I had recovered from the cabin of the helicopter. Emboldened by the apparent absence of anyone wanting to kill me, I approached the sliding glass doors that gave access to the saloon. Some unseen sensor recognized my wish, and the doors slid soundlessly open revealing the prairie of white carpet.

Again, the space was empty, and I wondered how long my good luck would continue. Wading quickly through the deep pile of carpet towards the front of the saloon, I was aware that I didn't really have any clue where Jess might be held. There must be plenty of places on a yacht this size, able to hold someone. Not having any better idea, I decided to go down the marble staircase which I had seen on my last trip through the boat, hoping it would lead to the guest accommodation. As good a place as any to start looking.

The stairs changed direction twice before ejecting me into a wide corridor with more lacquered wood and deep carpets. I was probably right in thinking this was a guest area. The décor could have been taken straight out of gentleman's club in Mayfair. Wall panelling was festooned with pictures of classic sailing yachts illuminated by discreet spotlights. The atmosphere down here, if you ignored the impolite pitching and yawing as the weather outside deteriorated, was one of calm, order, and wealth. Which was markedly at odds with the way the day was shaping up - except for the wealth part, I suppose.

The changes in direction on the stairs had left me disorientated, not completely sure which way led forward or aft. Figuring it didn't matter much either way, I turned right and followed the short corridor to where it terminated at a door. Cracking the door open slowly, I entered what could only be the master cabin. Gold fittings abounded. Light switches, cupboard handles, even the remote control for the flat screen T.V. appeared to be plated in the stuff. A bed the size of a small pacific island was immaculately made and showed no evidence of recent use.

Thinking I was wasting my time here, I nevertheless made a quick search of the *en suite* bathroom. Yet more gold, and towels folded in the shape of swans stood guard over a jewel encrusted manicure set. But no sign of Jess. Retracing my steps, I passed the stairs and headed in the other direction. Leading away from me, the corridor widened and offered two doors on each side before terminating with a fifth at the far end.

The first door I opened turned out to be a storage cupboard. Futuristic looking cordless vacuum cleaners clipped into charging sockets competed for space with trays of cleaning products, an ironing board and bizarrely, a collapsible ladder. The next door revealed a miniature version of the master cabin. It had the same plush décor, and multiple towels masquerading as wildlife, but with marginally less space to roam around in. I tried the third door, but it was locked. Banging hard on it, I called out.

"Jess? Are you there?" I could hear nothing from behind the door but saw no reason for it to be locked. I crashed my shoulder into it, tentatively at first, to see if there would be any give. Encouraged by the sound of splintering wood, I gave it all I had and on the fourth attempt the door swung open and clicked into a retaining clip, presumably there to stop the door from banging about in a rough sea.

The room was dark. A frantic moaning noise reached me as I fumbled for the light switch. The *click*, when it came, revealed this cabin to be the twin of the last I had visited. Seemingly identical in every way, it differed only by the presence of a figure sat in a wooden chair, arms cable-tied behind her. The same restraints held her ankles firmly against the legs of the chair. A black hood covered her head.

I stepped towards her pulling the hood from her head looking in shock into the Jess's distressed face. A silver strip of *Duct Tape* had been stuck across her mouth. Working to remove it, my anger grew, but it was no match for Jess's when I finally managed to tear of the tape.

"Fucking hell, Matt!"

I didn't know what to say. 'Sorry' hardly seemed adequate considering the danger we were still in.

"I will get us out of this."

"Well you had better hurry up about it." The slight improvement in her situation that came with the removal of the hood and tape wasn't enough to keep the anger and frustration from her voice. “Where are those fucking Russians?!" she demanded.

"One of them, Vladimir, I shot with a spear gun, but I don't know if he is out of action. Last I saw, he was on my boat, which is tied alongside. The other one, Victor, I don't know."

She strained against the ties. Her wrists were bloodied and bruised from repeated efforts to break free.

"What the hell is this about?

I began to explain the events of the last few days to her as I hunted around desperately for something to cut the cable ties.

She didn't seem overly impressed at my explanation, but I suppose that was to be expected.

“Cut me free and give *me* a fucking speargun!" Jess said, straining her head around to look at me as I pulled open drawers and rummaged around in desperation. A defiant look was simmering behind the green eyes, but the overriding image on her tear stained face was one of fear. "The man who grabbed me is deranged."

"I know."

Nothing capable of cutting the tough cable ties presented itself in the drawers and cupboards of this cabin, but as I moved into the *en suite* bathroom, the same jewel encrusted manicure set I had seen in the *Master* cabin was sat on the marble surface between two sinks. Tipping the contents out and rummaging around, a pair of tiny nail scissors offered the best hope.

***

The swim platform was still grinding and smashing its way towards freedom as Victor entered the garage by means of the watertight door from the engine room. Ignoring the water slopping in the stern and the sound of hinges being ripped out of the fibreglass, Victor squeezed his bulk behind the racks of water sports equipment and reached for the ventilated fuel locker.

Bending awkwardly in the narrow space, he lifted out one of the four red, plastic petrol containers which were neatly lined up there. With the container held at his side, Victor navigated his way back past the racks of skis and wakeboards.

Pausing only to pick up a small self-igniting blow torch from the workbench in the engineer's office, he took the wooden stairs leading upwards and entered the saloon through a small door disguised to look like just another ornate panel. Setting the canister down on the carpet, the knurled black cap was rotated off and discarded on the floor. Moving methodically, he glugged a trail of petrol through the saloon, lingering a little longer at the sofas and armchairs as he went. The container was half empty by the time he reached the forward end of the saloon and stepped into the lobby.

Engrossed as he was in his work, some instinct still managed to break through, making him glance back before stepping onto the first tread of the marble stairs. Through the tinted glass of the saloon's aft sliding doors, he saw a black semi-rigid inflatable boat cresting the last few waves between it and the stern of *Natasha*. With no time now to descend the stairs and continue the dousing, Victor laid the canister on its side; allowing the remaining liquid to gurgle its way down the stairway and soak into the carpet of the corridor. Pistol in one hand, blowtorch in the other, he raced back through the saloon where the doors respectfully opened as he approached.

The black boat was no more than fifty meters away, slowly sinking down off the plane as the helmsmen judged his approach. Ignoring it for the moment, Victor knelt on the teak deck as he lit the blow torch and lobbed it, grenade like, through the still open doors in the direction of the nearest sofa. Enough petrol vapour had mixed with air to ignite with a *crump* of concussion. As the initial mini explosion died away, only the areas still soggy with petrol remained burning. But it wouldn't be long before the hungry flames expanded their territory like a pillaging army, consuming and growing stronger.

The guest areas of *Natasha* held no fire suppression system, no glass phials to burst in the heat and sprays of high-pressure water to dilute and cool. *'Too much valuable artwork to risk accidental activation'* had been the rationale, discussed at length by the designers. A decision that ensured, in a few short moments, the interior of the yacht would be a nonsurvivable hell of heat and toxic smoke.

His orders complete, Victor continued to ignore the boat closing up on the stern and rushed to the side of the yacht where *First Light* had been moored. His blank eyes took in the details, giving nothing away. They saw the frayed black mooring lines trailing down the side of the clean white hull. They also saw, when raised to the horizon, the last glimpse of *First Light*, her stern bucking skywards to the rhythm of the waves as it was swallowed up behind the curtain of a squall.

Victor turned away - the hard edges of his rage dulled by resignation. He had been privy to enough treachery and deception in his life to know this outcome had always been a possibility, if not an inevitability. Still, he was a soldier at his core. Giving up whilst still breathing and armed didn't even cross his mind.

Returning to the aft deck, not bothering to crouch this time, the raised pistol in his hand, he fired a salvo of shots in the direction of the oncoming boat. The black inflatable boat continued its cautious approach, undeterred by the sound of bullets shredding the air above it. Crouching in the bow and preparing to make the jump across to the *Natasha* as soon as contact was made, Victor could see the policeman who had been poking around yesterday. In his hands he held what looked like an MP5 sub machine gun. The unstable platform of the small inflatable appeared to be the only thing stopping him from returning fire.

Victor knew he was out gunned, with only a handful of rounds left in his pistol. Loosing off one more shot in the general direction of the policeman in the hope of slowing him down, he dropped out of view, crawling towards the staircase leading up to the bridge deck. The elegantly curved structure kept him out of sight as he scrambled upwards. Deserted by Vladimir and with a boat load of police approaching, he figured his one slim chance of getting off the yacht alive and not in handcuffs, was the jet ski, strapped to its cradle on the deck above him. Launching it in these conditions though, was going to be a challenge.

TWENTY-FOUR

My fingers would not fit through the handle of the small nail scissors, so I was reduced to holding them with both hands, each circular handle gripped between finger and thumb. It took some time, and a stream of expletive laden winces from Jess, but finally I had her hands free and began working on the ties that held her legs to those of the chair. She painfully flexed her wrists, shaking them to get the blood flow back into her white fingers.

"Is that smoke?" Jess asked, craning her neck towards the cabin door, where tendrils of thin black smoke were streaming in at head height and expanding across the cabin's ceiling. The sight spurred me to intensify my efforts on the final cable ties around her ankles, and at last she was free.

In the distance a high-pitched siren, that could only be a fire alarm, was sounding. Familiar popping and crackling sounds greeted me as I looked out of the cabin and back down the corridor. The stairs I had come down were hidden behind a wall of flame. Smoke was beginning to boil along the ceiling towards me. Already I felt the radiated heat from the fire on my face and as I looked, an oil painting depicting a racing yacht of a bygone era ignited from the heat, crackling as it was devoured. The faint odour of petrol was carried to me in the smoke, and I felt naked without my fire kit.

The view out in the corridor was a familiar one to me in many respects. Certainly no different from many of the domestic fires I had attended. But, in those fires, the bread and butter of my career, I was clad in the best protective clothing, holding the best equipment and breathing clean cold air from my B.A set. Being in a fire without those defences, those appendages which allowed life to continue and useful work to be done, was likely to be a painful and short-lived experience. Jess joined me in the doorway.

"Please tell me they build these things with emergency escapes."

I searched the top of the corridor for any sign of an escape hatch. There was no chance of seeing anything at the fire end of the corridor, but to my right where the smoke was still relatively thin, I could make out the distinct lines of a square, set into the larger panels of the ceiling. It was well out of reach though.

"That could be it," I said, pointing up at the square. "But there is a door at the end we should try first."

We both ventured out of the cabin, crouching low, but the heat was painful, and the smoke caused us to start coughing. A few quick strides took us to the door, but it proved to be locked and didn't flex at all when we both slammed our shoulders against it. Our crashing into it though did result in some muffled shouting coming from the other side, not loud or distinct enough to make out any words, but definitely the sound of more than one person.

I pulled Jess away from the door, and we retreated to the cabin. The smoke was much thicker now, every hot breath we took producing painful coughs as our lungs tried to reject the scorching particulates. Jess eyed me expectantly, her mouth shielded by the inside of her elbow, but coughs racking her frame, nonetheless.

"That must be the crew quarters," I declared.

"They're locked up in there, by the sound of it." Jess spoke between bouts of coughing.

"We aren't going to break that door down Jess, it didn't want to give. Let's hope that it *is* a hatch in the ceiling."

"How the hell are we supposed to get up there?" she asked. Even as she spoke, the memory of the cleaning supplies cupboard and its collapsible ladder rushed back to me.

"Stay here, I will be back in two seconds. And lay down on the floor, there will be less smoke down there."

Crawling out of the cabin and down the corridor on my belly towards the fire, conditions were already bordering on intolerable. Breathing, even with my face a few inches off the carpet, was little more than a painful exchange of hot gases - a scavenging for rare oxygen which came up short at every breath. I knew that if I couldn't find a way out of here in the next few minutes, another person who I cared about would die because of the decisions I had made. I felt the unwelcome return of crushing paralysis, the fear and guilt rising up from some dark place within me. Tears began to well up in my eyes as the image of Sophie in that warehouse, her impaled head on the spike, body still quivering, filled my mind.

Another scene: This one, a detached view of myself, held *together only by the crispness of my dress uniform as I sat in the austere coroner's office, staring blankly at a government issue clock. The second hand, long ago separated from its more plodding work mates, was lying trapped like a dead insect behind the glass.*

Words reached me across the desk but did not penetrate. Spoken softly, they were dipped in a protective layer of varnish, designed to insulate the speaker from the grief and sadness which was inescapable in this room. The seconds passed, unmeasured by the clock. A polite cough announced the time had arrived for me to summon some strength, catch the words, and hold them up loosely for examination before allowing them to trickle away. The process left me wishing that they had evaded my grasp.

If only those words had not stuck, had not settled in my conscious, like windblown seeds on fertile soil. If they had passed me by unheard, settled on barren ground, I would not have had to deal with the knowledge that Sophie's quivering body had held the beginnings of our child.

I rested my face on the deep pile of the carpet. The temptation to leave it there and let the fire do what it does was overwhelming. Its insatiable appetite could consume me - at least then, the sadness and guilt in my head would forever disappear into the smoke.

The harshness of Jess's coughing pierced into my thoughts as I lay unmoving, my face in the carpet. The sound spurred me to lift my head. Looking back towards the cabin, I saw Jess lying in the doorway, staring at me between violent bouts of coughing. At that moment, I knew a window of opportunity was still open. She was not Sophie. Jess was not yet lost.

A determination, at first weak and faltering, rapidly grew into something tangible. A strength which I could cling to as it changed shape into the realization that I owed it to them both not to give up - that I was not ready to give up. Only by moving forward, fighting, could I hope to change the course of events which were in no small part of my own making. Perhaps I was not at fault for Sophie's death, enough people had certainly tried to convince me so. But without a doubt, Jess's predicament was my fault and only my continued fighting would give her a chance of survival. If I were to die here, it should be with movement, a purpose. Not face down, defeated on some asshole's Axminster.

***

The ladder was surprisingly flimsy, perhaps because of an expectation it would never be needed- 'let's spend the money on eighteenth century art instead.' I hoped it would be up to the job. When I pushed the release buttons on the side, it telescoped somewhat wobbly out to its full length. Pushing the top of the ladder hard against the inset square panel above me resulted in it flapping upwards on a hinge, revealing a steel hatch held closed with an oversized lever. I jammed the extended ladder into the recess below the hatch, before dropping to the floor and crawling back to Jess.

"Time to go."

"No shit."

Her face was blackened by smoke and the coughing was continuous, but a spark of spirit glimmered in her eyes. Together we crawled to the foot of the ladder and I motioned her upwards. She didn't need telling twice, racing upwards and slamming the lever open with the side of her fist. Unlatched, the hatch smoothly opened by itself, courtesy of a spring-loaded hinge. Whoever had overseen hatch purchasing had obviously thought enough was enough in the art department.

Jess turned to make sure I was following her before entering the crawl-way which led, I hoped, forward towards the bow. The space was relatively clear of smoke and dimly lit by a series of emergency lights. An irregular banging was reverberating in the enclosed crawl-way. Shutting the hatch behind me, and greedily gulping in the cleaner air, I hurried after Jess. The space we found ourselves in was only big enough to enable progress on hands and knees. As we shuffled along, the banging grew louder, reaching its peak as we passed a hatch similar to the one we had just climbed through.

This one was securely locked with a robust heavy-duty padlock. I gave a few heavy blows to the hatch, resulting in renewed banging and muffled shouts. There was nothing I could do about that padlock though, so I was reluctantly forced to keep moving forward, trying not to think about the people trapped below on a burning boat. Our passage was ultimately blocked by a more substantial hatch, its multiple locking arms and operating wheel suggesting it was a watertight door, which I desperately hoped opened into fresh air.

"Open it up, Jess!" I shouted from my position behind her. I tried to keep the anxiety from my voice, in contrast to my internal monologue which was screaming- *'please don't' be locked, please don't be locked!'*

A heavy sigh of relief escaped me as the central wheel spun in her hands, retracting the locking arms. Oversized gas struts raised the hatch smoothly skywards, revealing wind driven rain slanting onto *Natasha's* empty foredeck. Empty of people at, least. A large portion of the deck was owned by an elaborate anchor windlass, a confusion of shiny wheels, drums and brakes which looked like a degree in mechanical engineering was the minimum required for its operation.

I followed Jess awkwardly out of the hatchway, momentarily enjoying the freshness of the rain stinging my face. Behind us, the superstructure sloped upwards towards the bridge deck, the panoramic expanse of bridge windows blinded by the black smoke behind them. Our coughing eased, and I tried not to think about what toxic particles may still be clinging to the moist linings of our lungs.

Lowering my gaze, I scanned the surrounding sea. A full-on winter storm was building, waves collapsing upon themselves, the resulting white foam whisked away in long streaks by the gale. In the midst of this confusion, intermittently rising into view between the waves was a semi-rigid boat, the figures of two people indistinct in the flying spray. Its deep 'V' hull topped with black inflatable tubes appeared to be coping well in the conditions. We both frantically waved our arms overhead trying to attract their attention.

Behind us, up on the bridge, windows started to fail in the heat, cracking with a sound like pistol shots, reminding me I still had no idea as to the whereabouts of Vladimir and Victor. From my position on the foredeck it was impossible to see all the way back along the side of the hull, and I didn't know if *First Light* was still nearby. I highly doubted she could still be alongside in these conditions - she would have ripped free long ago.

Jess continued to wave and shout towards the small boat, which was edging closer, the figures onboard braced against the motion. Our world had contracted to the small area of the bow. The option of moving aft was receding as flames began to impinge on the side decks. Heading that way, whilst still possible, brought with it the risk of encountering Victor, a scenario I was keen to avoid.

The failed windows of the bridge had allowed smoke to vent out, the blackness inside transitioning into a pulsating redness. I could see no way of gaining access to the upper deck where the white boxes containing life rafts sat poised and ready - requiring only the pulling of a release pin to send them plunging into the sea. Turning my attention back to our immediate surroundings, I took a more detailed look around.

Next to the hatch that had ejected us on the deck were two lockers, both tightly secured against the weather with a series of closing levers. One was anonymous, displaying no clue as to its contents. The other was not so shy, with bold words depicted in fluorescent red paint proclaiming it to be a FIRE LOCKER. The long process of releasing the multiple levers revealed neatly stacked and secured, some familiar tools of my trade.

Two breathing apparatus sets were mounted on quick release brackets behind a roll of fire hose. One end of the hose had its brass coupling firmly screwed into a hydrant outlet. The other terminated in a complicated looking nozzle. With little in the way of expectation, I opened the tap on the hydrant with the lack of success that I had already anticipated - presumably, a pump would require starting somewhere to produce the desired result. A serious-looking fire axe hung by its head against the rear bulkhead. Beneath the axe, two sets of firefighting clothing, neatly rolled down over rubber boots and topped off with helmets, completed the inventory. What the space did not contain were the bolt cutters which I had desperately hoped would be there.

"Come over here, Jess!"

Reluctantly turning away from the high flared side of the bow, Jess joined me in front of the locker.

"They have seen us." She looked at me, then aft, at the inferno creeping steadily towards us. I lifted one of the B.A sets out of its rack, setting it down on the deck at my feet.

"I'm going to try to get the crew out."

"Is there time?" she asked apprehensively, looking at me then back at the encroaching fire.

I shrugged, swinging the set across my shoulders, and feeling the familiar comfortable weight as it settled into place. There was definitely no time for me to strip out of the clinging dry suit and put on the full fire-fighting kit, but at least the suit would provide some level of protection.

"I have to try."

Jess didn't question me, only a searching look at my face followed by; "What can I do?"

"Try shouting down to the boat. Tell them they will need to pick us up from the stern. There's no way, other than us jumping into the sea, that we can get down to them from here in these conditions."

"Can we even make it to the stern?"

I walked the few steps required to take me to the starboard side. *Natasha's* anchor had broken free of the bottom, and we were now rolling and heaving, beam on to the wind and waves. It was a deeply unpleasant motion but had resulted in the wind keeping the starboard deck, running back aft, relatively clear of smoke and flame. For the moment, at least.

"Probably, if this doesn't take too long," I reassured her. I didn't add, *'and if Victor or Vladimir are not waiting there to shoot us.'*

Further conversation was forestalled as I pulled the mask over my head taking the first deep inhalation to trigger the unit into delivering as much air as each breath demanded. The fire axe lifted cleanly from its housing and I turned back towards the open escape hatch, bracing myself against the rolling deck.

***

With the cylinder scraping against the top of the crawl-way and the axe held awkwardly down one side, I shuffled along until reaching the padlocked hatch. There was no room to challenge the padlock with the axe, so I continued along the passage, mentally revisiting the frustration of the lack of bolt cutters. I was still cursing into my mask as the end of crawl-way arrived. My hand found the hatch opening lever, hot to the touch of my gloveless hand, and my cursing dialled up a notch.

Nothing good was going to happen when, *and if,* I opened the hatch. Every instinct was screaming at me to leave it closed. With a cooling spray of water, dressed in the correct kit, maybe, just maybe, opening that hatch could be seen as a calculated risk. With no fire hose and clad only in a dry suit, the only calculation going through my mind was how much it was going to hurt. A lot, as it turned out.

I tried to move as quickly as possible, releasing the hatch to pop open against its spring at the same time as dropping the axe down through the billowing smoke. Squeezing myself around until I faced backwards, my flailing feet searched for the top rung of the ladder. The heat drove any coherent thoughts from my head as I half climbed, half fell, down the rickety steps, coming to a horizontal rest, the hard, angular axe between me and the carpet.

The corridor was now completely smoke logged, right down to the floor and the radiated heat of the fire began to burn my exposed skin. But as I painfully rose to my knees, the now open escape hatch started to vent some of the smoke and heat, allowing it passage towards the open air of the bow. It was a slow process, but visibility improved to the point where I was now able to match the crackling popping sound of fire to the flames which had nearly reached this end of the corridor.

The door was not lightly constructed. Blow after frantic blow, with little to show for my effort. A few brown splinters fell towards my feet, but the door stayed resolutely shut. Each hissing breath of compressed air in my mask punctuated with the sound of the axe smashing away at the wood. Fatigue weighed down my arms and I wondered how much longer I could function. The last twenty-four hours had sapped me of all but the dregs of my willpower, which this door appeared more than capable of withstanding.

Somehow the axe kept at its work and the door, splinter by splinter, reluctantly, begrudgingly even, swung open mere seconds before I was about to concede defeat and re-join Jess on the bow. I had a brief view of silver washing machines and tumble dryers lining the walls, before five agitated crew members pushed past me and began clambering up the ladder and into the escape hatch.

"You're welcome," I mouthed into my mask.

Squatting down against the wall, still sucking down huge lungful's of blessedly cool air to counter my exhaustion, I waited patiently as the last crew member climbed the ladder. As his feet disappeared above me, I wasted no time in following him up- flames licking at my heels. Shutting the hatch behind me, I closed right up behind him, determined that we spill out onto the bow as one. I didn't think they would close the hatch on me but wasn't prepared to give them the benefit of the doubt, given the welcome I had so far received on their boat.

With a wary eye, I looked at the crew on the fore deck as I re-entered the fresh air. Jess helped me shake off the B.A set which was hot to the touch. The crew were stunned at the sight which had greeted them on the foredeck, flames and billowing black smoke as their workplace and accommodation disappeared before their eyes, the smoke adding to already heavy sky. Jess pulled me over to the side.

"They're waving to us!" she exclaimed, pointing down. Below us, a semi-rigid boat containing what appeared to be two very wet police officers was tossing around under the bow, the helmsman managing with some difficulty to hold position close to the rearing yacht. A figure in the boat was gesticulating back towards *Natasha's* stern. Turning to the crew, I pointed down the side of the yacht, as the small boat turned and wallowed its way aft, disappearing from view.

"We've got to get to the stern. Keep down and follow me."

TWENTY-FIVE

Jake's day had not started particularly well. Swinging his feet out of the lumpy bed, he had longed for the memory foam mattress of his London apartment. Nothing else seemed capable of cosseting the aches and pains of his soldiering past. Picking up his phone from the bedside table where it had spent the night, he was faced with a resolutely blank screen. At some point in the night, the old sloppy wall socket of his government budget bed and breakfast accommodation had ejected the phone's charger onto the threadbare carpet.

He was showered and dressed by the time the battery had recovered enough to throw a multitude of electronic pings across the room at him. Listening to the voice messages with a growing sense of alarm, he strode quickly towards the door.

"I'm down at the port now, Ma'am. *Natasha* and the fireman's boat, *First Light* are gone," Jake told her, after first explaining the messages he had received from Matt.

Deborah listened to him, with the same sense that things had taken a significant turn for the worse.

"What assets are available there to go after them?"

Jake thought for a moment, before answering.

"The nearest tactical team we could mobilize would be in Plymouth. I will text you the position where I think the *Natasha* will be. But a quicker option might be the Royal Naval College here in Dartmouth. It has some fast ribs, and they usually have some well-trained people floating about on standby. There may even be a couple of SBS guys skulking around. With your authority I should be able to dig up a team and get out there long before anyone could arrive from Plymouth."

Deborah hadn't got where she was through indecisiveness.

"Do it," she instructed. "I will set the Plymouth side in motion. Keep me updated as much as you can. I am going to drive down there as soon as I can."

***

Barely three hours after being given the green light by Deborah, Jake was bracing himself against the pounding in the bow of the inflatable, with the blunt stern of the *Natasha* approaching fast. He was surprised at how quickly old habits flooded back. As the rounds from *Natasha* whined overhead, Victor was not the only one keeping a mental tally. Calculations of range, angles, options, came back as naturally as breathing. The MP5 in his hands, '*don't lose it, for fuck's sake mate,' as it was thrust towards him*, felt as balanced and capable as the day he had last slid one back across the counter to the armourer in Hereford.

Victor had disappeared from sight as the rubber tube of the inflatable boat squeaked hard against the lurching swim platform. Jake leapt nimbly over the bow onto the teak. The next wave carried the small boat away before he could be joined by the two SBS troopers, who had eagerly swapped the boredom of security detail at the college for the chance of some action.

Not waiting for the boat to reposition itself, Jake quickly stepped into the garage, the loaned MP5 leading the way. It was soon apparent that the garage was clear, and so he made his way forward to where the tender was stored, latching the watertight door open as he progressed. Searching the tender garage was trickier and slowed him down. With the *Riva* in place, its bulk provided plenty of cover to anyone intent on concealment. After methodically confirming that only the tender was in residence, Jake began to progress forward towards the engineer's office and engine room. As he moved, the earpiece in his right ear crackled into life.

"We are on board, but the boat can't stay here. It's too rough. They're going to make a circuit or two while they standby. Where are you?"

Jake replied to the trooper, speaking softly.

"Move forward through the tender garage. It's clear. I'm just forward of there, outside the engineer's office. I couldn't see where the shooter went, so we will clear down here first, then go up to the next deck."

"Copy."

Jake paused momentarily to allow the troopers to join him before continuing on, as loosely grouped as the space allowed.

***

Even as he clipped the crane's hook into the lifting cradle of the jet ski, Victor knew that launching it at all, let alone undamaged, was likely to be impossible. *Natasha* was rolling heavily, the movement amplified by the height of the deck above the sea. Once lifted clear of its chocks, the jet ski would swing wildly. The more it was lowered, the greater the swing would be and crashing it repeatedly into the superstructure and hull of the yacht on the way down, was unavoidable. Victor knew all this, but out of options, his thumb pushed the *Up* button on the cranes control box anyway and lifted the jet ski free of its chocks.

Initially, he was able to hold the jet ski with his free hand and reduce the swing. But once he had rotated the crane outboard, and began to lower, the swinging became progressively more violent. Pushing the down button and hoping for the best, Victor watched helplessly as the jet ski slammed into the side of *Natasha*.

The first crunching impact seemed to result in little damage, but the jet ski sat a bit more nose high in its cradle. It swung away from the point of impact, pausing at the extremity of its arc before returning with a vengeance. The second impact completed the process of dislodging the jet ski from its lifting cradle, dropping it stern first into the sea below. Released of its charge, the empty cradle continued to flail around in the wind, but Victor's eyes were on the jet ski, somehow still afloat, slowly drifting towards the stern. Still thinking it was his best option, he turned and raced for the stairs.

***

Jake's earpiece came alive with the voice of the rib's helmsman.

"We have multiple persons coming down the starboard side deck. It looks like they are heading to the swim platform. There is also someone trying to launch a jet ski from the bridge deck, do you copy?"

Jake was already moving back through the tender garage as he replied, "Copy. Where are you?"

"We are holding off the stern. Standing by to move in and take these people from the swim platform."

"Copy. Coming back towards you now."

***

The route aft along the starboard side was not too bad so long as we kept moving on bent knees. Flames had found their way out of the saloon through the windows, but the wind was doing a good job of keeping this side of the yacht relatively clear. As the narrow passageway widened into the aft deck, I once again saw the rugged black box, seemingly abandoned.

"Bring that." I pointed at the box. The crew, still avoiding eye contact, did as I asked without question, scooping it up, as we filed down the steps to the swim platform.

Oil from the overworked hydraulic arms was squirting out onto the teak with each upward movement of the platform. I was amazed it was still attached given the beating it was taking. The black rib surged in close enough for Jess and two of the crew to clamber inelegantly onboard, before being pushed away by the wind and waves. As we waited for the boat to approach again, a jet ski drifted unexpectedly into view from the port side. I was wondering where it had come from, when the bullet slammed into my back.

Its impact spun me around and toppled me backwards into the sea. The last image my mind recorded before the water closed over my head and colours faded into speckled greyness, was of a red mist erupting from the side of Victors head as he deflated to the deck. On the periphery of this scene was Jake, crouching low in the opening of the garage, his weapon still pointing at the crumpled heap.

TWENTY-SIX

Deborah stood in the shelter of the ambulance on the town quay, watching the small, overloaded boat approach. A collapsible umbrella in her hand showed signs of imminent failure as the gusts swirled around her. Gulls floated overhead, working hard in the blustery conditions. Behind the ambulance, a police minibus waited expectantly for its damp cargo, which was now clambering gratefully onto the quay.

She watched with interest as the person she assumed was Matt, was slid horizontally into the awaiting mouth of the ambulance. The doors slammed shut and it pulled away - the first of its painful decibels hitting Debora's ears as she turned and walked towards Jake. He was in the process of un-slinging the MP5 from his shoulder, passing it somewhat reluctantly back to the SBS trooper stood nearby.

"Thanks for the loan."

"Any time, Jake." The trooper instinctively ran the weapon through the 'make-safe' procedure, even though Jake had already done it, before switching his attention away from the MP5 and back to Jake. "Have fun with the paperwork."

Debora raised an inquiring eyebrow.

"Let me ask one of these local officers to seal that in an evidence bag," -Jake pointed at the black box recovered from the aft deck of the yacht- "then I can fill you in on the details in the car."

The wet winter greenness of the Devon countryside had given way to the equally wet greyness of Plymouth by the time Jake had bought his boss up to speed. Deborah had remained silent as he had described how the events on the *Natasha* had unfolded, her first question catching him a little by surprise.

"Are you okay? I know your background, obviously, but it has been a while since you were at the sharp end like that."

"I'm fine Ma'am, thanks for asking though."

Deborah continued to look at her officer, remaining quiet until Jake broke into the silence. "Really, I'm fine."

And in truth, he was. Taking down clear-cut evil had never given him any sleepless nights. The sleepless nights he *did* have, came from the confusion of the battleground, the indiscriminate mayhem of a fragmentation grenade lobbed into a village compound. Or the knowledge that the hut you had just lit up with a laser, guidance for the soon to be impacting missile, contained more than just the evil needing to be snuffed out. But killing the likes of Victor? No, that was just a good morning's work in his book.

***

An hour later, Debora was sitting at a battered metal desk, an array of paperwork strewn in front of her when Jake opened the door and joined her. An untouched mug of tea was gradually adding its dwindling heat to the chilly interview room. Fresh from a shower and dressed in a borrowed boiler suit, Jake sat down opposite her wondering what the papers contained to be able to put such a worried look on her face.

"Was this the only box?" Deborah asked, looking enquiringly across the desk at him.

"The only one we found, yes. If there are any more, they are either still down in the wreckage of the helicopter, on board the *Natasha*, or, more likely on *First Light* - Matt Curtis's boat. Which has disappeared," he added.

"That's a pity."

Jake picked up a piece of paper from the pile and looked at it.

"What are these?"

Deborah reached across and plucked it from his hand, placing it back down on the stack it had come from.

"They're documents which appear to detail various aspects of Dimitri Petrovitch's business affairs. They should be invaluable in helping to piece together where his wealth came from and how he managed to avoid prosecution for so many years."

The worried look that remained on Deborah's face suggested to Jake that some part of the box's contents went further than that, but it had been made clear he would not be privy to the details.

"I need to get them back to London immediately." Deborah stood, the frown still in place.

Between them they repacked the box and placed it back in the plastic evidence bag. Deborah was worried with good reason. Even the cursory look at the paperwork the box held, had thrown up names that were familiar to her. Familiar to a lot of people, in fact. She knew enough about Dimitri's business practices to know that if genuine, the contents of the innocuous looking black box, when tipped out into the spotlight of public scrutiny, had the potential to be highly damaging to certain individuals. Deborah was political enough to know that if handled correctly, the documents could lead to her own position and aspirations being considerably strengthened. She was also smart enough to realize that the opposite was equally true, especial given one of the names that had leapt out at her of the pages.

A polite knock preceded the opening of the interview room door as a uniformed policeman stepped in.

"Just to let you know, our police launch, and the Plymouth all-weather lifeboat are in the last known position you gave us for the yacht. She sank before they managed to get near. But there wasn't a lot left of her before she went down, the fire was intense. If you give me your email, I can forward you some of the pictures taken as they approached."

"Thank you."

Deborah plucked a card from her bag, passing it over and waiting for the policeman to retreat.

Turning to Jake, she summarized; "So, Dimitri's helicopter and yacht are both at the bottom of the English Channel. We believe Vladimir and or Victor may have murdered the crew of the *Southern Cross*. Victor is dead and Vladimir-

"Is nowhere to be found," Jake interjected.

"Maybe Vladimir died on the yacht, but it's equally possible he slipped away in Matt's boat, *First Light*, before you arrived on the scene. Correct?"

"That's about the crux of it, Ma'am, yes."

Deborah sighed as she sat on the deliberately uncomfortable chair screwed to the floor on the interviewee's side of the desk.

"Can you stay down here for a little longer?" she asked.

Jake nodded in affirmation, his back silently groaning at the idea of more nights on the lumpy mattress.

"I will have you relieved as soon as I can get someone else up to speed. In the meantime, keep on top of what the divers find on the two sites when the weather lets up. Whilst waiting for that, you can debrief this Matt chap. Quite frankly I am amazed he is still alive after meddling with that pair."

Jake was of the same mind, wondering how Matt had survived, albeit by the skin of his teeth. He was looking forward to hearing Matt's account. Deborah squirmed uncomfortably in the hard seat before continuing.

"And keep your ear to the ground regarding *First Light*. If she turns up somewhere, it suggests Vladimir used her to get away," she concluded, reaching across the desk for the neglected mug of tea. She tentatively sipped, unsure what to expect.

The grimace told Jake it had been a long time since she had had to suffer through cold, over sweetened, police station tea. The thought of institutional tea caused his mind to wander-back to the night when the informant he was supposed to be meeting had managed to get himself murdered, right under Jake's nose.

"Ma'am, about the Albion Syndicate-" he started.

Deborah stopped him with a raised hand.

"It was not your fault," she interjected. "Operation Albion was running with far too few resources. You know how stretched things are. There was no way just the two of you could have kept that guy under surveillance twenty-four hours a day."

Jake took a different view on that but remained quiet.

"Yes, it's a shame," she continued. "Because what he could have told us would probably gone a long way to disrupting the drug trade in this corner of the UK quite dramatically for some time to come. But we don't win them all, Jake. We never have. At least this time it was one of their own that they killed. Like you, I'm fine with that."

He digested her words with another nod. Not in the habit of seeking absolution, Jake knew he had done the best he could under the circumstances. It hadn't even been *his* lapse in concentration which had allowed his informant's murderer to somehow enter the house. He still wasn't sure why he had remained silent on the subject. The only words spoken about the failing, had been a short, private conversation uttered with one hand around his colleague's throat.

Deborah set the cup back down.

"Something you may not know, is the Constable you were with that night asked for you to be charged with assault."

Jake looked at Deborah, seeing the beginnings of a grin pulling at the side of her mouth and wondered where this was going.

"Obviously, this created a need for him to explain why you assaulted him - which he was eventually persuaded to do."

"And?" Jake queried.

"Well, I'm not completely sure, but I heard a rumour that he's likely to end up working in the fresh fruit and vegetable section at *Tesco*.

***

Jake's gaze followed the Range Rover containing Deborah and the problematic box glide out of the police station car park to begin its trek back to London. Knowing the boss had his back regarding the botched surveillance on the house was a bonus, but the frustration of losing the informant, whose information could have crippled a drug ring, had not been entirely dispelled by her words.

TWENTY-SEVEN

I finally decided the square of light could only be a window. With the sound of my breathing keeping time with a soft electronic beeping, I waited patiently for the appearance of features that a room with a window must surely also contain. They did not come. Slowly the square and the beeping faded away leaving me in the darkness.

The second time around, with the beeping still there, I was convinced that the square was definitely a window. I congratulated myself on my perception. A shape moved across the square, detracting from its pleasing symmetry. Probably a person, I thought, but held back from committing to a firm opinion in the absence of further clarity. In the end it was the voice which provided the toehold back to full consciousness.

"Matt....*Matt*." More insistence this time. I was lying on my back, head to one side. Blurred shapes slowly sharpened into focus; a fog bank burned away by the sun.

Jess sat near my head, silhouetted by the last of the afternoon daylight from the window behind her. The fingers of a firm hand intertwined with mine.

"Hey."

I got a reassuring squeeze in return.

"Hospital?" I asked. To be fair, the earlier *beeping* had given me a clue.

"Yes. Torquay," she answered. "Hang on, I'm supposed to call someone now that you are awake."

Jess disappeared through the door of my small cubicle, returning almost immediately with a nurse.

"Ah...awake. Finally. Good sleep?" The nurse didn't wait for a response, but began fussing with various bits of equipment, before jotting down a lengthy note on the clipboard at the foot of my bed. Her abrupt manner made me look at her, searching for signs of a family resemblance to Kemp.

"The doctor will be in to see you shortly, and its four P.M. Visiting time is over I am afraid," she directed at Jess. "You can come back tomorrow if you want."

I noticed Jess beginning to bristle and interjected, "How long have I been here?"

"A day, give or take," the nurse replied.

Looking back at Jess, memories of the events on *Natasha's* swim platform came unbidden.

"You're okay?" I asked her.

"I'm fine. You're the one with the bullet in you," she said, smiling. "Actually, it's not in you anymore. They took it out as soon as you got here."

I thought about those last seconds on the *Natasha.* The searing heat of the bullet as it had ploughed into me. The cloud of red produced by Victors head.

"How did I get out of the sea?"

Jess smiled again, leading me to wonder how I had survived the pre-smile days.

"It was unlikely two highly trained Special Boat Squadron troopers wouldn't have been able to drag your sorry ass out of the water," she said. "I would say you owe them a beer...or ten."

I wouldn't argue with that.

"Sorry, I got you into this mess Jess... I bit off way more than I knew when I got involved with them."

"I'm good, Matt. I'm likely to have a few nightmares for a while, but I can deal with them."

A white-jacketed man in sensible shoes and his mid-fifties came unannounced through the door. The stethoscope around his neck and a handful of notes clutched in one hand completed the look.

"Time to go, Luv." The nurse began herding Jess towards the door. Scowling at the nurse, she nonetheless allowed herself to be evicted without further hostilities.

"I will come back tomorrow. Hope you have a good night."

I watched her leave, casting a final smile at me from the doorway. I didn't know what, *if any,* pain killers I may be on; but with that smile, I was fairly sure they could reduce the dose.

"How are you feeling?" the Doctor looked down on me with a kindly face.

I mentally ran through a check list from head to toe. The only points which seemed worthy of mention, were a numbness in my chest and a so far suppressed desire to cough.

The Doctor nodded sagely.

"Well, all things considered, you aren't in too bad a shape." Stealing a quick glance at his notes, he continued. "The bullet we pulled out of you clipped the side of your lung, but just barely. A couple of ribs which got in the way were the only issue we could see. You didn't even lose a lot of blood, thanks to the clotting agent those soldiers carried with them. Amazing stuff."

The Doctor paused, before adding, "I do have a slight concern some sea water entered your lungs, which could cause infection, but we are pumping you full of antibiotics which will hopefully reduce that risk. You also have some burns on the neck and arms which will be a bit sore." He reached down and lifted my left forearm, showing me the tubes that had been stabbed into my veins and held in place with tape.

"We put in a line in that can give you painkiller on demand."

Draped over the metal railing which ran around the bed was a pen sized device with a button on one end, the other trailing a wire which disappeared into the trolley-full of electronics pushed up against the wall. Lowering my arm back down to the bed, he picked up pen thingy and gave me a closer look at the button.

"You can push this once if the pain gets too bad. But don't make a habit of it," he said, glancing at me to see if he had wasted the line.

"Funny." I got the impression he had been waiting a while for that opportunity to arise, it would have been churlish of me to let it go unrecognized. "Thanks, Doc."

I think I saw him stiffen at the foreshortening of his title and tried to make amends. After all, tired jokes aside, he *had* probably saved my life.

"*Doctor*, any idea how long before I can be up and about?"

Placated, the Doctor responded, "You need to stay here for a week or so, with the chance of infection being so high. The wound made by the bullet also needs time to heal before you move around. After that, well, that's going to be dependent on your pain threshold. The smashed ribs are going to hurt considerably for some time. But as soon as you feel up to it, we can arrange for a physiotherapist to give you some exercises which you can do in bed, so you don't get too weak with all the lying around."

I thanked him, watching as he studied the monitors on the trolley. Apparently satisfied at what he saw, his last task was to check the notes at the foot of my bed, before assuring me he would return in the morning and closing the door behind him. It opened again, almost immediately. Just the Doctor's head reappeared.

"A number of people wanted to come and see you, but I want you to have a good night's rest before letting them in. I told them to come back tomorrow."

"Sure, thanks, Doctor. Good of you to let Jess in though."

"Yes, well, that young lady wouldn't take *no* for an answer. And some battles are best left unfought, I have found. See you tomorrow."

The head disappeared and the door closed, leaving me to ponder my predicament. At the top of my list of things to worry about, was the whereabouts of *First Light*.

***

As promised, Jess was my first visitor, after a restless, uncomfortable night. I looked on in disbelief as she knocked and entered the cubicle, closely followed by the dragon nurse of yesterday. The nurse was holding a tray of tea and biscuits. Setting it down on the bedside table, she smiled at Jess.

"I'm just down the hall. Shout out if you need a top up."

Jess smiled sweetly. "Thanks Cheryl."

"What just happened?" I asked, as soon as '*Cheryl*' had left.

"We had a chat, that's all. She's actually really nice once you get to know her."

"Got any other superpowers we can use?"

Jess grinned cheekily at me. "Well, yes. But they are going to have to wait until you're a bit more mobile."

The sleepless night forgotten, I resolved to ask the Doctor about physiotherapy at the first opportunity. Jess settled in on the chair near the head of my bed, and we talked about the last few days. She appeared, outwardly at least, to be coping well with being kidnapped, threatened with execution, and nearly dying in a fire. There were sure to be some tough moments in front of her, but surprisingly, it seemed the hardest thing to deal with was Victor killing Andrew's dog.

"Is Andrew around?" I asked.

"He should be here any minute." A heavy look replaced the smile on her face.

"The dog was not your fault."

"I know. But I am struggling to get the image out of my mind. He didn't need to kill him."

I remained silent. The memory would surely fade with time. Nothing I could say would help with that. The fact that Victor had got what he deserved would provide some comfort as well, I was sure.

We were both quiet with our thoughts when Andrew strode through the door. His eyes were blood-shot, and stubble lined his jaw. He looked from one of us to the other for a moment before dropping a newspaper onto my bed and turning to Jess.

"Are you okay?"

Tears were welling up in Jess's eyes as she replied, "I'm fine. But I'm so sorry about your dog."

Andrew gave her a quick hug as he reiterated my point.

"You can't blame yourself for the actions of that psychopath, Jess. I'm just glad you are alright. Things could have turned out quite different for the pair of you."

I was looking at the newspaper lying face up across my legs. Above a grainy picture of a fishing boat, the headline read, '*Hopes fade as search for local trawler called off.*'

"That had to have been Vladimir." I sighed heavily.

Turning to me, Andrew asked, "What the hell happened out there?"

He listened patiently as I told him. When I got to the part about Vladimir finding the box we had tried to hide, he gave a shrug of acceptance.

"Easy come, easy go, as they say."

In truth, I was struggling to take such a philosophical view about that, but continued with the sorry tale, to its bullet punctuated end. Andrew listened, occasionally shaking his head in disbelief.

"You're both lucky to be alive. And what about Vladimir and your boat?" he asked.

"I can answer that," Jake said as he slipped unexpectedly through the doorway; the privacy provided by the thin door to my cubicle only going so far apparently.

"Jake. Good to see you." I shuffled my upper body to a more vertical position against the head of the bed before gingerly reaching out to shake his hand. "Thanks for turning up when you did."

Jake carefully shook my hand.

“You’re welcome,” -he pulled up the remaining chair and placing it alongside Jess, he sat down- “although I thought we had left it a little too late when they pulled you out of the sea. I didn't get your message straight away, and it was a bit of a scramble getting out there." He reached across to the table and plucked a biscuit from the plate. "I need to take a statement from you, if you're up to it?" Jake looked across at Andrew and Jess as he spoke.

Always quick on the uptake, Andrew rose to his feet.

"Come on, Jess, let's leave them to it. We will come back this afternoon and bring you some grapes or something."

I received a soft peck on the check from Jess and a raised eyebrow from Andrew, before the door closed behind them. Jake pulled a recording device from a pocket and turning it on placed it on the table next to the plate of biscuits.

"Tell me what happened."

Starting from the time I had arrived back onboard *First Light* to find Vladimir waiting to greet me, I recounted the events. Jake stopped me when I reached the part regarding the removal of the boxes from the helicopter and how we floated them to the surface.

"So, there were six boxes' in total? Can you describe them?"

I saw no reason to hold back, explaining to Jake that five of them were extremely heavy and at least one of them was stuffed full of one-ounce gold bars. It took a few minutes to explain exactly how I knew that before Jake would let me move on. I finished with my assumption that, except for the black one left behind, all the boxes had ended up on *First Light*, wherever she might now be.

Jake sat back in his chair, digesting what I had told him, along with another biscuit. "Well, that certainly explains your tenacity."

"So, what was in the black box?" I asked.

"Nothing as glamorous as gold, I'm afraid. Just a bunch of paperwork."

Bringing the conversation back to a point which I already knew I wasn't going to like hearing, I asked, "And my boat?"

Jake looked at me, a candid expression on his face.

"I'm sorry Matt, but I was informed this morning that the French Gendarme found the burned-out hull of *First Light* abandoned in a creek, somewhere near Morlaix. There was no sign of our friend Vladimir, or any boxes. And it seems the locals had picked it clean of anything not destroyed by the fire."

I sank deeper into the pillows behind my back and closed my eyes. So, that was that. My 'tenacity' had cost me my home and everything in it, as well as nearly costing me and Jess our lives. Even the consolation prize, stuffed into the pockets of the two buoyancy compensators was not to be. I began to feel a bit of a chump.

"Was your boat insured?" asked Jake, before reading the answer on my face.

"What happens now?" I spoke in the hope of distracting myself from the predicament I was now in.

"We will keep looking for Vladimir. But given his skills and the resources he may now have; I'm not going to hold my breath. When the weather calms down, the Navy will recover the pilot's body from the helicopter, maybe even raise the entire wreckage. And I'm sure they will take a good look through what's left of the *Natasha*, when they find it. But other than that, I think the excitement is over."

I digested Jake's words in silence.

"What will you do, once you are out of here?" Jake asked, glancing around the small cubicle.

I answered with a good deal more optimism than I felt. "I'll be fine. Once I am back on my feet, I'll find a place ashore to live and go back to work."

Jake's expression told me he hadn't fallen for my upbeat assessment of my future. The mention of work reminded me of the thumb drive in my locker.

"Can I ask one thing, before you go? The house fire I saw you at, what was that all about?"

Jake sighed. "I can't really say much about it, other than some mistakes were made, and a lot of useful information was lost."

"The sort of information that might be held on a memory stick?"

He looked at me, a quizzical expression on his face, but remained silent.

"It's in my locker at the fire station. When I picked up the body that night, I found it underneath and dropped it into my pocket. I forgot about it until the other day when I was going through my kit."

"Did you look at it?"

No point in denying I had, he already had ample evidence of my inquisitiveness.

"Yes. I took a quick look. A lot of names and addresses. And what might have been bank details. Some other stuff that I didn't recognize."

"That's great. A big help." Jake looked as if a weight had been lifted. "I'm going to need to get it today."

"Feel free. Kemp, the Station Manager, is usually there. I'm sure he will let you in. The combination to my locker padlock is 2727, not that I suppose you would have any trouble opening it without the code."

Jake rose and shook my hand again.

"Thanks Matt. I will be gone tomorrow. Someone else will be here to oversee the last of this, but I will leave my number, for when you get a new phone. Keep in touch. And if anymore get-rich-quick schemes come your way, give me a call. I'll do my best to talk you out of them."

And that was pretty much that. Except for the infection.

TWENTY-EIGHT

Ten miserable days passed before my body began to return to some semblance of normality. Bouts of coughing dwindled, each heave of my chest incrementally becoming less eye-watering, until a combination of my temperature and the notes at the foot of my bed at last decreed that I could be discharged.

Dressed in unfamiliar, borrowed clothes which were loose on my frame, the hospital's entrance doors slid open revealing the dull greyness of a winters evening. Boxes of medication, their sharp edges beginning to tear through the thin paper bag clutched in my right hand represented the sum total of my possessions; if you didn't count the motorbike which was presumably still brooding under its cover. It was going to be some months before I would be fit enough to throw my leg over it, hopefully by that time I would have worked out how to start it without the key.

"The car is just over there," Jess said, pointing towards Andrew's car, idling at the nearby curb.

In the driver's seat, Andrew’s attention was held by a squirming, black puppy as we approached. It was determined not to miss an inch with its licking. Jess opened the door for me, watching with a concerned expression as I awkwardly manoeuvred myself into the rear seat.

"Thanks for coming to fetch me," I told Andrew, his hands still full with the dog.

"No trouble. Meet *Django*." He lifted the puppy up, holding its writhing body with some difficulty. Jess slid in next to me and reached forward to take Django from Andrew.

"Cute." I envied its mobility.

My ribs noted every bump on the long drive back to Dartmouth, but I would take them any time over having to remain even one more day in hospital. At least the pain distracted me from thoughts of my future, which was looking somewhat limited for the time being. My already deflated spirits sank further as we boarded the car ferry for the brief crossing to Dartmouth. The sight of the river, without *First Light* on her mooring, was an unwelcome reminder of my situation.

A short drive after bouncing painfully off the ferries ramp, Andrew pulled up outside Jess's modest house, the middle one of a terrace. Set back from the towns small market square, the houses were small and neat, empty window boxes and hooks for hanging baskets awaiting the spring. Jess dug around at her feet, coming up with a small wicker travel basket. The puppy's frivolity turned to whining as its freedom was curtailed. Fair enough.

Andrew twisted round from the driver's seat and took the basket, placing it on the passenger seat. The whining moderated a little, but affront was clear in the puppy's eyes.

Probably for the tenth time, I asked, "You're sure this is okay, Jess?"

"I'm sure, Matt. Stop asking. If you turn out not to be house-trained, it's only a short walk for you around to Andrew's."

Shuffling myself carefully from the car, I turned to see Andrew's window sliding open as he gradually pulled away from the curb.

"Be ready at nine tomorrow morning, there's somewhere we need to go." With that, the window slid closed and the car turned out of sight at the end of the road.

***

Jess's home was everything I had expected. Warm and welcoming, with the furniture having an emphasis on comfort over style.

"This is for you." Jess handed me a rectangular white cardboard box which was on top of a pile of unopened letters on the hallway table.

"Jess," I began to protest, but she stopped me firmly, with a finger on my lips. "It's a gift. You need a new phone, so don't upset me by making a fuss about it."

I put my arms around her and squeezed my thanks, as hard as my wound would allow.

"Besides, if you upset me, I won't help you set it up and I'm pretty sure you are going to need help with that." The cheeky grin which I was growing so used to flashed again, as she darted nimbly out of reach. Not that she needed to move so quickly. It was going to be a long while before I would be able to give chase, unfortunately.

The first evening out of the hospital was a real pleasure. A dinner was rustled up from a fridge full of leftovers with seemingly little effort and eased on its way with a chilled glass of wine - *Sorry Doc, couldn't help myself.* Shortly after that, I was ensconced in a comfortable armchair which immediately gave the impression it was unlikely to release me without a fuss. The small wood burner flickering away in the corner of the compact sitting room, gave a warmth and light that were a world apart from the clinical sterility of my hospital cubicle.

Jess looked on in amusement as I unpacked the new mobile phone from its incredibly over engineered packaging. I did my best with the setup, unwilling to concede defeat. But it wasn't long before she took pity on me.

"Chuck it over here, you Luddite. It's too painful to watch you."

After a few minutes of her attention, fingers tapping away in a blur, she passed the phone back to me. It even had the same screen saver photo as the one it was replacing.

"Wow, thanks."

"You know the numbers one to eight don't really constitute a decent password, right?"

We discussed my lackadaisical approach to online security, among other things, for the remainder of the evening. In the background my new phone pinged regularly as it caught up on its work. Over in the corner, the last log in the wood burner collapsed on itself with a shower of sparks, as good a signal as any that it was time to fight my way out of the armchair and go to bed.

I awoke having slept through the night for the first time in a long while. The warm indentation in the mattress which had previously contained Jess was disappointingly empty, but footsteps coming up the wooden stairs gave a clue as to her whereabouts. Placing a cup of coffee on the bedside table she kissed me good morning.

"Got to go to work. Make yourself at home. See you later."

I watched her turn and leave before easing myself carefully upright. Reaching for the coffee, I wondered where Andrew wanted to take me today. Hopefully not to his office to discuss outstanding mooring fees.

Whilst the coffee went about its work, I picked up my new phone, scrolling idly through the back log of messages. Most where short texts, wishing me well, as well as one from Kemp telling me to call him so he could start the process of trying to get me some sick pay. I sighed at the reminder of my financial situation. The only remaining message of any note, was from Jake, sent two days ago. The enigmatic wording contained three pieces of information; an address in Plymouth, which I didn't recognize; today's date, which I did; and the instruction: '*Be there at ten thirty*'.

***

Nine o'clock found me sat in Andrew's car - no dog, imprisoned or otherwise today - showing him the message from Jake.

"I have no idea what this is all about. But is there any chance you'd drive me there?"

"I got the same message. Very enigmatic."

An hour later we turned down a dead-end alleyway and pulled into the narrow, cobbled gateway of a business in the Barbican area declaring itself to be '*The best Auction house in the south-west. Guaranteed.*' Easing ourselves out of the car we looked around at the premises. The cobbled courtyard ran all the way up to the front façade of a large dilapidated warehouse.

One of two full height sliding doors had been slid open on a rusty track, affording a view of mostly tatty looking household goods, double stacked in places. Random objects were dotted between the predominantly brown furniture. Out of style bicycles with flat tires, fridge freezers, their doors wide open and the shelves piled with yet more random items gave the impression of a junk shop, at odds with the bold claim of the sign above the gate. The office proved to be a *Portakabin* pushed up into the lee of the warehouse. An assortment of concrete blocks were doing their best to hold it off the ground for the time being.

As we approached, the office door groaned open, revealing a rotund lady of indeterminate age. The beige cardigan buttoned up to her neck hung loosely from her shoulders, any history of shape long since washed away. One outstretched hand clasped a clip board which served to balance her as she stepped carefully down onto the upturned milk crate moonlighting as a step.

"Here for the auction?" As she spoke, her eyes scanned the courtyard with a resigned look. I got the impression that dribs and drabs were the norm here.

Not at all sure *why* we were there, I nonetheless answered with a questioning; "Uh, yes?"

"Well you had better come in and register before the rush starts," she snorted slightly through her nose, as if the idea of a rush was preposterous.

Inside the *Portakabin* she sagged into residence, the ancient office chair squeaking in protest. In front of her a collapsible table served as a desk, as well as storage for discarded fast food wrappers. Multi-functional, or messy, depending on which side of the table you happened to be.

"We haven't been given the police auction before," she offered.

We remained silent. Not our place to comment why that might be.

"But the bulk of the items are to be auctioned next week," she continued. "I hope you have not wasted your time. Today is just for some boat. I guess the mooring fees don't stop adding up and the police want it gone, pronto." She tossed a folder towards us. It cleared a pile of pizza boxes in the manner of an under powered aeroplane scraping over the Alps.

Andrew and I looked at the photograph which had spilled out on transit. It showed a classic motor launch, bigger than *First Light*, but not stupidly so. Neatly tied up alongside in a swanky looking marina, everything about it was pristine; from the highly polished brass deck fittings to the coach-house varnish which reflected in the photograph like glass.

"If you are interested in the houses and cars, you will have to come back next week. I think there is even a Lamborghini included in the lot." She sighed again, wistfully. "That won't make you seasick."

"No, we are here for the boat," Andrew told her, not looking at me.

"What's the story behind these items?" I piped up.

"Proceeds of crime. Some major drug ring around here somewhere got busted recently." The woman stood and picked her way to the window looking hopefully out into the still deserted courtyard. With a yet another sigh she turned back to face us.

"Well, looks like just you two. Make me a bid, so I can go get some lunch."

I reached out, poking Andrew's arm. "However cheap it is, I can't afford it."

He ignored me.

"What's the reserve?" he addressed the woman instead.

"I'm not supposed to tell you that."

Andrew continued to stare at her until she finally relented. Pointing at the photograph in my hands, she made a rotating motion with her finger. Turning the photo over revealed a handwritten notation. *RES 5000*. I stared, surely it was a mistake. The boat in the picture was worth way more than that. But even as my hopes lifted at the ridiculously low figure, I knew even that amount was well beyond my reach.

"I bid five thousand." Andrew had raised his finger to accentuate his statement.

"You are aware there are buyers' fees to be added?"

"Yes."

"Sold."

Andrew ignored my protests and I stared in disbelief as documents were signed and stamped. When banking details had been exchanged the woman informed us, "She's lying in

Mayflower Marina. Once your bank transfer hits our account, you will receive the ownership document. But the marina fees are down to you, as of today."

Andrew nodded his acceptance, and we exited the musty *Portakabin* into the damp air of the courtyard.

Settling into the car I said, "Thanks. I think. I have no idea how to pay you back. Or even cover the marina fees."

"I'm sure you'll be back on your feet in no time." Pulling out of the courtyard, he changed the subject. "I wonder what that's doing there?" Andrew gestured in the direction of a police car jammed into the alleyway like a cork in a bottle. As we approached, it started its engine and pulled away.

***

I spent the journey back to Dartmouth alternating between euphoria at having a boat again and worrying about how I was going to pay the bills on two boats. The loss of *First Light* would not stop the loan company from wanting their money, and the payment deadline was merely days away.

Andrew remained for the most part silent until we arrived back in Dartmouth and pulled up outside his storage unit. I noticed it had a much more sophisticated padlock on it compared to when I had last been here to dig out his speargun.

"What are we doing here?" I asked, puzzled.

"Come on." Andrew ignored my question as he slammed his car door shut and dug around in his pocket for a key.

Once inside the storage unit, I stood perplexed as Andrew pushed aside a wall cabinet to reveal a shallow recess in the brickwork behind. Two black bags sat in the hollow, on top of the dusty red bricks. Picking one up, he dropped it at my feet. Reaching down to unzip it, the familiar plastic sleeves with their golden glow looked up at me; the stomach clenching gold rush no less powerful than the last time I had laid eyes on them.

"But, how...?" I stopped, forcing myself to think about the chronology.

Andrew waited for the gears to mesh, a grin on his face. It dawned on me that he must have removed the gold from the dive sets before heading out of town for his reunion.

"I couldn't sleep all that night. Knowing the gold was there, not more than a few hundred meters from Vladimir. With you being on call for the fire station and me going to Scotland, the idea of leaving it on your boat just didn't seem sensible."

"But the padlock on the dive locker... It was still there when I got back on board in the evening."

"Come on Matt, you've been using that same combination for everything since the day I met you. I bet your bank card pin code is even 2727! But I took some bolt cutters from work with me, just in case."

"Jesus, Andrew, you could have let me know!"

"I sent you a text telling you to call me, but we kept missing each other. The next time I was able to speak with you, you were in the hospital. Sure, I could have told you then, but this is so much better, don't you think?" He was grinning from ear to ear, and I was torn between throwing something at him and, well, throwing something at him.

Andrew's grin became infectious and I begrudgingly forgave him the delay in telling me he had moved the gold. He was right, this was a heck of a feeling, much better than if he had told me while flat out on my hospital bed coughing up phlegm every few minutes.

"There is just one thing though." Andrew's countenance turned serious as he looked at me.

"What?"

"How about you pay me back for your boat now?"

***

Not yet fit enough to ride my bike, I borrowed Andrew's car and spent the next week converting a small percentage of our haul into cash. There was no shortage of '*We Buy GOLD*! signs in the dozens of towns I passed through as I criss-crossed the South of England. Selling one or two bars at each location seemed the sensible way to go about it, even though I was rarely offered anything like a fair price.

After seven days of hotels and haggling, the cash in my backpack had accrued to a level which would comfortably cover immediate needs and more. I pointed the car back in the direction of the West Country, making a quick stop as evening fell at the sign writers' studio, on the outskirts of Dartmouth.

"Is it ready yet"? I asked.

"Here you go," the shop owner said, his paint stained fingers passing me the oblong mahogany board. "Nice name for a boat."

***

Jess was at the helm as we slipped out of Mayflower Marina and out into Plymouth Sound, the freshly varnished name plate screwed into place on the transom. The weather was kind to us, with just a gentle swell under the hull as we spent the day progressing along the coast getting to know the boat. It didn't disappoint.

The *well looked after* impression we had got from the auctioneer's picture was accurate. From the recently painted, oil free bilges, to recently overhauled engines, it was clear that no expense had been spared in maintaining her. Even the interior styling was muted and comfortable, not at all what I had expected given its previous owner's vocation. I saw with satisfaction that there was a space on the saloon bulkhead just the right size to take the soon to be arriving *Monet* print.

Evening was falling as we glided into the river mouth, and I couldn't help grinning as Andrew's voice crackled out over the VHF radio.

"*Golden Horizon, Golden Horizon,* this is Dart Harbour Authority, do you require a mooring? Over."

EPILOGUE

The plan had been to stay for just a few days. Standing on the dock at Peter Island waiting for the golf cart to pick him up, he had watched the resort's launch begin its return journey across the Sir Francis Drake channel towards Tortola and thought he had made a good choice.

The small Caribbean island's luxury resort provided the level of isolation and anonymity that he desired, the independent villa he had booked proving to be just a short walk along the gravel path from the amenities of the main complex.

But it wasn't the high-end spa, or top-quality food options that kept him place longer than was prudent. It was the beach.

The golden sand and turquoise water of Deadman's Bay called to him from the moment the resort's golf cart had deposited him outside his villa. It was with some difficulty that he curbed his impatience as the concierge dropped his bags in the cavernous main bedroom. A ceiling fan, shiny metal blades gently mixing the air caused his mind to briefly wander, as the concierge droned on about the various features of his temporary home. Fifty dollars cut short the detailed explanations. He was fairly certain that he could figure out how to operate the shower without the input. Pausing only to change into swimming shorts, he was soon in the water, pulling long powerful strokes out into the bay. After a dozen or so such strokes he had turned to look back at the shore, treading water to give his shoulder a rest.

The yellow curve of sand was separated from the water by a thin line of white froth nibbling at its edge. Overlooked by lush tropical greenery, the beach held no more than a handful of overweight guests giving their sun loungers a workout. He saw a pretty, dark-skinned girl, pushing her trolley on oversized wheels over the sand. A jauntily positioned parasol shaded her and the trolley's cargo of cold drinks and local delicacies as she plied her trade. Each transaction produced a wide, white smile and tinkle of laughter that reached him across the water.

Two days spent alternating between swimming and sunbathing had started to ease the pain in his shoulder and push back the pallor of his northern climes skin. Skilfully, the trolley with its parasol and pretty vendor, managed to time their arrivals with his, as each muscle fatiguing swim brought him back to the sand. Cool coconut water, handed over with a smile, became a ritual. Those initial two days expanded into four, then a week had passed.

On the morning of the eight day, he knew it was time to move on. His body was a golden brown and the long swims were no longer accompanied by pain in his shoulder. Donning his swimming shorts for the last time he headed for the water.

The scene from his viewpoint in the centre of the bay was unchanged. His eyes drank it in, reluctant to swim back to the beach and begin packing. Eventually though, his feet grounded, soft sand squeezed up through his toes as he transitioned back to land.

A different hand passed him the coconut water today, disconcerting for no other reason than he had become used to the routine, but confirmation, if any were needed, that it was time to be moving on.

"No Celine?" he inquired, taking the proffered coconut, and quaffing its contents with relish.

"No, today you got me."

Looking at the woman, he detected a slightly bitter taste in his mouth from the coconut water. Her eyes were watching him, searching for some sign, he thought. She was pretty enough in her own way, carrying herself with the confidence of an athlete. The arm that passed him the drink was sleek and sinewy in a way that only regular, hard exercise could produce.

He continued to stare at her with interest, noting that her skin was not dark like Celine, and had the beginnings of sunburn appearing at the edges of her T-shirt. The sight of the reddened skin jarred with the notion that she was a *local.* Alarm bells started to ring in his subconscious. He lifted his gaze to her face seeing the eyes staring back at him held the same, blank look that faced him every day from the mirror. A feeling of dread crept over him.

Apparently satisfied at what she saw, the woman lifted the hotel branded apron over her head discarding it on the sand.

"Goodbye, Vladimir."

Turning away and heading up the beach, she looked back only once, seeing him leaning against the abandoned trolley, one hand reaching up to claw at his throat.

***

Five thousand miles away, a telephone rang. The *icons* on the wall looked on, observing everything but saying nothing.

"Yes?"

"It's done."

ACKNOWLEDGMENTS

Special thanks to Gene du Plessis for the awesome cover art and working tirelessly to get it *just so.*

Thanks to my friends, and especially my family, for their proofreading, encouragement, and feedback.

ABOUT THE AUTHOR

NICK BOHNET

Born and raised in Dartmouth, England, Nick has led an eclectic life all over the world. A *Jack of All Trades*, Nick draws from his own experiences as a fire fighter, super yacht captain, tree surgeon, sailing instructor, farm hand and a poker player, to create colourful characters in his stories. As a licensed pilot, he flies helicopters, light aircraft, paramotors and gyrocopters. Nick has crossed Europe on motorbikes; skippered yachts worldwide; and explored, dived, gold panned and volunteered in Central America.

Trained in Maritime Anti-Piracy Techniques and Firearms, *skill's that have come in handy on several occasions*, he serves part-time as captain for the marine conservation group, *Sea Shepherd,* on anti-poaching campaigns. Nick's wit and varied lifestyle is apparent in his writing and can be enjoyed in his action-adventure novel, *Golden Horizon.*

To see Nick's current and upcoming books and writing projects, visit www.nickbohnet.com

AFTERWORD

This book is formatted for British English. It has been edited and proofed, but typos are sneaky little buggers. If you spot a typo, please let me know through the Contact Page of my website: www.nickbohnet.com.

And please sign up to know when I release new books. I welcome your thoughts on, *Golden Horizon*. Leave a review a *Like,* or a comment on my website or social media pages.

Thanks,

Nick

Printed by Amazon Italia Logistica S.r.l.
Torrazza Piemonte (TO), Italy

16808819R00169